Loaded Dice

Loaded Dice

James Swain

LARGE PRINT

This large print edition published in 2004 by
RB Large Print
A division of Recorded Books
A Haights Cross Communications Company
270 Skipjack Road
Prince Frederick, MD 20678

Published by arrangement with Ballantine Books, an imprint of
Random House Publishing Group

Publisher's Cataloging In Publication Data
(Prepared by Donohue Group, Inc.)

Swain, James.
  Loaded dice / James Swain.

  p. (large print) ; cm.

  ISBN: 1-4025-9558-1

1. Valentine, Tony (Fictitious character)—Fiction. 2. Private investigators—New
Jersey—Atlantic City—Fiction. 3. Gambling and crime—Nevada—Las Vegas—Fiction.
4. Card dealers—Nevada—Las Vegas—Fiction. 5. Blackjack—Fiction. 6. Terrorists—
Fiction. 7. Large type books. 8. Las Vegas (Nev.)—Fiction. 9. Mystery fiction. 10. Suspense
fiction. I. Title.

PS3569.W225 L63 2004b
813/.6

Printed in the United States of America

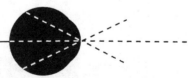

**This Large Print Book carries the
Seal of Approval of N.A.V.H.**

For Steve Forte

ACKNOWLEDGMENTS

The author would like to gratefully thank the following people for their help in writing this novel: Chris Calhoun, Dana Isaacson, Michele Jaffe, Linda Marrow, Fred Rea, Deborah Redmond, Charles and Margaret Swain, and Laura Swain.

The biggest and first crap game is mentioned in Greek mythology. Zeus, Poseidon, and Hades rolled dice for shares of the Universe.

Poseidon won the Oceans.

Hades won the Underworld.

Zeus won the Heavens and is suspected of having used loaded dice.

MARIO PUZO
Inside Las Vegas

LOADED DICE

PREFACE

He had left Arlington Heights early that morning, knowing there would be traffic, and had not been disappointed.

The long line of cars on I-395 headed toward Washington had stopped moving, and he hit his brakes. Then he glanced nervously at the cell phone lying on the passenger seat beside him. He'd left the radio turned off so he would not miss the call when it came.

Traffic started to move, and he lightly tapped the accelerator. Normally, he liked to listen to the area's local shock jocks rant and rave. Even when he didn't understand what they were talking about, he still fed off their anger.

He saw the sign for his exit and merged into the left lane. Putting his indicator on, he kept left at the fork in the ramp, then took a right onto C Street.

A Texaco station sat on the corner. Inside, he bought a sixteen-ounce cup of coffee. Paying for it with the change in his pocket, he saw the manager stare.

"Where did you get that, buddy?" the manager asked.

He stared at the handful of coins in his palm. With the quarters and dimes was a casino chip. It was brown, what gamblers called a chocolate chip.

"Gambling," he replied.

"No kidding." The manager leaned over the counter. "I've seen purples and yellows, but never one that color before. How much is it worth?"

He started to tell him that it was worth five thousand dollars. Only he didn't. He was dressed in crummy street clothes, and didn't look like someone who'd won that much money.

"Nothing," he said. "It was a souvenir."

"Pretty neat," the manager said.

He sat in his van and sipped the coffee until it turned cold. Finally, the cell phone on the seat beside him rang.

"Yes?" he answered.

It was Ziad.

"It's time," his cousin said.

The line went dead. He took the chocolate chip from his pocket. Staring at it, he thought of all that had happened, and all that was about to happen. Then he thought of his parents and family back in Pakistan. What would they think of him? He could only hope they would be proud of what he was about to do.

He left the gas station and drove onto First Street. At a traffic light he stopped and realized his hands were trembling. He unzipped his windbreaker and stared at the three hand grenades strapped around his waist.

4

The light turned green. Closing his jacket, he took a right on Independence, heading the van toward Pennsylvania Avenue and the White House.

TWO AND A HALF YEARS LATER

CHAPTER 1

The most desirable women in Las Vegas didn't live there.

They lived in southern California and worked as dental hygienists, aerobic instructors, and nurses. They lived regular, nine-to-five lives. Then, on the weekend, they flew to Las Vegas—usually on Southwest, because it had the most flights—got off the plane, and became different people. Their names changed, and so did their hairstyles and their clothes. It was as if a magic wand had been waved over them, although the change was anything but magical.

They became strippers in the gentlemen's clubs that hung on the periphery of the Las Vegas Strip. They paid the club owners two hundred bucks a night and made the money back in twenty minutes from drunken men wanting a friction dance. On a good night, they took home a grand.

It wasn't that these women were *more* beautiful than the women who lived in Las Vegas. Vegas was filled with knockouts. What made them different was that they weren't used to being treated like garbage, which was how most women in Vegas got treated. No, these women still had dreams. They lived in la-la land, and it came through on their faces every time they smiled.

Her name was Kris, and she danced at the Pink Pony.

Lieutenant Pete Longo of the Metro Las Vegas Police Department had met Kris while responding to a call about a fight. Normally, he would have let a uniform deal with it, only the prospect of seeing naked women dancing against a backdrop of sporting events projected on a colossal screen had propelled him into action. That, and not having to see his wife for another hour.

The fight was between a drunk and a bouncer, and it was over Kris. The drunk was a big, corn-fed kid from the Midwest who'd trapped Kris in a VIP booth. She was naked save a G-string and looked scared out of her wits. Petite, blond hair, great figure, and her own breasts. Not the prettiest woman he'd ever seen, but damn close.

Longo had acknowledged her with a thin smile. Then he'd tried to arrest the drunk. The drunk had responded by spitting on him.

Longo was pretty fat. His mother called him chubby, but that was his mother. Beneath the flab was some real muscle. In the gym, he could bench-press his weight. Most guys his size couldn't do that. And he knew how to fight.

He knocked the drunk out with two punches. It had impressed the hell out of the bouncer, an

African American kid whose Italian suit had gotten torn in the scuffle. And it had impressed the gaggle of patrons and strippers standing nearby. But who it impressed the most was Kris.

"Ohhh," she'd squealed as the Midwest Mauler fell.

Longo made the bouncer sit on him. Then he'd taken off his jacket and draped it over Kris's shoulders.

"You okay?" he asked.

She closed the jacket around her and nodded her head.

"Did he hurt you?"

She shook her head. "That was really cool," she said.

"What's your name?"

"Starr," she said.

"Your real name."

That had gotten her. The hint of a smile crossed her lips. "Kris."

"You're not from around here, are you?" he said.

That had been six weeks ago. Pulling into the driveway of Kris's townhouse in his brand-new Ford Explorer, Longo found himself shaking his head. It felt like they'd known each other six years. Every time they'd gotten together—every single encounter—had been the stuff dreams were made of. Beeping his horn, he looked expectantly at the front door.

A minute passed. He rolled down his window

and sucked in the brisk desert air. It was early April, his favorite time of year. Warm days, cool nights; perfect sleeping weather. He tapped his horn again.

When she didn't come out, he slipped out of the SUV. The garage door was open, his old Mustang convertible sitting in the space. He'd given it to Kris so she'd have wheels on the week-ends. He'd concocted an elaborate story for his wife, only she'd never asked him what he'd done with the car. Too happy with the new Ford Explorer, he guessed.

Cindi was funny that way. Since their marriage had gone on the rocks, she had stopped ques-tioning where the money was coming from. They went on nice vacations twice a year, drove new cars, and had money in the bank. All on his crummy detective's salary.

The front door was locked, and he trudged around back. Taking the spare key out of the flow-erpot, he unlocked the back door. He waited expectantly for the alarm's piercing whine. When it didn't sound, he went in.

"Hey, Kris, it's me. They stop serving breakfast at nine. We need to hurry."

Still no answer. Probably in the bathroom, doing her hair. Kris looked like a cheerleader when she wasn't stripping. She was a stickler about keeping the place clean, and he slipped off his shoes and padded silently into the living room.

Right away he knew something was wrong. The

air smelled funny, and he spied a half-smoked cigarette lying on the glass coffee table. Kris had flown in the night before and called him from the club. Said she was going to dance until three AM, then go to the townhouse. He was to pick her up at eight thirty for breakfast. A simple plan, although he now realized that someone had come home with her.

Lifting his eyes, he stared at the hallway that led to her bedroom. Were they in there, sound asleep?

He took a deep breath. Being a cop twenty years, he'd come to know the seven deadly sins pretty well. Betrayal was the worst. It shattered everything you held to be true, and was as damaging as a bullet to the flesh.

He cracked her bedroom door and peeked inside. Kris lay beneath a leopard-skin blanket, eyes shut, her wheat-gold hair displayed luxuriously on a pillow. His heartbeat quickened. Every time he saw her, he felt like a high school senior with his life stretched out before him, not some fat, forty-five-year-old bozo with two kids and a wife he couldn't stand.

Longo opened the door fully and stared at the bathroom door. Was her friend with the cigarette in there? His eyes canvassed the room and spotted Kris's clothes folded neatly on a chair. It was a little ritual she performed whenever they made love. It always made him smile.

"Kris?"

Her eyelids remained shut. He stepped into the

room. His instinct told him to check the bathroom first, and his heart told him to check her. His instinct won out, and he kicked the bathroom door open. Empty.

He sat on the edge of the bed. It was a motionless water bed, so comfortable that they'd once slept for ten hours straight. He looked down at her. The color was draining from her face, her exquisite features turning hard.

"Kris?"

He didn't want to believe she was gone, his heart winning out over his instincts. He lifted the blanket with the tip of his finger and saw where the bullet had entered her body, and taken her life.

Her killer had been kind. He'd shot her through the heart, and he guessed she'd died instantly. Lowering the blanket, he rose from the bed, looked at the ceiling, and tried not to sob.

Only one thing to do. Get in the Explorer and burn rubber. He couldn't be caught here. He looked down at her a final time.

"I love you so much," he whispered.

Putting his shoes on in the kitchen, Longo stared at a pair of socks sitting on the table. He'd left the socks here last weekend. In typical Kris-fashion, she'd washed and folded them. As he picked up the socks, the words *Oh, no,* escaped his mouth.

How many more of his things were in the townhouse? And what about his fingerprints? They were probably on every doorknob and light fixture. And

Kris's phone bills, the investigating detectives would surely look at those. All trails would lead directly back to him.

He pulled a chair out from the table and dropped his massive bulk into it. He was about to become a suspect in a murder investigation. The detectives in charge would not be his friends. They would look at his lifestyle, questioning his expensive vacations and the new cars he bought every year. What was he going to tell them? That he found a bag of money behind a casino?

Or would he tell them about the department's secret slush fund, and how money was being siphoned from the bank accounts of well-known wise guys. The wise guys weren't shouting about it, knowing a bribe when they saw one.

He couldn't do that. That would be suicide.

He would lie about the money.

"Jesus Christ," he said aloud.

He'd get thrown off the force, and Cindi would surely leave him. His teenage daughters would shun him, and his parents wouldn't be too thrilled, either. His life was about to be ruined. And all because he'd gone and fallen in love.

Standing, he slid the chair beneath the table. The leg hit something soft, and he looked beneath the table and saw a black gym bag. The bag was open and stuffed with casino chips from several different casinos. He pulled it out and let his fingers run through the chips. Reds, greens, purples, and yellows. There was even a brown chip. You didn't see those very often.

He blew his cheeks out. There was twenty grand here, easy. This was worse than bad. He couldn't explain *this*. And if there was any part of the story the investigators would want explained, it was why twenty grand in casino chips was in Kris's townhouse.

Zipping the bag closed, he saw a sliver of paper tucked in a side pocket. He pulled it free. It was an embossed business card, and he stared at the raised lettering.

Grift Sense
International Gaming Consultant
Tony Valentine, President
727/591-5115

It was a small world. He knew Valentine. A retired Atlantic City detective who helped casinos catch cheaters. Had he blown into town, met Kris, and made her an offer she couldn't refuse?

Sticking the card into the bag, Longo searched the bag's other pockets and found a pack of Marlboros. He went into the living room and stared at the filter of the cigarette lying in the ashtray. It was a match.

Back in the kitchen, he grabbed the gym bag off the floor and exited through the back door. He went straight to the community trash area and buried the bag beneath a ton of garbage.

16

Coming back inside, he dialed the police station on the kitchen phone. An automated message greeted him. While he waited for an operator, he wondered how hard it would be to track Valentine down. Valentine was probably in town on a consulting job, staying at one of the nice joints on the Strip. A few phone calls at most, he decided.

His thoughts shifted to his dead girlfriend. Her memory was going to stay with him for the rest of his life. He was going to make Valentine pay for this, only he wouldn't be as kind as Valentine had been to her. There was no reason why he should be.

CHAPTER 2

Tony Valentine watched a police cruiser race down Maryland Parkway, the morning sunlight beating brightly off its roof. Distances were hard to determine in the desert, and he guessed the cruiser was five miles away. Back home in Florida, the landscape didn't play tricks with you like it did out here. But that was the appeal of Las Vegas: You didn't know what was real and what was an illusion.

He turned from the window. He was standing in a penthouse office of Sin, Las Vegas's newest casino. Three thousand guest rooms and a gaming area as big as an airport terminal. It was Vegas's second new casino this year, the public's appetite for throwing away their money knowing no bounds.

Three of the most powerful men in Nevada stood on the other side of the room: Shelly Michael, CEO of Michael Gaming, the country's largest casino chain, the man the *Wall Street Journal* called "a barracuda in pinstripes"; Rags Richardson, the African American owner of three Strip casinos and founder of BE BOP SHABAM

Records; and California beach boy Chance Newman, owner of Sin, who'd made his fortune in Silicon Valley before the tech bubble burst.

Crossing the room, he stuck out his hand. "Tony Valentine. Nice to meet you."

They all shook hands. Normally, Valentine didn't kowtow to *anyone*. Only these guys had made his day. They'd called yesterday and offered him twenty-five thousand dollars for a private demonstration. Even if he hadn't already been en route to Las Vegas to check up on his son Gerry, he still would have accepted the job.

Twenty-five grand was a lot of dough. More than he'd made his first years as a cop in Atlantic City. When he and his wife retired to Florida, he'd figured his earning years were over. Then Lois had died, and he'd opened a consulting business to help casinos catch cheats. It kept his mind off the past. And the pay was good.

He caught the three men smirking and guessed it was his clothes. The airline had lost his luggage, and he'd bought pants and a shirt in Sin's haberdashery for the meeting. The pants had set him back three hundred bucks and didn't fit worth a damn.

A blackjack table sat in the center of the room, along with four stools and a dealer from the casino. Hitching up his trousers, he crossed the room and pulled a stool out from the table. "Care to join me?" he asked.

The three men elbowed up to the table. Shelly

Michael had an annoying habit of continually looking at his watch. Valentine saw him do it again.

"Got a train to catch?"

Shelly glared at him. He wore an exquisite silk suit that was offset by a toupee too flat for his head. He also wore a wedding ring, and Valentine wondered why his wife hadn't bothered to tell him how ridiculous he looked.

"You may begin," Shelly said.

Valentine had a feeling that he wouldn't be getting any jobs from Michael Gaming after today. That was okay. He had to draw the line in the sand somewhere.

"As you know, blackjack is the favorite table game of every casino in the world," he began. "It is also, unfortunately, the game that's most susceptible to cheating. I personally know of a hundred ways to cheat at blackjack, and that doesn't include card-counting. That's why casinos monitor their blackjack tables so zealously."

He shifted his attention to the dealer behind the table, a good-looking Italian kid named Sal Dickinson. They'd talked briefly in the elevator. Sal was an A dealer, which meant he got to work the high-roller salon and made good tips.

"Sal," Valentine said, "please shuffle up."

Sal removed six decks of playing cards from a plastic shoe on the table and began to shuffle. Valentine turned his attention to the three casino executives.

"For every method of cheating at blackjack,

casinos have devised a way to beat it. Computers, cameras, mirrors, daub, you name it, and the casinos have figured out how to stop it. Then something called Deadlock appeared on the scene."

"So it does exist," Shelly said.

"That's right."

"You've seen it, or just heard about it?" Shelly asked.

The challenge in his voice was unmistakable. Valentine could hear the soft purr of the cards being shuffled behind his back. "I own one," he replied.

Chance Newman acted surprised. He wore hip designer threads and moved like he'd spent his life on a dance floor. "I thought they were impossible to get," he said.

"They are," Valentine replied.

"Then how did *you* get one?" Shelly demanded.

Valentine's face burned. Shelly's mother had obviously left him in diapers for too long. Taking out a pack of Marlboros, he banged one out and stuck it between his lips. Leaving it unlit, he said, "A casino in the Philippines I was doing a job for gave it to me. The casino's security department raided the room of a gang of suspected cheaters. They found the device in a suitcase and thought it was a card-counting computer."

"And you taught yourself how to use it," Shelly Michael said.

"That's right."

Chance Newman placed his hand on Valentine's shoulder. "Tony's the best in the business. That's why I asked him to give us this demonstration. If anyone is going to understand how Deadlock works, it's him."

Valentine turned to face Sal. The six decks were ready to be cut. He picked up the laminated cut card sitting on the table and jammed it in. Sal separated the cards at the spot and fitted them into the plastic shoe.

Then Sal started to deal.

Valentine played all seven hands at the table, a hundred dollars a bet. Within twenty minutes, the shoe was exhausted and he was down ten thousand dollars.

"This is cheating?" Shelly asked sarcastically.

Shelly was watching him like a hawk. So were Chance and Rags, only Shelly had breath that could melt your glasses. Valentine wondered if he knew how bad his breath was. That was the problem with rich people. No one was honest with them.

"It sure is," Valentine said.

"But you're down ten grand."

"That's right. I'm splashing."

"You're what?"

"Splashing. It's a hustler's term. I'm throwing money around, setting you up."

"How so?"

"I've made you think I'm a sucker."

Valentine placed his unlit cigarette in the ashtray

on the table. Picking the ashtray up, he moved it next to the plastic discard tray where Sal put the cards after each hand was dealt. Beneath the ashtray, Valentine secretly held a "lug"—a piece of rubber band tied in a knot with its ends snipped off. With his middle finger, he shot the lug into the discard tray. Sal immediately put some cards above the lug. Then he removed all the cards from the discard tray and began to shuffle them.

Valentine turned around on his stool, effectively shielding Sal from the three men.

"What should make us think otherwise?" Shelly asked.

"My behavior," Valentine said. "I lost ten grand, and didn't start pissing and moaning."

Shelly didn't get it. Neither did Chance. But Rags was all smiles, his gold teeth glittering. In and out of prison as a kid, he knew the ways of street people, and said, "That's a tell."

"Sure is," Valentine said.

"So what are you telling us?"

"That I'm about to rip you off."

Rags grinned. "Sure you are."

Valentine had been counting time in his head. Twenty seconds had passed, and he turned around and watched Sal finish shuffling. So did the other three men.

When Sal was done, he offered the cards to be cut. Valentine picked up a laminated cut card lying on the table and stuck it into the break in the cards created by the lug.

Sal watched him with a bored look on his face, playing his part perfectly. It had taken Valentine no time to explain the scam to him in the elevator. It was one of the things that made Deadlock so deceptive. A dealer could be easily recruited.

Sal fitted the cards into the plastic shoe and started dealing.

Valentine played all seven hands, a thousand dollars a bet. After ten minutes, he'd won his ten grand back, as well as twenty thousand of the house's money.

"What the hell you doing?" Rags yelled at him. He was hanging on the table rail, staring in disbelief as Valentine won every single hand he played.

"Cheating," he replied.

"Ain't possible," Rags said, looking at his peers for support. "Is it?"

"That, or he can walk on water," Chance said, shaking his head in disbelief.

Shelly glared at him, refusing to acknowledge he was beaten. Valentine played another round, winning all seven hands. Rags slapped the table incredulously.

"Are you going to show us what you're doing, or do we have to lie on our backs and say *Uncle*?" Shelly finally asked.

Shelly's timing was perfect. The cards that Valentine was using to win had been exhausted. He *couldn't* cheat anymore, not that he planned to tell Shelly that.

"Be happy to," Valentine said.

Standing, he undid his belt and let his ill-fitting, three-hundred-dollar slacks fall to his ankles. The three men instinctively stepped backward. They stared at his white jockeys and the keypad strapped to his thigh. It was the size of a PalmPilot and had wires that ran beneath his shirt. Valentine lifted his shirt and let them see the small black box taped to his side.

"Gentlemen, allow me to introduce Deadlock," he said.

"A couple of years ago, a group of supersmart college students in Japan pulled a little prank," Valentine said after he'd removed the apparatus and laid it on the blackjack table. Pulling his pants up, he continued. "They read in the newspaper that U.S. reconnaissance jets were flying over their country while monitoring North Korea. So these students made some alterations on a computer in the math department at their school.

"One day, while a U.S. jet was flying over their country, the students sent a beam up from the computer and downloaded all the intelligence in the jet's computer that had been gathered about North Korea. They e-mailed the information to everyone they knew.

"Needless to say, they got in trouble, and apologized for what they'd done. After a while, things calmed down. Then one day, a guy from Nevada shows up at their school. A gambler.

"This gambler had participated in a blackjack scam in Atlantic City years ago that used a computer hidden in a van, and a gang of accomplices. He explained the scam to the students and challenged them to come up with something that would re-create it, using less equipment and no accomplices. He also offered to pay them extremely well if they succeeded."

"And Deadlock was born," Shelly said.

"That's right." Valentine picked up the equipment from the table. "In the beginning, the students had some problems, mainly because they didn't understand how blackjack was played. But eventually they caught on. Here's how Deadlock works.

"The keypad is strapped to my thigh. With my right fingers, I input the values of the first hundred and twenty cards played through the fabric of my pants. Because my right hand is beneath the table, the security cameras won't see this. Neither will anyone else at the table.

"Deadlock takes this known sequence of cards, plays out all possible drawing sequences, then outputs the strategy that wins the most money."

"How many sequences are we talking about?" Shelly asked.

"Millions."

"How quickly?"

"Ten seconds at most. Deadlock also adjusts for player mistakes, and legitimate players entering the game, all on the fly." He picked up Deadlock

26

and pointed at the red light on the keypad. Pressing the 1, he made the light come on. "This means Deadlock is ready to pass the information on to me." He pointed at his right ear. "I'm wearing an intracanal earpiece. In a few seconds, Deadlock will tell me how to play the first round."

"It will *tell* you?" Rags said incredulously.

"That's right. Deadlock speaks with an automated voice. The instructions are always crystal clear."

"Wait a minute," Shelly said, unable to hide his anger. "These cards were shuffled. They were in a *random* order."

Valentine shook his head. "Afraid not."

"What do you mean?"

He glanced at Sal. "I had some help. That was one thing the Japanese whiz kids couldn't solve. The scam needs two people."

It took a long moment before the words sunk in. Then Shelly erupted. With venom in his eye, he stared across the blackjack table at Sal. "You tricked us!"

Sal was a classy guy and held his ground. "Mister Newman told me I was to do whatever Mister Valentine wanted. Mister Valentine asked me to help him demonstrate the scam. So I helped him."

"Sal didn't shuffle the first one hundred and twenty cards," Valentine explained. "He only pretended to, while I was distracting you. He shuffled the *rest* of the cards, which was what you saw, and remembered. When I cut the cards, I brought the unshuffled cards to the top."

"That won't work in a casino," Shelly said.

"Of course it will," Valentine replied.

"Now *this* I've got to see," Rags Richardson said.

"It's called putting the eye to sleep," Valentine explained. "The average surveillance technician in a casino watches forty different video monitors. He tends to focus on things that attract his eye. Like a guy betting heavy. Or a pretty woman. Things that most casinos are filled with. Especially at night.

"The cheater knows this. So he plays like a dummy for a few hours, splashes money around. He's not seen as a threat, so the technician stops watching him. That's when the scam happens."

"What if the tapes were watched later on?" Shelly said, still not believing him. "Wouldn't they see that the cards weren't shuffled?"

Valentine looked at Sal. "Sal, would you please demonstrate the zero shuffle?"

Sal slid a deck across the felt, broke it in two, and prepared to shuffle the cards together. Only he didn't interweave the cards. He simply ran his thumbs up the sides of the decks, while leaving one half atop the other. Then he squared them.

"Looks stupid, doesn't it?" Valentine said. "The only eye it will fool is the one in the ceiling. To the camera, this shuffle looks legitimate."

Shelly climbed up on a stool and had Sal do the shuffle again. Chance and Rags got on their stools as well.

"That does look good," Rags admitted.

"Radical," Chance added.

Valentine had Sal do the zero shuffle again. From above, it looked perfect, and that was all that mattered.

"Jesus!" Chance exclaimed.

"Impressive, huh?" Valentine said.

"I'm not talking about that," Chance said, pointing at the picture window on the other side of the penthouse. "Looks like we've got a jumper."

The three men turned and stared. Next door was a dump called the Acropolis. On its top floor, an attractive woman stood on a balcony on the wrong side of the guardrail. They hurried across the room just as she started to cross herself.

Valentine put his face to the glass. Then he swallowed the lump rising in his throat. The woman looked like his late wife, right down to the short dark hair and the way her dress clung to her slender frame as the wind whipped it around her body. His wife, whom he missed more than anyone in the world.

"Call the police," he said.

Then he ran out of the penthouse as fast as his pants would let him.

CHAPTER 3

Reaching Sin's lobby, he flagged down a security guard on a bicycle. One of the annoying things about Las Vegas was that nothing was close. The city's architects had somehow forgotten how difficult it was to get around in the desert, and had spaced the casinos far apart from each other.

"There's a jumper next door," he told the guard. "I need your bike."

The guard was a red-haired guy with a face that looked like a swarm of bees. "You a cop?" he asked.

Valentine had been a cop so long that being retired was something of a joke. "Yeah," he said.

The guard relinquished his bike. Valentine hopped on and sped through the casino's front doors. As he pedaled furiously down the front entrance, he looked straight up, and saw the woman that resembled Lois standing on the edge of the balcony, getting ready to take a swan dive into the great beyond.

He rounded the corner and rode up the Acropolis's entrance, still staring at the sky. The woman saw him, and he waved to her, hoping to get her attention. That was key: Get her thinking about something besides dying. He'd dealt with jumpers in Atlantic City several times. A couple he'd saved, a few he hadn't. There was no magic to it.

He passed the Acropolis's famous fountains and got sprayed with water. Nick Nicocropolis, the hardheaded little jerk who owned the place, had erected toga-clad statues of his voluptuous ex-wives—a stripper, two showgirls, two beauty queens, and a retired hooker who'd run for mayor and gotten six votes—and bathed them in orgasmic bursts of water. A seventh statue had been added, the beautiful Nola Briggs. Nola was a blackjack dealer who'd stolen Nick's heart, while her boyfriend, a cheater named Frank Fontaine, had nearly stolen Nick's casino.

He parked at the valet stand and ran inside. The lobby was jammed, and his eyes scanned the crowd's faces. He worked for Nick often and knew most of his security people by first name. He didn't see anyone he knew.

An elevator reached the lobby and opened its doors. He jumped in and held out his palm as others tried to board. "Police. This is an emergency."

No one argued with him. The doors shut, and he hit the button marked PH. The Acropolis wasn't one of those fancy joints where a special key was needed to reach the top floor. Rich and poor rode together here.

At the penthouse floor he got out. He knew which suite the jumper was staying in: It was the same suite Nick had put him in two years ago.

The door was locked. He raised his right leg, put all his weight and momentum into his heel, and kicked it above the knob. Thirty years ago, he could take a door down with one good kick. Now it took several. He went in.

"Don't come in here," a woman wailed from the balcony.

He looked around the suite and tried to imagine where she was. He decided she was right behind the wall he was staring at.

"I'm not the police," he called out.

"I don't care," she shrieked.

He searched the living room for something with her name on it. The room was still furnished in loud LeRoy Neiman paintings and chrome furniture, the color scheme painful to the eye. On the coffee table he spied a suicide note, her name at the bottom of the page. Lucy Price.

He stepped into the dining room, and through the slider saw her sitting on the balcony railing. She'd closed the slider behind her when she'd gone out, another bad sign.

"Lucy Price," he said.

She swung her head around. Early fifties, Italian, with a slender nose, high cheekbones, and dark, penetrating eyes. Not his wife, but from the same tree.

"Stay away from me!" she shouted.

He crossed the room and opened the slider. Sticking his head out, he said, "I need to talk to you."

"Didn't you hear what I just said?"

She was glued to the railing, the wind whipping her skirt up into her face. Embarrassed, she tried to flatten her skirt out, lost her balance, and started to scream.

He stepped onto the balcony and stuck his hand out. He'd known a cop in Atlantic City who'd grabbed a jumper, and they'd both ended up falling to their deaths. He braced himself. "Take my hand," he said.

She regained her balance and glared at him. "They stole my money! I finally got my life sorted out, and they stole my *money*."

"Who?"

"The bastards that run this place!"

He didn't believe it. Nick was a lot of things—womanizer, foulmouthed thug, Neanderthal—but not a crook. Down below, he saw six firemen inflate a giant mattress and position it directly beneath where Lucy stood. He stepped forward.

"Take my hand. You don't want to die."

"Yes, I do."

"No, you don't."

"But they ruined my life . . . ," she sobbed.

He was close enough to grab her. Their eyes met, and he saw an emptiness where her soul had once been. The desire to kill herself was real, and he realized that if he didn't act right now, she was going to jump. He reached out and took her arm.

"Everything's going to be okay," he said.

He made her face him. The railing was waist-high, and he pointed at it. "I want you to swing your legs over, one at a time. I'll hold you steady."

She started to say something. A helicopter came around the building, and drowned her out. It sounded lighter than a police chopper, and Valentine guessed it was from a local TV station. Lucy shook her fist at it.

"Leave me alone!"

She lost her balance and let out another scream. Shooting her hand through the railing's bars, she grabbed the waist of his pants. They fell down, and a cool breeze shot through his jockeys.

He envisioned them both going over. Grabbing her by the shoulders, he lifted her clean over the railing. She was crying, and looked terribly ashamed.

He pulled up his pants. The TV helicopter came around the building again. He lifted his head and saw a grinning cameraman in the copter's open doorway give him a thumbs-up.

Valentine flipped him the bird.

CHAPTER 4

Chance Newman stepped away from the window as the TV helicopter flew by. The last thing he needed was to be seen on the news, leering at a suicide.

In the window's reflection he saw Rags and Shelly standing behind him, their faces set in stone. Sal, the blackjack dealer, remained at his post on the other side of the room.

"You can leave now," Chance told him.

Sal departed. Moments later, the door to Chance's study opened, and a shaven-headed man in his late forties emerged. Dressed entirely in black, he was thin to the point of being unhealthy, his once handsome face marred by a zipper scar running from cheek to jowl. He approached the three casino executives.

"This is Frank Fontaine," Chance said.

Shelly and Rags nodded stiffly. Fontaine sized each man up, then crossed the suite and picked up the Deadlock equipment sitting on the black-jack table. He shook his head.

"Shit," he said.

"Shit is right," Shelly practically shouted.

Coming over to the blackjack table, he wagged his finger in Fontaine's face. "You told us that nobody in North America knew anything about Deadlock. You said it was a cinch. So we invest a million bucks to buy ten of these fucking things, only to find out that you were wrong."

Fontaine realized that Shelly was staring at his scar. Up close, it bordered on hideous. A few months ago, while serving a life sentence in the federal pen, he'd gotten his face slit for dealing off the bottom during a poker game. The doctors who'd sewn him back together had never expected him to walk free, so they'd made him look like Frankenstein.

"I was wrong," Fontaine said.

"That's it? You were wrong?" Shelly looked at Rags and Chance in disbelief. "Can you believe this guy? He was *wrong*. He's gone and wasted our money, and he acts like it doesn't matter."

"I think we're entitled to compensation for our loss," Rags said. He crossed his arms and puffed up his chest. "Know what I mean?"

Fontaine went to the window and stared next door. He found the statue of Nola Briggs in the fountains and felt a fist go tight in his chest. They had nearly pulled off the heist of the century; then Tony Valentine had stepped in and ruined everything.

"Not really," Fontaine said.

"We hired you to shut the Acropolis down," Rags said. "Do that, and we'll be square."

"Is that what you want me to do?"

Fontaine saw the three men nod in the glass's reflection, and laughed silently to himself. He'd heard they wanted Nick to go under, so he'd made them an offer. He'd bankrupt the Acropolis if they'd fund him. All he'd wanted was capital. Not once had he said exactly how much it would cost.

"You're saying I should work for free," Fontaine said.

"That's right," Rags said.

Fontaine eyes shifted to the dumpy Acropolis and he felt himself smile. Nick's casino was directly between Sin and two casinos owned by Shelly Michael and Rags Richardson. He'd always been good at figuring out puzzles. It was what had gotten him out of the joint. And now he'd figured out why these greedy pricks wanted Nick Nicocropolis gone.

"Isn't that something," Fontaine said. "I just noticed how Nick's casino stands between your casinos. Did you guys ever notice that?" He turned from the window and gave them his best prison-yard stare. "You want to build a walkway between your casinos, don't you? Keep the suckers all to yourselves. That way, you can't lose them to a competitor."

"Stay out of our business," Rags said.

Rags's tone had a real threat behind it. Fontaine looked him over. A big black guy dressed like an African prince, his clothes all shiny. Rags wouldn't last a week in the place he'd just come from.

Fontaine removed a square of paper from his pocket and unfolded it. It had been torn from the infamous Nevada Black Book. The book contained mug shots of individuals who'd cheated Vegas's casinos, and were barred from entering any gaming establishment. He raised the paper to eye level, letting them see his picture.

"So?" Rags said.

"I'm not allowed in any Nevada casino, yet here I am. Know why?"

The three men shook their heads.

"Because the FBI wants me here, that's why." He paused to look each man in the eye. "I've got the tiger by the balls, boys. Welch on this deal, and I'll *fuck* you permanently. Understand?"

Fontaine saw the fight leave their faces. Mentioning the FBI had done the trick. They had become Nevada's casinos worse nightmare, and had every owner in town shitting in his pants. He went to the door. "I'll call you in a few days."

"What about Valentine?" Shelly said.

"What about him?"

"You two have a history. He's not going to ignore you if you run into each other at the Acropolis."

A history. That was a nice way to put it. He'd killed Valentine's brother-in-law twenty years ago, and Valentine had paid him back by getting Nola sent to prison, where she'd gotten sick and died. No, he and Valentine had a lifetime together.

"I'll take care of him," Fontaine said.

"Will we be funding that as well?" Shelly asked.

The question was on each man's face. That was the beauty of Las Vegas. No matter what it was about, it was *always* about money.

"On the house," he replied.

CHAPTER 5

Valentine felt like he was dancing.

Lucy Price was as light as a feather in his arms. As she pulled away from him, her chin grazed his. Their eyes met, and she said, "You're not a cop?"

"No."

"Then why did you save me?"

Because you remind me of her, he nearly said. Through the slider, he saw that the suite had filled with security people. He escorted Lucy inside and let Wily, the casino's head of security, take over. Wily couldn't connect life's dots if he had a blueprint, yet had managed to stay in Nick's employ for fifteen years. He wore a sharkskin suit—the norm for casino management these days—and had spiked his hair with mousse. Lucy tried to scratch his eyes out.

Wily wrestled with her briefly, then handed her over to a pair of security guards. She left the suite kicking and screaming. Wily brushed himself off, then shot Valentine a loopy grin.

"For an old guy, you sure attract the dames."

"Shut up," Valentine said, tucking in his shirt.

"What's wrong with your pants?"

"They don't fit. The airline lost my luggage."

"Why did you buy a pair that doesn't fit?"

"I like wasting money."

"I guess so."

Valentine tried tightening his belt, only it made him look like a circus clown. Out in the hallway, he could hear Lucy putting up a fuss as she was dragged into an elevator.

"What's her beef, anyway?" he asked.

"That's a good question," Wily said. "Little Miss Lucy won twenty-five thousand bucks playing blackjack, so we comped her into a suite. She woke up this morning, and the money was gone from the room safe. She went ballistic, claimed we stole it."

"Did you?"

"Very funny," Wily said.

Wily offered to buy him coffee, and they took an elevator to the first floor. The Acropolis was not responsible for money left in room safes, he explained on the way down. Insurance didn't permit it, and there was a sign in every guest room.

"Lucy Price's money isn't our problem," Wily said.

They walked through the bustling casino. It was designed like the hub of a wagon wheel, with table games and slot and video poker machines in the center, and all other destinations flowing from that center. Once, all casinos had been designed this way, the idea being that people would drop a few dollars each time they passed by.

They entered Nick's Bar. Wily grabbed a table with a RESERVED tent and motioned to the hostess, a pretty woman in a toga. "Coffee for two. And make it fast, okay?"

The hostess left. At the next table, a group of intoxicated men were whooping it up. Behind the bar, two backlit screens contained shadows of topless dancers gyrating to blaring music. Valentine glanced at his watch. Ten in the morning.

"I saw Nola Briggs's statue in the fountains," Valentine said. "Is Nick still pining after her?"

"Yeah," Wily said. "He really loved that chick."

"When does she get out of prison?"

Wily gave him a somber look. "You didn't hear?"

"No. What?"

"Nola died in prison. Some sort of female thing. Bled to death internally. The doctors thought she had food poisoning."

Their coffee came. Valentine stared at the reflection in his cup. Nola hadn't been a bad person, just wounded, and he'd imagined her getting her life back together once she got out of prison. It made him feel bad to know that would never happen.

"So, what brings you to town?" Wily asked.

"Checking up on my son," he said. "He just started working for me. I wanted him to learn card-counting at blackjack, so I paid for him to attend Bart Calhoun's school."

"So you're spying on him," Wily said.

Valentine didn't answer him.

"I hope your son's not tempted too easily," Wily said.

"Why's that?"

"A lot of newbies form teams. Being new, we don't have their faces in our computers. A new team took Harrah's for two hundred grand last month."

Valentine sipped his coffee. It sounded exactly like something Gerry might try. His son had been on the wrong side of the law since he was a teenager. Now thirty-six, he'd recently decided to go legit, mainly because he was married to a wonderful woman named Yolanda, and there was a baby on the way. Only *legit* had a different meaning to Gerry than it did to most people.

Valentine stared at the drunks whooping it up at the next table and realized he'd made a big mistake. Vegas was Sin City. He should never have sent Gerry here.

He glanced across the table at Wily. "Any idea where Calhoun's school is? The phone number I've got is answered by a service."

"Calhoun is a hard guy to pin down. I'll put some feelers out for you, if you want."

"Thanks. I appreciate it."

Wily gulped down his coffee. "Remember those Asian cheaters I e-mailed you about? The ones beating us silly at baccarat?"

Valentine dredged his memory. He was on a monthly retainer for several dozen casinos and received distress calls constantly. Then he remembered. "Three males, early thirties, playing a thousand bucks a hand. Winning way too much."

"That's them," Wily said. "You told me they were probably nail-nicking the cards. Said it was an Asian specialty. Well, you were right."

"You caught them?"

Wily slapped the table. "It was absolutely beautiful. One of the guys had really long fingernails. He had a tiny *razor* beneath one of them. He was slicing up the side of the cards, marking all the nines."

"A razor?"

"Yeah. He baked it in an oven, made it pliable."

"How did you catch them?"

Wily laughed, really enjoying himself now. "That's the best part. The guy must have realized we were on to him. He got scared and started tugging at his collar. Guess what happened?"

"He cut himself."

"Sliced a fucking artery," Wily roared. "Nearly bled to death right there on the baccarat table. Oh man, you should have been there."

"You thought this was funny?"

Wily was holding his sides and appeared ready to fall out of his chair. The guys sitting at the adjacent table had overheard the conversation and decided to leave; so did several other patrons.

Wily was oblivious to their departure, his face beet red.

"I've got it on tape, you want to see it," he choked. "It's priceless."

CHAPTER 6

Gerry Valentine was sweating like a hooker teaching a Sunday school class. His cell phone, which was on buzzer mode and sat in his pocket, had gone off twelve times in the past hour. Three times he'd pulled it out and glanced at the face.

His wife.

Something was wrong, and he thought he knew what. Yolanda had found the grocery bag stuffed with bills he'd hidden under the bed. That, or a creditor had started calling the house and was threatening her.

Gerry owed a lot. How much, he wasn't entirely sure. Which was why going into his father's business had seemed like a good idea.

His old man made some serious coin. He was pretty tight, but Gerry had a feeling that becoming a grandfather might loosen the purse strings. Then Gerry would touch him for a loan, and get the wolves away from the door.

He wiped at his brow and saw his classmates giving him funny looks. Four other people were enrolled in Bart Calhoun's school along with him.

Tara, a legal secretary from Boston who was super-smart; Getty, a gay stockbroker from San Francisco who believed ripping off casinos was more ethical than robbing pension funds; and Amin and Pash, the Indian brothers whose parents back in Bombay thought they were enrolled in UNLV's hotel management program. *They* weren't sweating, and Gerry guessed he was making a spectacle of himself.

"You with us, Gerry?" their teacher asked.

"Yeah, I'm here," Gerry replied.

"Good. I was getting worried." Calhoun pointed a crooked finger at the blackboard at the front of the room. He'd been barred from every casino in Nevada because of his ability to card-count. He was a cowboy and wore denim shirts with pocket flaps, and wide silver belt buckles. "Today our topic is Flying Under the Radar. I'd suggest taking notes, as this gets a little detailed."

Gerry stared at the blackboard. As schools went, Calhoun's was pretty basic. There was a black-board with each day's topic written on it, a blackjack table where they could practice their lessons, and that was it. Students were expected to bring their own paper and writing instruments. And Calhoun didn't tolerate interruptions, unless someone was dying.

"Flying Under the Radar is probably the most important thing I'm going to teach you," he said, leaning against the wall and firing up a cigarette.

"Anyone can learn to count cards. All it takes is practice. The hard part is getting away with it.

"The enemy is the casino's surveillance department. Most surveillance people learn to count. If a deck is rich in high cards, and you increase your bet, they'll know you're card-counting. Right?"

He blew two purple plumes of smoke through his nostrils. Part of the entertainment included tricks with cigarettes. So far, he hadn't repeated himself.

"Wrong!" he exclaimed. "Surveillance won't know you're a card-counter if they're not watching you. And surveillance hardly ever watches certain types of people. This includes women over seventy, drunks, and people with a history of losing. Those people fly under the radar. They're there, but they're not noticed."

"What about me and my brother?" Amin, the older Indian, asked.

"What about you?"

"We cannot disguise ourselves to look like women, and our religion prohibits us from touching alcohol. How do we fly under the radar?"

Calhoun scrunched his face up. "Bunch of ways. Disguises, although from what your brother's told me, you're pretty good at those."

Amin nodded. He and Pash were experienced counters. They had enrolled in Calhoun's school to sharpen their skills and pick up a few pointers.

"You *could* use a ham radio to jam the frequency of the surveillance cameras, but that will only work once," Calhoun said. "It would also mean smuggling a ham radio into the casino, which is a serious offense if you get caught.

"You can learn to know when surveillance is watching you. The cameras beneath the smoky domes have tiny red lights. If the camera is on, so is the red light. If you see the light, it means the camera is looking in the opposite direction."

Amin scribbled furiously, his pen never leaving his yellow legal pad.

"You need to rethink the alcohol thing," Calhoun said, puffing on his cigarette. "Here's an idea. Bring a beer bottle filled with water into the casino with you. It's a great way to blend in. Just don't do like one dumb ass did over at the Tropicana and come in with a Corona bottle. They're see-through, so everyone *knew* it was water."

Pash slapped his desk. "Very good!"

Everyone in the room laughed. Pash was a funny kid, a perfect counterpart to Amin, who was often sullen and brooding. Calhoun smiled and said, "Here's another jewel. Every surveillance department has something called 'blind time.' That's when the department switches the tapes in the VCRs. This can take anywhere from several minutes to over an hour in some of the larger joints. You want to fly under the radar, that's the time to do it."

Amin put down his writing instrument. "That is brilliant."

Calhoun's leathery face seemed to crack as he smiled. "Thanks."

"But how would you get such information? You can't just ask them."

Calhoun used the cigarette to light another. "Bunch of ways, actually. Check the want ads in the papers when the new casino job listings are posted. Most surveillance departments say they're looking for technicians or investigators, instead of running blind ads. If it says, 'Come visit our HR department for immediate consideration,' you know they're desperate. Go interview."

Calhoun paused to puff heavily on his cigarette. Gerry was convinced that everyone in America walked around believing they were someone they'd seen on TV. For Calhoun, it was the Marlboro Man.

"And?" Amin said expectantly.

"Ask for a tour of the surveillance control room. This won't sound unreasonable coming from a job applicant. After all, you have a right to see the work environment."

"And then you ask them," Amin interrupted.

"No, no, you don't ask a thing," Calhoun said.

"But how—"

"Easy," Calhoun said. "Ask to see the room where the VCRs are stored. It's usually pretty big, and kept cool so the tapes won't spoil. When you go in, glance at the VCRs. On the face is an LED or LCD meter that's constantly advancing in one-second increments. The casinos all stretch their tapes to eight hours to save money, so look at the meter and remember the time. If the meter says 4:00, you know the tape will be pulled in four hours. Add four hours to the present time, and you'll have all their tape-change times."

Amin seemed perplexed. "Please, explain."

Calhoun looked at his watch. "The present time is eleven AM. Let's say the time you saw on the LED was 4:00. That means in four hours, the tapes will be changed. Which means the casino changes tapes at three PM, eleven PM, and seven AM. That's their blind time. Like I said, if it's a big casino, it's usually substantial."

Amin looked at his brother and said something in his native tongue. Pash grinned.

"Very good," Pash said in English.

Gerry's cell phone was buzzing. Card-counting was hard enough without having to remember all this crap. He pulled the phone out of his pocket and stared at its face.

It was Yolanda.

He felt himself start to panic. Was she having the baby early? The women in her family had a history of that. What if she was calling to tell him that he was a father, and like a coward he was hiding from her? He'd never live it down.

Gerry looked up and saw his teacher giving him the evil eye. Calhoun hated cell phones almost as much as he hated interruptions. Gerry stood up.

"Excuse me, but I need to take this."

Then Gerry walked out of the room.

★   ★   ★

Calhoun ran his classes out of his house, a ramshackle structure on the outskirts of Henderson, a town bordered on three sides by the desert. Gerry walked down the dirt driveway to where his rental car was parked, got in, and fired up the engine.

Out on the open road, he pushed the rental up to ninety and felt his anxiety slip away. Ever since he was a kid, he'd been good at getting out of jams: Why should this time be any different? Pulling into a mini mart, he bought a Slurpee and a bag of chips, then called Yolanda when he was back behind the wheel.

"Hey beautiful," he said by way of greeting.

"Oh, my God, Gerry, what have you done?" his wife wailed.

He closed his eyes. With his lips he found the Slurpee's straw and took a deep pull. "I haven't done anything. What's wrong? You having the baby?"

"Didn't you get my messages?"

"I'm incognito, remember?"

"I'm your wife, goddamn it!"

Gerry felt the icy drink shoot up the back of his head. "You're not having the baby."

"No."

"So what's so catastrophic that you had to call me twelve times?"

The line went quiet. *That was a stupid thing to say,* he thought. He opened his eyes and stared at the painted landscape. The desert led to mountains, which pointed at the endless sky. He could understand how people fell in love with it out here. Every time he looked out the window, it made him feel better. "Sorry," he said.

Yolanda said, "I called because a collection agency is calling every hour, and the bank is calling because you bounced ten checks—including one to my mother in San Juan—and I found a stack of bills underneath the bed, and I wanted to know how you planned to support us when the baby is born."

The straw in his Slurpee made an offensive sound as he sucked his drink dry.

"What was that?" she snapped.

"The car," he replied. "Look, I spoke to the bank, and I'm going to wire them the money. It's no big deal. I sent the bill collector the money two weeks ago—why he hasn't gotten the check, I have no idea."

"What about all these bills?"

"It's under control," he said calmly. "You need to relax, stop worrying about this stuff. I'll admit things are a little tight, but once I start pulling my weight with my father, we'll be swimming in dough."

"Oh, God, Gerry, I hope you're telling the truth."

"Why wouldn't I be telling you the truth?"

"Gerry, my mother was crying when she called. She *lives* on the money we send her."

Gerry stared at the midday sun. It was a pale

disk in a creamy vanilla sky. He watched rays of light dance on the snow-covered mountaintops. Yolanda was a doctor. Her parents had nearly gone broke putting her through medical school. By knocking her up, he had inherited her financial obligation to keep them afloat. It hadn't seemed like such a scary proposition, until now.

"I overnighted you money yesterday," he said. "When you get it, send some to your mother."

"Oh, Gerry," Yolanda said, "what are you doing out there? You don't return my calls, and now you're sending money? Where did you get it?"

Gerry felt his cheeks burn. He loved Yolanda more than anything else in the world, but he had to get off the phone right now.

"I've got to get back to class."

"Why won't you answer me?"

"I did answer you. Everything is under control. You've gotta trust me."

"I love you," his wife said, suddenly sounding frightened.

"I love you, too. Good-bye."

He killed the connection. Soon he was on the highway driving back toward Calhoun's house. This time he kept under the speed limit while his mind wrestled with his situation. In the last six months, he'd maxed out ten different credit cards. On top of that, there was the overdue mortgage and car payments. He guessed he owed fifty grand on top of what he'd sent Yolanda yesterday.

He took a deep breath as he pulled down

Calhoun's bumpy driveway. He could get his hands on the money, but it wouldn't be easy.

It never was.

CHAPTER 7

Wily and Valentine finished their coffee and walked to the front of the Acropolis. By the front doors was the garishly lit alcove that housed One-Armed Billy, the world's biggest slot machine. A bus tour of blue-hairs stood on line, waiting to take a crack at the thirty-million-dollar jackpot.

"You know," Wily said, "the best thing that ever happened to us was Nola Briggs and Frank Fontaine trying to rip Billy off."

"Business that good?"

"Billy's is. The tour buses bring a thousand retirees a day. You're a hero to these people."

Valentine laughed. The attempted heist had been made into an asinine TV movie. A young Hollywood actor with wavy hair and bulging muscles had played Valentine's role. He had watched half the program before turning it off.

They entered the alcove. Joe Smith—all seven feet, three hundred pounds of him—sat on a stool next to Billy. Joe had been there during the heist and been diverted away from Billy by a staged fight in the casino. Joe had gotten to play himself in the TV movie and looked like he was enjoying his newfound celebrity. Eight-by-ten glossies, signed and framed, were on sale on a table beside him.

"Hey Joe, how's it going?" he said.

Joe smiled. He was getting his picture taken with an elderly fan. Picking up a mike off a table, he said, "Ladies and gentlemen, we have a special guest with us. The man responsible for stopping the heist in the movie *Grift Sense*. The one and only Tony Valentine."

The line of retirees ohhed and ahhed. The elderly fan clapped her hands together in delight. Brushing past Valentine, she disappeared into the casino lobby.

"What brings you to town?" Joe asked.

"He just saved our ass again," Wily piped in.

Joe scratched his chin like a great thinker. "Let me guess. You stopped the jumper."

Valentine acknowledged that he had. "You like being famous?"

"Beats working," Joe replied.

The elderly fan returned to the alcove, looking annoyed. "Tony Valentine wasn't in the lobby," she said. "Where is he?"

Joe pointed at the real McCoy. She looked Valentine over from head to toe.

"Really?" she asked skeptically.

"People can be cruel," Wily said as they walked outside. The fountains had just come on, the statues of Nick's ex-loves getting their midday shower. Wily's cell phone went off. Ripping it from his pocket, he stared at its face.

"The boss," he said. Turning it on, he said, "Hey Nick, what's up?"

Valentine mouthed the words *See you* and started to walk away. Wily motioned with his hand for him to stop. "Yeah, Valentine's right here," he said into the phone. "I know he saved the day. You want him to come over?" Wily covered the mouthpiece. "Nick wants to thank you in person."

"I need to go find my son."

"Nick's got spies all over town," Wily said. "If anyone can track Bart Calhoun down, it's him. Come on."

Valentine considered it. Nick had been in Las Vegas forever and knew everybody. He was also usually good for a few laughs.

"For lunch?" he asked.

Wily took his hand away from the phone. "Valentine wants to know if you're going to feed him." The head of security covered the phone. "Nick says sure, if you'll promise to tell the story of how you caught Nola and Frank Fontaine."

"To who?" Valentine asked.

"Nick's new wife."

Nick's bride was named Wanda Lovesong. According to Wily, the English language did not contain enough adjectives to describe what she looked like. Driving to Nick's palatial estate on the outskirts of town, Wily explained how she and Nick had met.

"You know how Nick's a sucker for beautiful women," Wily said.

"His Achilles' heel," Valentine said.

"There you go. Well, he gets a distress call a few months ago from a promoter named Santo Bruno. Seems Santo is staging the Miss Nude World contest, and his venue backed out on him at the last minute."

"The Miss what?"

"You heard me," Wily said, grinning as he stared at the highway. "The hundred best strippers and exotic dancers in the country compete for prizes. It's a real scene."

"What's the grand prize? A new wardrobe?"

Wily slapped the wheel. "That's a good one. Anyway, Santo asked Nick to hold the event at the Acropolis, *and* be a judge. Well, you know Nick's weakness for naked broads. He said yeah, and we got to host the event. Craziest weekend of my entire life."

"Did you see the contest?"

"Wouldn't have missed it if the place was on fire. The talent show was amazing."

Nick's place was up ahead, a lush, sprawling estate surrounded by other sprawling estates, all in the middle of nowhere. That was the thing about Las Vegas: Being in the desert, *everything* was in the middle of nowhere.

Wily drove down the elongated driveway without

slowing down. Two cars sat beneath the pillared front entrance: Nick's black Cadillac and a pink Jaguar convertible with a vanity plate that said LITLMISS. As they approached the front door, Valentine said, "So how did Nick end up getting hitched?"

Wily pressed the front doorbell. Moments later, the door buzzed, and Wily grabbed the handle then glanced at him. "One hundred of the best strippers in America were at the Acropolis. Wanda stayed."

They entered the ten-thousand-square-foot monstrosity that Nick had salvaged through six messy divorces. The place had changed, the paintings of nymphs engaged in orgies replaced with classic English landscapes. Gone, too, were the anatomically enhanced statues of the famous Greek gods. Valentine's favorite piece of furniture—the marble bar shaped like a cock—had been whittled down, and now resembled a lima bean. Grabbing two sodas from the bar, Wily headed down a long hallway toward the back.

"Nick's in the bedroom. He's always in the bedroom."

"One question," Valentine said.

"Shoot."

"Did Wanda win the contest?"

Wily stopped at the double mahogany doors to Nick's bedroom. Lifting his hand to knock, he said, "You're kidding, right?" and rapped loudly.

★　　★　　★

"We're all friends here," a voice called from within.

They entered the master bedroom. Nick's bachelor pad had been transformed into a Laura Ashley showroom, and the little Greek lay propped up on pillows on his gigantic bed. He was dressed in a satin robe, and as he jumped out of bed, his manhood was displayed for all the world to see.

"Tony, how you been?" he said, whacking Valentine on the arm while pulling his robe together. He smelled like cheap perfume, and Valentine gagged on his reply.

"No complaints. I hear you tied the knot."

"Yeah. They say number seven's the charm."

Valentine heard the bathroom door open, and a pair of feet approach. He turned slowly, expecting to be overwhelmed, and was not disappointed when he laid eyes on Nick's bride. Wanda Lovesong was a shade under six feet, with flaxen blond hair, too much makeup, and a body worth fighting a war over. That she wore a toga like the women in Nick's casino only added to the allure. Valentine realized his mouth was hanging open, and he snapped it shut. Wanda demurely offered her hand. He took it.

"I saw you on TV earlier," she said breathlessly. "That took courage to do what you did."

She flashed a smile, and Valentine smiled back. It was shameless flirting, and it helped erase the sting of the woman at the Acropolis who'd found him too old. Out of the corner of his eye, he saw Nick grimace, not enjoying being upstaged.

61

"A real hero, except his pants fell down," Nick said.

"Airline lost his luggage," Wily explained.

"You need pants, I've got pants," Nick said. Crossing the room, he flung open the door to his clothes closet and motioned for Valentine to follow him inside. Nick was short, and Valentine didn't think he'd have anything that fit, but saw no point in rubbing it in. As he entered, Nick said, "What's your waist size?"

"Thirty-five."

"Stop bragging."

Nick nosed around his seemingly endless collection of clothes, then stuck his head through the open closet door. "We may be a few minutes," he told Wanda. "Why don't you and Wily go whip something up."

"You hungry, honey?" his bride asked.

"Just for you, baby."

"Want a Wanda sandwich?"

Nick said *Heh, heh, heh* under his breath. As they departed and Valentine started to look through the pants, he heard Nick come up behind him.

"Hey," Nick said.

Valentine turned and found his host standing next to him. The fun had gone out of the little Greek's eyes. "None of these clothes fit you," he said.

Valentine nearly said *No kidding* but decided to shelve it.

"You going to tell me what the hell's going on?"

"I don't know what you're talking about," Valentine said.

Nick stuck his arm behind a rack of silk jackets and pulled out a baseball bat. It was a Louisville Slugger, and had Mark McGwire's name on the throat. Nick gripped the bat with both hands, his eyes never leaving Valentine's face.

"Want me to beat it out of you?"

"You're serious," Valentine said.

"Dead serious," his host replied.

CHAPTER 8

As a cop, Valentine had never done well with threats. People brandishing weapons particularly annoyed him. Knives, guns, baseball bats, they were all throwbacks to the good old days when people lived in caves and settled their differences through violence and bloodshed.

Stepping forward, he grabbed Nick's wrists, wrenched the baseball bat from his grasp, and within seconds had him writhing on the closet floor.

"Let me go! Let me go!" Nick begged, gnashing his teeth.

"Promise you won't threaten me again."

"I promise I won't threaten you again!"

Of all the casino owners in Las Vegas, Nick's word meant something. Valentine released him, and Nick sat on the floor rubbing his wrists. Then he tried to stand, only his balance wasn't there. Agewise, they were about the same, only Nick hid his through dyed hair, dyed eyebrows, and cosmetic surgery that made his face look like he'd gotten caught in a wind tunnel. Valentine pulled him to his feet.

"Why did you do that?" he asked, still holding the bat.

"It's a long story," Nick replied.

"I love long stories."

They went into the bedroom. Nick pointed at the couch in the room's main sitting area. Valentine lay the bat on the floor, then sat down and watched his host pull up a chair. When Nick spoke, his tone was somber. "Things have been kind of hairy lately."

"Is that an apology?"

"Yeah."

"Mind explaining?"

Nick leaned in close. "I got a call this morning from the FBI. A stripper at the Pink Pony got murdered last night. She used to come into my casino and cash in chips. Claimed guys gave them to her for dances.

"FBI says they want to come in and review all my surveillance tapes, which means closing down my surveillance control room for a few days. They specifically want to see if this stripper ever cashed in a chocolate chip."

"A five-thousand-dollar chip?"

"Yeah. The Acropolis doesn't hand many of those out. I told the FBI that. Know what they said? If I didn't cooperate, they'd take my gaming license away."

"Can they do that?"

Nick threw his arms in the air. "That's a good fucking question. FBI says that the U.S. Patriot

Act gives them the right to shut me down if I don't cooperate."

"You going to do it?"

"I don't have any other choice," Nick said. "I talked them into waiting until Monday, so I don't lose my weekend business."

"You the only casino in town they called?"

"They're threatening a bunch of us. And all over the same thing. Chocolate chips."

"So she was laundering them."

"That would be my guess," Nick said.

Valentine looked at the baseball bat lying on the floor. Then he looked at Nick. "Why did you threaten me, anyway?"

"You once told me you were tight with the FBI. I figured they sent you to check up on me."

It was funny how people interpreted things. Valentine had never been tight with the FBI. He'd known Peter Fuller, the bureau's director, since his early days in Atlantic City. He couldn't utter Fuller's name without cursing, and he guessed Nick had misconstrued that to mean they were tight.

"I'd never spy on you," Valentine said.

Nick leaned back in his chair. "Want to do a job for me?"

"Not really." His host grimaced, and Valentine said, "I need to find my son."

"Where is he?"

"Bart Calhoun's card-counting school. Wherever that is."

Nick scratched his chin. "Calhoun is a hard man to pin down. I'll make you a deal. I'll find Calhoun if you figure out how Lucy Price ripped me off."

"You think she's a cheater?"

"She's a slot queen and has a history of losing. This is the first time she's played blackjack, and she won twenty-five grand. Those don't go together."

Valentine thought back to his encounter with Lucy Price. He would not have pegged her a cheater. He said, "I'll look at the surveillance tapes, if you think it will do any good."

"So we have a deal?"

He nodded, then said, "I could also use a room in your hotel."

"Done," Nick said.

They sealed the deal with a handshake. There was a light tapping on the bedroom door. Nick said, "Do you mind, we're having sex?" and a giggling Wanda entered balancing a tray of food on her upturned palm.

"Here you go, Nicky," she said proudly. "Campbell's chicken noodle soup, and baloney sandwiches with the crusts cut off. Your favorite lunch."

She placed the tray on the coffee table, and Valentine noticed that her breasts, which were barely contained by her low-slung top, had several bread crumbs sprinkled on them. Nick pointed at the crumbs and said, "Is that dessert, baby?"

A harsh look clouded Wanda's face. Leaning

over, she gave him a resounding slap in the puss, then marched out. Nick blushed as he picked up one of the soup bowls.

"She doesn't like it when I talk crude around company. Pass the salt, will you?"

CHAPTER 9

At one o'clock that afternoon, Pete Longo was released under his own recognizance by the Metro Las Vegas Police Department, having been suspended without pay from the force, and having been advised that he was considered a prime suspect in the murder of Kris Blake, the stripper he'd been having an affair with.

Being named a suspect didn't surprise Longo. His alibi from the previous night had yet to check out. It would, since it involved two other cops he'd been drinking with. They would corroborate that he hadn't been at Kris's townhouse at the time of her killing. And then he'd be clean.

Only clean was a relative term. The shame would be still there. From that, he knew there was no escape.

He lived halfway between Las Vegas and Henderson, in a new development a stone's throw off the Boulder Highway. It was a decent neighborhood, with monthly block parties and friendly dogs that didn't need to be tied to chains. And the schools were good. Both his daughters had seen their grades go up.

He lived at the end of a cul-de-sac. Pulling up the driveway, he felt his face go flush. He'd called Cindi from the station house and spilled his guts to her. Better for him to tell her than some newspaper reporter, he'd thought at the time.

Now he wasn't so sure. His clothes were piled in the middle of the front yard. Next to them was an open suitcase. The message was clear. *Leave.*

He got out and started to pack his things. At the bottom of the pile he found his one good suit all balled up. Cindi was really pissed.

He put his knee to the suitcase to shut it and realized he was shaking. Except for the time he'd puked in the punch bowl at his high school prom, he'd never been more humiliated in his life. The curtains over the living room window were fluttering, and he glanced up. Were his daughters inside spying on him? He tried to imagine what they were thinking. *Dad's a real piece of shit* was all that came to mind.

Back on the highway, he started to calm down. His daughters would eventually come around. They'd forgiven Clinton, hadn't they? Cindi was a different story. He couldn't see them mending this bridge.

He drove into Henderson. It was one of Las Vegas's bedroom communities, with shopping malls and subdivisions sprouting out of the desert every week. It also had casinos, but they didn't make much money. The locals knew better.

He pulled into a fast-food drive-through. Ahead of him, two punks in a BMW were razzing an employee inside the restaurant. He punched his horn, and the driver sauntered over. A sixteen-year-old wearing designer clothes. "What's eating you?" he snarled.

Longo showed his badge. "You are. Leave."

"But we haven't gotten our food."

"That's the price for being assholes."

Longo ate lunch in the parking lot. He loved Vegas, couldn't imagine living anywhere else. But it could happen. Somehow it had never occurred to him that by having an affair, he could lose everything in his life that mattered.

His cell phone went off. He pulled it out of his pocket and stared at its face. It was Jimmy Burns, his former partner.

"Do you have any idea how much trouble you're in?" Jimmy asked.

"Yeah," he said wearily. "I sure do."

They met up in the men's room of Main Street Station, an old-time casino on Fremont Street.

The men's room had two unique features. The first was the urinals, which were set against a graffiti-covered piece of the Berlin Wall and had been sprayed by every drunk who'd ever set foot in the place. The second was the hidden entrance that only a few people knew of. He pumped Jimmy's hand.

"Hey, shrimp."

"Hey, fat boy."

"Thanks for coming."

"It's been a slow day."

Jimmy ran the city's elite Homicide Division, wore tailored suits, and got his hair cut every few weeks. For a town into image, Jimmy projected a good one, and it was no secret that he was being groomed to one day run the show.

The hidden entrance was covered by a large mirror. Jimmy pushed the mirror inward and stepped through the space. Longo followed him down a darkened hallway and out the casino's back door.

As they neared Fremont Street, both men instinctively glanced over their shoulders. No one was following them, and they crossed under a gigantic steel canopy called the Fremont Street Experience.

The Experience was a seventy-million-dollar gamble designed to draw tourists to old downtown. Every hour, the canopy was transformed into a ballet of mesmerizing images created by two million multicolored synchronized lights. It was a blast to watch, yet the only people who ever came were kids.

"How about Fitzgerald's," Jimmy suggested.

"Sounds like a plan."

Fitzgerald's was a smoky, low-ceilinged joint with penny slot machines, nickel roulette, and sixteen-ounce margaritas for a buck. Locals went to Fitzgerald's when they found themselves longing for the good old days. An escalator took them upstairs, and they grabbed the last table at a bar called Lucky's Lookout.

A waitress appeared before their asses hit their seats. A big gal, with monster arms. Jimmy ordered two drafts. She left, and Longo put his elbows on the table.

"What are you hearing?"

"Bad stuff. How well did you know this stripper?"

"I met her six weeks ago."

"She was under investigation by the FBI."

Longo felt an invisible weight press down on his shoulders. FBI meant wiretaps and tails. How many pictures of them did they have? And phone calls?

"What's she suspected of doing?"

Jimmy lowered his eyes to the water-marked table, then lifted them slightly so there was no mistaking his seriousness. "Money laundering. They searched your girlfriend's townhouse, and the grounds. They found a gym bag with casino chips in a Dumpster."

Longo shifted uncomfortably. The waitress brought their beers and saved him, but only for a minute. Had he wiped the gym bag clean of prints? No, he hadn't.

"I found the bag under the kitchen table," he said.

Jimmy let out a little shudder. It was a habit he'd picked up after he'd become a homicide detective. "So you knew about it?"

"No, I didn't know about it. I found it this morning, right after I discovered her."

"Why did you hide it?"

"I knew it would lead to questions I couldn't answer."

"You don't know what she was doing?"

Longo shook his head. He'd been 100 percent right. Nobody cared about Kris's murder. All they cared about were the casino chips beneath her kitchen table.

"You didn't think you were being used?" Jimmy asked him.

"Used how?"

"Like a shield she could hide behind."

"No."

He saw Jimmy gaze out the window and up the street past the El Cortez Hotel, an area filled with psycho panhandlers, porno palaces, pickpockets, and the world's most depressing strip of cockroach-infested motels. It had been their first beat together and seemed like another lifetime ago. Jimmy's gaze returned.

"You want to save your ass?"

"Of course I want to save my ass."

"Then here's the deal," Jimmy said. "The department is going to close ranks around you. You had an affair with this chick, and that's it. The FBI may haul you in, so don't stray from your story. We're not offering you up as a sacrificial lamb."

Longo stared at the foam cresting the lip of his mug. He was going to keep his job, and some semblance of his old life. He wanted to lean across the table and give Jimmy a bear hug. Instead, he said, "Thanks, man."

Jimmy sipped his beer. "There's something I need to ask you."

"What's that," Longo said.

"You looked through the gym bag, didn't you?"

Longo nodded that he had.

"Did you find any chocolate chips?"

Longo pushed his chair back. "You accusing me of something?"

Jimmy gave him a mean stare. "Three different cops touched that bag after you put it in the Dumpster. The FBI needs to know, Pete. Did you find any chocolate chips?"

So that was why Jimmy had called him. The fucking FBI. From his pocket Longo removed the five-thousand-dollar chip he'd pilfered from the bag and tossed it to his ex-partner.

"Just one," he said.

Jimmy pocketed the chip. Then he threw down a five-spot for the beers. The waitress hit the table like a shark, and didn't ask if he wanted change. Jimmy rose from his chair. "You see who the gym bag belonged to?"

"Yeah, I saw it," Longo said.

"Know him?"

"A little."

"Stay away from him, if you know what's good for you," Jimmy said, and then walked out of the bar.

★　　★　　★

Longo stayed in his chair and drank his beer. Then he drank Jimmy's beer. The waitress circled the table, wanting to give it to another couple.

"No," he said firmly.

She gave him a hostile look and left. Out on the street, a man's recorded voice filled the air. The Fremont Street Experience was about to begin. Longo shifted his chair to watch and heard his cell phone ring. He pulled it out and stared at the face. The caller was Lou Snyder, a guy in town who was wired in the hospitality business.

"Hey," Longo said. "Find anything?"

"Valentine stayed at Sin last night," Lou said. "He checked out this morning. I think he's still in town, though."

"Why do you think that?"

"I accessed the airlines' computers, couldn't find his name on any departing flights," Lou said. "He also still has his rental car."

The Experience's light show had started and was accompanied by blaring *Star Wars* music. It was the kind of goofy thing that Kris loved. He thought about calling her, then remembered she was dead. He swiped at his eyes with his sleeve.

"My guess is, Valentine's staying at the Acropolis," Lou went on. "Word on the street is that he and Nick Nicocropolis are tight. If you want, I can call over there, find out what room he's in."

Longo thought about Jimmy's warning and decided to ignore it. He wanted to know why

Valentine had shot her. What had Kris done to deserve that? The police wouldn't ask him, because the police didn't give a shit. All they cared about were the chips.

"Do it," he said.

CHAPTER 10

Valentine finished eating lunch with Nick, then rode back to town with Wily. He hadn't talked to Mabel all day, and he pulled out his cell phone and called her.

Mabel Struck was the most important woman in his life. An attractive southern lady who'd befriended him after Lois had died, she now ran his business, solved an occasional minor scam, and fed him when she thought he needed a home-cooked meal. Next to his late wife, he'd never known a better person.

"Grift Sense," she answered cheerfully.

"Is this a rare coin shop?"

"There you are! I was starting to get worried about you."

"You holding down the fort without me?"

"I got a Federal Express package this morning from the Yeslenti Indian tribe in northern California," Mabel said. "They also sent a certi-fied check with your usual fee."

"What's the problem?"

Mabel read from a letter included in the package. The Yeslentis had opened a casino twelve months ago. It was nothing more than a giant circus tent in the middle of a parking lot, and had none of the hysterical architecture of Las Vegas or Atlantic City, yet it had already pulled in a hundred million bucks.

The problem the Yeslentis were having was at their blackjack games. A pair of gamblers had been winning regularly, and the tribe suspected marked cards. Finishing the letter, Mabel said, "They sent six decks of cards from the casino."

"Did you look at them?"

She hesitated. One of the great things about Mabel was that she wasn't afraid to take the initiative. Admitting it was another matter, and he said, "You did."

"Well, yes."

"Find anything?"

"I put the decks under the ultraviolet light on your desk. They haven't been treated with luminous paint. There aren't any obvious marks or nicks, either. I know you said there are marked decks that are nearly invisible to the naked eye, but I don't think these cards are marked like that."

"Why not?"

"I went onto the tribe's Web site and looked at their setup. The lighting in those tents is horrible. You start squinting at the backs of the cards, people are going to get suspicious. I think the marks are there, but somehow I can't see them."

Valentine closed his eyes and thought for a few moments. "Are the cards Bees?"

79

She let out a laugh. "Why yes, how did you know?"

"It's an old trick, dates back to the Wild West. The cards aren't marked, but a cheater can tell what value they are."

"That's some trick," Mabel said.

"Open up the center drawer on my desk," he said. "There should be a brand-new deck of Bees. Take it out and put it next to the cards the Yeslentis sent you."

He waited while Mabel found the deck. Through the car's windshield he could see the surreal skyline of the Las Vegas Strip. Wily had been driving for ten minutes, yet didn't seem any closer to their destination.

"Done," Mabel said. "Well, would you look at that! It's the sides of the cards that are different. Your deck has lines running up the sides that are in perfect alignment. The deck from the reservation casino has irregular lines running up the sides. How clever."

"They're called sorts," he said. "A deck of cards is cut from a sheet. That way, all the cards have identical markings on the backs and the sides. To construct a deck of sorts, the cheater buys a few cases of Bees and finds decks that are cut off-center. He removes the high-valued cards from an off-center deck, and mixes them with low-valued cards from a regular deck. That's all he needs to know."

"Who should the Yeslentis arrest?"

"They need to determine who's bringing the cards to the table. It might be a pit boss, or a shift manager. They should watch him for a few days, see who he's tight with. For all they know, he may be the ringleader of a gang."

Mabel wrote down what he'd said, then read it back to him. It sounded better than anything he could write, and he told her so. Then he said, "How's Yolanda? How's the baby?"

"Yolanda is coming over later. Baby's still cooking."

"Tell her I said hi."

They had reached the Strip. He started to say good-bye, then remembered that he'd called Mabel for a reason. Instead of spending a few hours looking at surveillance tapes of Lucy Price, why not have Mabel find out if she was a cheater?

"I need you to look up a woman in Creep File. She may be a blackjack cheater. I'll give you her profile." Closing his eyes, he described the woman he'd talked out of committing suicide that morning.

"You sound like you got a good look at her," Mabel said.

He opened his eyes. He detected a hint of jealousy in his neighbor's voice. That's wasn't like her, and he said, "We were on TV together. Talk to you later."

Mabel hung up the phone with a smile on her face. Leave it to Tony to end the conversation with a puzzle. *On TV doing what?* she'd wanted to ask.

She booted up the computer on his desk. The study was her favorite room in Tony's house, its walls lined with a treasure trove of crooked gambling equipment and gambling books. But when it came to catching cheaters, the most important thing in the room was a computer program called Creep File. The program contained the names of five thousand cheaters and con artists whom Tony had tangled with during his twenty years policing Atlantic City's casinos. When it came to catching cheaters, there was nothing like it.

Pulling up a blank profile, she typed in Lucy Price's particulars. Then she ran it against the other profiles in Creep File. No matches came up.

She reread what she'd typed, just to be sure she'd filled in all the boxes. There was something unusual about Lucy Price's profile, only she couldn't figure out what it was.

Then she had an idea. Tony said the best way to tell if something wasn't right was to compare it to something that *was* right. She went into the database and pulled out a profile of Patty Layne, one of the greatest casino cheaters of all time. She compared it to Lucy Price's profile and immediately saw the difference.

For the heck of it, she pulled up three more women. And saw the same thing.

Tony had known Lucy Price's height, weight,

and age. For the other four women, he had put in estimates. He hadn't known exactly, so he'd guessed.

He hadn't guessed on Lucy Price.

Tony was old-fashioned when it came to the opposite sex. And he rarely talked to strange women when he was working. Too fearful of being set up, she guessed. So how had he known so much about Lucy Price? There could only be one explanation. He was attracted to her.

She shook her head sadly. She loved her boss, but had also accepted that he didn't quite love her. Not that he didn't treat her well; he was an absolute prince in that department. He paid her a wonderful salary with terrific benefits, made her laugh every day, took her out to meals and to the movies, and was willing to share just about everything he knew. But he didn't love her. And there wasn't a damn thing she could do about it.

Hearing the front door chime, she went to greet her visitor.

Yolanda stood on the stoop, clutching a paper bag to her pregnant belly. Her eyes were bloodshot, and Mabel realized she'd been crying. It was a nasty day; rain pelted her shoulders like stones thrown by wicked little boys. She ushered her inside.

"Drink it," Mabel said, offering her a glass of milk in the kitchen. "It will make you feel better."

Yolanda drank the milk in one big gulp. She had

put the paper bag between her legs. It fell forward, the mail spilling across the faded linoleum floor. Leaning down, Mabel squinted at the return addresses on the envelopes. Credit card companies. Lots and lots of credit card companies.

"Bills?"

Yolanda nodded. Eight months' pregnant and she still looked intoxicatingly beautiful. Beneath the pretty face and figure was a wonderful person: a doctor who sent money to her elderly parents in Puerto Rico. She and Gerry had moved across the street a month ago, and Gerry had gone to work for Tony. Not an easy arrangement, but so far it seemed to be working. Mabel refilled Yolanda's glass and one for herself.

"Gerry's in trouble," Yolanda said.

"Did you talk to him?"

"Yes, this morning."

"How did it go?"

"All he did was lie to me." Yolanda's eyes shifted to her pregnant belly and she smiled. "The baby's doing the cha-cha. Mark my words, kid's going to be a dancer." She lifted her eyes, and met Mabel's stare. "Gerry never lies to me. It's why I've stayed with him. Gerry's no angel, but deep down he's a decent person. You know what I mean?"

"Of course," Mabel said.

"But he's not acting so decent anymore," Yolanda said. "I just got a call from a lady at American Express. She'd seen a lot of activity on Gerry's credit card and wanted to be sure he was making the charges. I asked her to read me what he'd bought."

Yolanda put her glass on the table's edge and leaned forward. "He bought a gun."

"In Las Vegas?"

"Yes. A Smith and Wesson Model Sixty-five." Yolanda fished a square of paper from the pocket of her blouse. "I went on the Internet to a gun dealer's Web site. This is what I found posted about it. 'The Model Sixty-five is made of stainless steel. It has a serrated front ramp sight, exposed hammer, and holds six rounds of three fifty-seven ammo. It is a hefty, solid piece of American steel, built to handle the violent three fifty-seven round. Shot at night, the unburned powder from the bullet will make a huge yellow flash and a noise you don't want to hear inside a building without protection. This gun is an attention-getter.' "

"Oh, my," Mabel said.

Yolanda let the paper float to the floor. It did a butterfly spiral and landed atop the bills. She shook her head in the way that people do when they've given up hope.

"Gerry is in real trouble," she said. "I can feel it in my bones."

Mabel remembered her two pregnancies, when the hormones raging in her body during her last trimester had been on the verge of going out of control. *The more Yolanda stresses,* she thought, *the more it's going to affect the baby.*

"This is terrible, Yolanda. I'm going to tell Tony."

"I hope . . ." She let her voice trail off.

"What?"

"It's not too late."

Mabel patted her arm reassuringly. "Don't worry. Tony's gotten Gerry out of plenty of jams before."

CHAPTER 11

The first thing Valentine did when he reached the Acropolis was call Gerry. He hadn't told his son he was coming to Las Vegas, and realized it might come as a shock when they eventually did hook up. So he decided to break it to him gently.

"Hey, Gerry, this is Pop," he said, getting his son's voice mail. "I was thinking about coming out to Vegas. What do you say we hook up? Call me on my cell."

He hung up feeling guilty as hell. They hadn't done much together when Gerry was growing up, and trying to sound chummy felt awkward. He hoped Gerry's relationship with his own kid was different than theirs had been.

The next thing he did was look for his luggage. He pedaled the bike he'd borrowed that morning over to Sin and inquired at the concierge desk.

"It hasn't arrived yet," the concierge said, staring at her computer screen.

"You can still keep the bike," he said.

She frowned, not getting the joke. He started to

leave, then halted at the glass front doors. He was forgetting something. Something *really* important.

His fee.

Mabel was always chiding him about not collecting his money. Maybe it was because he'd lived most of his life broke and never put much value in it. He went back to the concierge and explained the situation. The woman on duty called upstairs to Chance Newman's office.

"Go to the cashier's cage on the south side of the casino," she said, drawing a map as complicated as a football play on a sheet of paper. "Hugo, Mister Newman's bodyguard, will meet you there. He'll have the money, and your equipment."

Valentine entered Sin's casino with the map in his outstretched hand. The casino was enormous, its motif a boozy interpretation of ancient Rome. As he walked, he imagined he was giving the boys upstairs in surveillance fits. He'd come in on a bike and was now doing a serpentine stroll. Seeing a smoky dome in the ceiling, he waved.

Hugo awaited him at the cage. He had a wrestler's body and the face of a mad Bulgarian. He opened a leather bag and let Valentine see the stacks of money and Deadlock equipment lying inside.

"Your fee and your equipment," Hugo said.

"Count it," Valentine said.

Hugo's face turned an Eastern European mean. "I already did that."

Valentine thought he'd seen Hugo playing

volleyball with the nuns, but asked him to count it again anyway. Then added, "If you don't mind."

Hugo was wearing a walkie-talkie setup that was practically invisible. Valentine sensed that someone was talking to him, and he watched him hand the bag through the bars to the cashier.

"Do it," Hugo said.

The cashier counted the money. It was all there. Valentine took the Deadlock from the bag and made sure the guts hadn't been ripped out. Then he signed a receipt for the money.

"How long you been out of the slammer?"

Hugo's mouth opened, then snapped shut.

"You didn't get those muscles hitting the gym a few nights a week."

"You are a Webster," Hugo said.

A *Webster* was casino slang for a floor person who thought he knew everything. Valentine said, "I want you to tell Chance Newman something."

"What's that?"

"Tell him I'm no pigeon. You know what that is?"

Hugo smiled. "Everyone's favorite customer."

"That's right. Chance thought that by making me walk the casino, I might stop on my way out, make a few bets, and he'd win his money back. Maybe he put a plant at a table to lure me."

"A plant?"

"A house girl, a hooker. Know what those are?"

Hugo touched his lapel. Valentine realized he was turning his walkie-talkie off.

"Get out of the casino, or I'll throw you out," the bodyguard said.

Valentine was impressed he'd strung all those words together himself. As he hoisted the bag off the counter, it occurred to him that something was wrong with this picture. Hugo hadn't touched him. Security *always* grabbed troublemakers. But why hadn't Hugo touched him? He looked like he could lift a car.

"Know what they say about guys who lift weights?"

Hugo shook his head.

"They say they have little dicks. If they had big dicks, they wouldn't spend so much time in the gym."

Hugo still didn't want to touch him. Valentine walked away shaking his head.

He checked into the Acropolis, put his twenty-five grand into the hotel vault, and rode the elevator still shaking his head. What good was a bodyguard who didn't like to fight?

Nick had comped him into a penthouse suite. In the Acropolis, that meant three high-ceilinged rooms filled with polished chrome and cushy leather, the bizarre color schemes reminiscent of *Rowan & Martin's Laugh-In*. That was the thing about Nick. He loved the old stuff.

He went into his suite and saw a chambermaid's cart sitting in the living room. Chambermaids *never* locked themselves into rooms, and he looked around the suite.

"Anybody home?"

He heard something. He stood by the dining room entrance and stared through a pair of sliding glass doors leading to the outside balcony. No one out there.

Taking off his shoes, he flung them into the dining room. The second shoe struck a flower vase and shattered it. He heard movement inside the kitchen. Picking up a marble ashtray, he walked into the dining room.

A fat guy wearing a stocking over his head came out of the kitchen. His hands were balled into fists, and for a few seconds they danced around each other. The guy looked like he tipped the scales at two-fifty. Big guys usually just ran over people. Not this guy. He had an attitude.

"I thought you knew how to fight," his intruder said.

Valentine held the ashtray like a Frisbee and shook his head.

"Guess that stuff in the movie was bullshit, huh?"

Valentine remembered Hugo's earlier hesitation. "Guess so," he said.

"You're just an old fuck with a dried-up dick, huh?"

He placed the ashtray on the dining room table. "Take your best shot, asshole."

"What did you say?"

"You heard me."

His intruder threw a right hook with a telegraph

attached. Valentine ducked the punch but didn't see the second shot coming, a sneaky uppercut that caught him in the side of the head. Falling backward, he shot his leg out and kicked his intruder squarely in the shin.

The shins were one of the body's weak spots. His intruder howled and danced on one leg. Valentine straightened and felt his head spin. He hadn't been sucker-punched in a long time.

He considered his options. He could sweep his intruder's legs out from under him, or he could flip him. Those were correct ways to deal with an attacker. Only the guy had pissed him off. So he punched him in the face.

His intruder staggered backward, hitting the glass doors leading to the balcony with his head. A thousand spiderwebs magically spread across the glass. He shakily drew a gun and pointed it at Valentine. It was a slimmed-down Glock .45, a weapon favored by detectives with the Metro LVPD.

"Why did you kill her?" he asked.

"Who?" Valentine said.

"Kris Blake. I found your stuff in her town-house. You brought her home from the Pink Pony last night and shot her. Why did you do it?"

"I don't know what you're talking about, pal."

"Tell me, goddamn it."

He sounded like a lovesick boyfriend, not someone who really wanted to shoot him. Valentine said, "My stuff couldn't be at your friend's place, buddy. I don't have any stuff. The airline lost it."

Blood seeped out of the stocking. "Bullshit."

Valentine pointed at the bedroom door on the other side of the suite. "I filled out a lost claim form for my luggage. It's on the night table, lying in the same sleeve as my airline ticket. For Christ's sake, *look* at it."

"If you're lying, I'm going to kill you," he said.

"I'm not lying."

His intruder crossed the dining room. As he opened the bedroom door, a uniformed chambermaid came out, kneed his groin, and ran out of the suite screaming at the top of her lungs. Valentine ducked into the kitchen and grabbed a steak knife from the utensil drawer. Then he glanced around the corner. His intruder was running away. He grabbed a cordless phone off the counter and punched zero.

"It's a beautiful day at the Acropolis," an operator said.

"Help!" he yelled.

Chasing someone with a gun was a stupid idea, and he hunkered down in the kitchen and waited for someone to rescue him. A minute later, Wily appeared, all out of breath. He slid the steak knife back in the drawer and came out of hiding.

"Did you catch him?"

"Who?" Wily said.

"The guy who broke into my room."

Wily shook his head, staring at the broken vase on the floor and the cracked sliding glass doors. "You get in a fight?"

"No, I was recording a sound effects record. Of course I was in a fight." He came over to where the head of security stood. "The guy was six-one, weighed about two fifty, and wore a stocking over his head. How could you miss him?"

Like most guys who ran casinos, Wily hated to be questioned, and he shrugged. "The casino is mobbed, and so is the hotel. You know how it is."

Valentine felt his heart racing. He had reached the age when bad things upset him in ways he could not control. He pulled a chair out from the dining-room table and sat down. After taking several deep breaths, he said, "No, I don't know how it is. Why don't you explain it to me?"

Picking up the phone, Wily called the hotel's maintenance department and ordered new sliding doors for the room. Hanging up, he said, "It's like this. The Acropolis has a hundred eye-in-the-sky cameras. That sounds like a lot, but they can't watch everything. So they watch one area of the casino, then they watch another."

"So?"

"Do the math," Wily said. "One hundred percent of the time, fifty percent of the casino floor isn't being watched. The same is true for the hotel. Things happen that don't get picked up. Like your guy."

"What about security on the floor?" Valentine said.

"What about them?"

"The guy was bleeding from the nose. Think they would have spotted that?"

"You pop him?"

"He's got a thing about heights. Yes, I popped him."

Wily called downstairs. The Acropolis employed ex-cops to patrol the floor. They were sharp guys, and when Wily hung up a few moments later shaking his head, Valentine had his answer. His intruder was someone the guys on the floor all knew.

"Must have disappeared," Wily said sarcastically.

Valentine rose from his chair. The side of his face really hurt. His intruder had said his girl-friend worked at the Pink Pony. So had the dead stripper Nick had told him about. Had to be the same woman.

It was time he paid Bill Higgins a visit. Bill was the director of the Nevada Gaming Control Board and one of the most powerful law enforcement figures in the state. If anyone would know what this was about, it was Bill.

He went into the hall, slammed the door, and listened as the broken sliders came down with a thunderous crash, followed by Wily's string of four-letter expletives. He smiled all the way down in the elevator.

CHAPTER 12

Valentine got his rental car from the Acropolis's valet. The vehicle was a real piece of junk. Roll-down windows, a sputtering heater, and a front seat with enough legroom for a circus midget, all for thirty-nine bucks a day.

Leaving the Acropolis, he followed the signs for Las Vegas Boulevard and soon was driving south into the desert. As the towering casinos grew small in his mirror, he felt himself relax. He'd been offered several lucrative full-time jobs in Las Vegas over the years and always turned them down. He needed to be rooted in reality, and this town was anything but that.

After five miles he hung a left on Cactus Boulevard, and a mile later a right on Hibiscus. It was a newer suburb, with roads seeing blacktop for the first time. Although he didn't remember Bill's address on Hibiscus, he was certain he'd recognize Bill's place when he saw it.

He powered up his cell phone. He considered cell phones one of life's great intrusions and rarely left his on. He had a message in voice mail and retrieved it.

"Tony, please call me," Mabel said. "It's an emergency."

He punched in his work number. His neighbor answered on the second ring.

"What's going on?"

"You must start leaving your cell phone on," she scolded him. "It's Gerry."

"Did you speak to him?"

"Yolanda did earlier. Gerry is involved with something very bad."

What's new, he nearly said.

"Yolanda got a call from American Express," Mabel went on. "They saw a lot of activity on Gerry's credit card. He bought a gun in Las Vegas."

"He did what?"

"A three fifty-seven Smith and Wesson. Yolanda is worried, and so am I."

He saw Bill's place up ahead, a single-story ranch house with a terra-cotta tile roof and all-natural landscaping. The colors were earthy and seemed to bleed beneath the bright sunlight. Slowing down, he said, "I need you to do something for me. Contact every casino boss in Nevada we do business with, and see if you can get the address of Bart Calhoun's school."

"Certainly. May I ask what you're going to do when you find Gerry?"

Wring his neck, he thought. "Bring him home."

"Can I tell Yolanda that?"

"You can tell her whatever you want."

Mabel was silent as he pulled into Bill's driveway. Venting his frustrations on her was juvenile, and he said, "Am I starting to sound like a cranky old man?"

"Yes. I think you need to pack your bags and come home."

"Once my bags get here and I find Gerry, I will."

"Wonderful. Just remember one thing."

"What's that?"

"Start leaving your cell phone on!"

As he got out of the rental, Bill emerged from the house, walking with a metal cane. Bill was a Navajo Indian, a shade under six feet, with a stony face offset by piercing eyes and a full head of hair. The gunshot wound he'd endured in Miami two months ago had been slow to heal, and he was still working from home.

They shook hands on the lawn. Valentine asked him how his leg was holding up. Bill said okay, then asked him about his ear. The same guy who'd shot Bill had blown off Valentine's left ear. Valentine showed him the replacement.

"Is that real skin?" his friend asked.

"Yeah. Don't ask where they grafted it from."

They went inside. Bill's house was U-shaped, the rooms facing a courtyard with a meticulously landscaped Japanese garden complete with a running waterfall and a pond filled with exotic goldfish. The back of the property was walled off, hiding everything from view. Bill and his partner,

Alex, liked it that way. On a coffee table in the living room sat a pitcher with lemon water, and a tray of glasses. Bill filled two, handed him one. They toasted each other's health.

"What brings you to Las Vegas?" Bill asked.

Valentine stared at the waterfall in the garden. Telling Bill he was looking for Gerry was not a good idea. If Gerry was breaking the law, Bill would have to do something about it. He didn't want to put his friend in that position, so instead he said, "I'm doing a consulting job. That's not why I came to see you, though."

Bill sipped his water, waiting for him to continue.

"A guy wearing a stocking paid me a visit earlier. Swore I'd killed his girlfriend, a stripper at the Pink Pony. We mixed it up, and he ran."

"You call the cops?"

"That's the bad part. I think he was a cop."

Bill raised an eyebrow.

"I had lunch with Nick Nicocropolis," Valentine said. "Nick told me about a call he got from the FBI regarding this same stripper. The FBI thinks she was laundering casino chips."

"Any idea how your name got tied up in this?"

"No. Have you heard about the case?"

"Yeah," Bill said. "But I can't talk about it."

"Not even to an old friend?"

It was a Navajo custom not to make eye contact during conversation. Only Bill was staring right at him. He said, "Not even to you. When the FBI contacts you—and trust me, they will—you need to play ball with them. Whatever they want to know, tell them. Otherwise, they'll make your life a living hell."

"But I don't know anything."

"Let them be the judge of that, okay?"

Valentine went back to sipping his water. Bill rarely lectured him. The FBI had him scared, just like they had Nick scared. The bureau had invaded Las Vegas right after 9/11 and, along with setting up an extensive surveillance operation, was watching the casinos' cash flows. They were Big Brother, and making everyone's life miserable.

Bill was still staring at him like a hawk.

"Whatever you say," Valentine said.

"Believe it or not, I was just about to call you," Bill said after they'd both emptied their glasses.

"You missed my cheery voice?"

"I'm reviewing a case, and I'm stumped."

They went to Bill's study in the back of the house. The walls were decorated with Native American artifacts and paintings from New Mexico where Bill's parents lived on a ranch. He was a teenager when his parents learned he was gay, and they sent him away to school. Somehow they had managed to reconcile, and their pictures were scattered around the room.

Bill picked up a remote and the TV on his desk came to life. "This is a tape of a robbery that happened last week. It went down so fast, the casino is convinced it's an inside job. They had their employees submit to polygraphs. Everyone came out clean."

The tape showed a woman in her fifties with a Dolly Parton hairdo standing inside the cage. Her job was to change chips into money when players wanted to cash out. A bearded man appeared at the cage's window and shoved a gun through the bars. The woman put her hands on her head as if to scream. The bearded man motioned with the gun, silencing her.

The woman opened a cash drawer and started pulling out bundles of bills, which she slipped through the bars. The man shoved the money into the pockets of his windbreaker, then sprinted away. The woman again put her hands on her head. Then she tripped an alarm, and all hell broke loose inside the casino.

Bill shut the tape off. "What do you think?"

"Did they polygraph her?" Valentine asked.

Bill broke custom again and stared at him. "The woman in the cage?"

"Yeah. My guess is, they didn't, considering the trauma she went through."

"You think she's involved?"

It seemed so obvious that Valentine paused before answering him. "I counted twelve cash drawers where she was standing. She went to the one with the big bills without the robber telling her to. She's part of it."

101

Bill rewound the tape, watched it again, and laughed out loud. "Now that you mention it, it does look kind of strange, doesn't it?"

It was nearly three o'clock, and Valentine realized he wasn't going to find his son by hanging out with Bill. He said good-bye and started to leave, then noticed a large Federal Express box sitting on Bill's desk. The shipper was a company in Japan, the receiver Chance Newman. The top was sliced open, and he glanced inside.

"That was intercepted yesterday by our friends at FedEx," Bill explained. "The shipping instructions say the contents are PalmPilots, only they're really card-counting computers. I called Chance Newman, asked him what was up. He said he's giving them to his surveillance people to help track counters."

Chance's explanation to Bill made perfect sense. The easiest way to spot card-counters was by tracking their play with a computer. There were several good ones on the market. Only the devices Chance had bought from Japan weren't computers. They were Deadlocks.

It had been a day filled with troubling questions, and now Valentine had another. Why had Chance paid him twenty-five thousand dollars to explain an illegal device that he obviously already knew about? That was a lot of money to blow, even for someone as rich as Chance.

He waited until Bill's back was turned. Taking

a Deadlock from the box, he slipped it into his pocket and showed himself to the door.

"Talk to you later," he said.

CHAPTER 13

"Hey Gerry, you ready to rumble?"

Gerry lifted his eyes from the men's magazine he was reading. Pash stood in the doorway that separated their motel rooms. He wore jeans and a football jersey that was so large he was swimming in it. Gerry had told him that they made jerseys in his size, but Pash had laughed at his suggestion.

"I want to feel like a gladiator," he said.

Rising from his chair, Gerry went to the window and shut the blinds, then flipped on the TV and blasted the volume. The hotel wasn't responsible for theft, so he'd started taking measures.

"Yeah, I'm ready."

He followed Pash into the adjacent bedroom. As usual, it was trashed. The maid came in the morning and made the beds. By late afternoon, it looked like a tornado had visited.

"Where's your brother?" Gerry asked.

"Getting a soda," Pash said. "We have a new member to our team I want you to meet. Hey Dean, you ready?"

The bathroom door swung open. Out stepped

a guy with a forked beard, glasses, and a baseball cap. He wore jeans and a denim work shirt with multiple food stains. He looked like what gamblers called a scellard, or a scale. A loser.

"Meet Dean Martin," Pash said.

Gerry stared at the disheveled stranger, then at Pash. "Dean Martin? This isn't Dean Martin. He's dead!"

Pash brought his hand to his mouth. "Oh, no!"

"You idiot," the stranger said to Pash. "I told you that was a bad name to use!"

"I didn't realize he was that popular," Pash said.

"Everybody knows Dean Martin," Gerry said. He got close to the stranger and said, "Amin, that you hiding in there?"

Something resembling a smile crossed Amin's lips. He didn't do that very often. For Amin it was no booze, no butts, and no staring at naked chicks. Real introspective, but also a real wizard with numbers. He could do basic math in his head as fast as a computer.

"I really fooled you, huh," Amin said.

Amin had flared his nostrils with pieces of plastic tubing, lowered his forehead by combing his hair straight down, and painted a mole where none had been before. He was a master of disguise, and he had to be. His face was in a data-base of known card-counters called FaceScan. For a fee, a casino could e-mail a player's picture to FaceScan and find out if the player was a counter.

"Sure did," Gerry said. "But you need another name. No more celebrities."

"But it has to be a name we can both remember," Pash chimed in. He had a problem with American names, except for those he'd seen in the movies. "How about James Dean?"

Gerry nixed that with a shake of his head. "That's going to attract attention. You want something that won't seem out of place. How about John Dean? He was a character in *All the President's Men*."

"Ohh," Pash said. "*John Dean*. Yes."

Amin worked his mouth up and down the way he did when he was thinking. He stepped in front of the dressing mirror that hung next to the bed and appraised himself.

"John Dean," he said. "Yeah, that will work."

That night, they took two cars into town. Pash and Amin shared one while Gerry followed in his rental.

Amin parked across the street from Mandalay Bay, and Pash hopped out. They did not want to be seen entering the casino together, or even being in the same car near the casino. Casino surveillance cameras were extremely powerful, especially those used on the outside of buildings. A license plate could be read from a block away.

Pash strolled over to the Glass Pool Inn and stopped to stare at the kidney-shaped, above-ground swimming pool in the parking lot. The pool had seven portholes, allowing bystanders to see the limbs of underwater swimmers. It had been used in many movies, all of which Pash had seen. Amin beeped his horn and drove away.

Gerry pulled off to the side of the road to wait. Tonight they were going to hit the MGM Grand, and the surveillance there was top-notch. Better to take his time. That way, he would not be seen with Pash or Amin until he was inside the casino.

Ten minutes later, he pulled into the MGM's valet area. It was twelve cars wide and looked like an auto show. While he waited for someone to take his car, he took out his cell phone and powered it up. There was a message in voice mail. He retrieved it.

His father, saying he was coming to Las Vegas.

"Just what I need," Gerry muttered.

He erased the message, then turned the phone off. He'd considered calling his father the last four nights. Each time he'd gone into a casino with Pash and Amin, he'd whipped his cell phone out and considered asking his old man to bail him out.

He hadn't made the call.

He wasn't sure why. Maybe it was the invisible pressure of fatherhood that had gotten a stranglehold over him the past few months as Yolanda had grown bigger, and his problems had started to include those that hadn't been born. What was his father's expression? It was time for Gerry to stop trying and start doing.

Maybe that was why he hadn't called his old man.

Gerry entered the lobby a few minutes later, and paused dutifully to stare at the wall of movie screens at the check-in that showed acts playing in the hotel. That was what everyone did, and he didn't want to appear any different.

He took his time, going first to the bar and ordering coffee, then heading across the casino, stopping occasionally to watch folks lose their money. Pash had picked the casino tonight, and now Gerry realized why he'd chosen this one. The MGM was owned by a movie studio, and the casino was filled with famous black and white movie stills.

Nearing the blackjack pit in the back, he saw Amin. Amin was playing third base—the last spot at the table. The seat next to him was open.

Gerry's seat.

"This seat open?" Gerry asked, putting his coffee down at the empty spot. The dealer nodded and so did Amin. Gerry took the seat and tossed two hundred dollars in wilted twenties onto the green felt.

"Changing two hundred," the dealer called out.

Soon Gerry was gambling, ten bucks a hand. He played Basic Strategy and never deviated. His role in the scam was simple. Try not to lose his money too quickly. That was all he had to do.

Amin, on the other hand, was on another

mission. He wasn't supposed to *win* too much. He could win thousands of dollars an hour if he wanted, but then the people staffing the eye in the sky would start studying him and, if they didn't like what they saw, place him under "Special Ops." They would scrutinize his every move, run it through a computer, maybe even start to harass him. It was as much fun as being chased by a police car.

So Amin played it safe and won five hundred dollars an hour. It was a grind, but it rarely drew heat. The system he used was called the Hi-Lo. By assigning +1 and −1 values to the dealt cards, he could determine when the game was favorable to the player, and when it was favorable to house. He would bet accordingly, and almost always come out ahead.

Amin executed Hi-Lo flawlessly. He *always* knew the game's exact count. Bart said even the best counters were only 70 percent accurate. Not Amin. The man was focused.

By ten PM, Gerry was down to fifty dollars and sweating through his clothes.

Amin was up. Way up. To hide his winnings—something gamblers called "rat-holing"—Amin had been palming his hundred-dollar chips, then dumping them in Gerry's half-filled coffee mug. If anyone in surveillance had been paying attention, they would have noticed that Gerry's drink was growing as the evening progressed.

Amin had also started dumping chips into Gerry's jacket pocket. That was okay, except there were so many that Gerry could feel the chips pulling down his coat. Amin was acting so blatant that Gerry almost felt like he was being set up. Finally, he rose from the table, leaving his remaining chips, and said to the dealer, "Where's the john?"

The dealer gave him instructions. Left, right, left, you can't miss it.

Gerry marched through the casino, holding his filled coffee cup, afraid to drink the liquid and expose the chips shimmering just below the surface.

The john had photos of famous Hollywood actors hanging on the walls. He found Pash standing at the urinals and sidled up next to him. Pash was staring at a photo of Cary Grant and said, "The first movie I ever saw was with Cary Grant. It was called *Gunga Din*. He played a character named Archibald Cutter. Have you seen it?"

Gerry shook his head. "Look, we need to talk about Amin."

"The theater was wonderful. You paid for a ticket, walked through a lobby, then went outside into a courtyard and watched the film beneath the stars. I was six years old. When I first saw Cary Grant, I thought to myself—*This is the man I want to grow up to be!*" He burst out laughing. "It was so funny. I thought that as I grew older, I could change my skin and hair color, and look like Cary Grant!"

"Your brother is fucking up," Gerry said through clenched teeth.

Pash pulled up his fly and glanced over his shoulder. The johns were the only place in the casino where there were no surveillance cameras. It was against the law. But that didn't stop people in security from occasionally popping their heads in and having a look around.

"How?" Pash asked.

Gerry showed him the chips in his pocket and his coffee cup.

"Is anyone else at the table winning?" Pash asked.

"No, and that's the problem," Gerry replied. "Everyone else is losing their shirts. But the dealer's tray is being depleted. Someone in surveillance is going to notice, and your brother and I will be fucked."

With one eye on the door, Pash took Gerry's chips and stuffed them into the fanny pack he was wearing. "Pick me up at the Glass Pool Inn in twenty minutes. I'll signal to my brother that we are leaving."

"I'll tell him," Gerry said. "I still haven't cashed out."

Gerry started to leave, and Pash touched his sleeve.

"I'm sorry," he said.

Gerry wanted to tell Pash that it was okay, only it wasn't okay. Amin was a known card-counter. If Gerry got pegged as a member of his team, he'd be photographed and have his face added to Face-Scan's database. He'd never be able to set foot inside a casino again, much less work for his father. He was mad, and Pash knew it.

"*Very* sorry," Pash added.

CHAPTER 14

Out of the corner of his eye, Amin watched Gerry come up to the table, grab his chips, wish everyone good luck, and walk away. Their eyes never met, yet Amin knew what was happening.

Gerry was running out on him.

Amin continued to play. Back in his country, men who broke their promises were made to pay, and often lost a hand, or an eye. Not here in America. It was the thing about Americans that he hated the most. They would change their minds, and their allegiances, whenever it suited them.

He glanced down at his chips. He'd been keeping a running track of his winnings in his head. Over six thousand dollars. It was a lot of money, but he needed to make up for the bag of chips he'd left in the stripper's townhouse the day before.

Kris. Another traitor. Like Gerry, her job had been simple. Every few days, she brought Amin's chips to the casinos and cashed them in at the cage. If anyone questioned her—and someone usually did—she would say that she received them as tips. Strippers did it all the time, and the casinos accepted it.

Only Kris had decided to pull a fast one. She wasn't willing to accept 10 percent as her take. She wanted 20. When Amin protested, she'd threatened him.

"My boyfriend will beat you up," she'd said, lying on the couch in her townhouse. She always wore crummy clothes when Amin came over, saving the G-string and slutty makeup for her customers. "He'll put the screws to you."

"Your boyfriend?" Amin had said skeptically.

"Yeah. Pete Longo. He's a cop."

Amin had tried to play it cool. He didn't think a cop would be stupid enough to date this woman. Sitting on the arm of the couch, he'd said, "Ten percent is standard. Come on."

"I want twenty."

"I can find another girl."

She lit up a joint and blew the disgustingly sweet smoke in his face. "Do that, and I'll tell Pete what you're doing."

"I don't believe you," he said. "There is no Pete Longo."

Kris went into the bedroom and returned with a digital camera. Loaded into its memory were a dozen pictures of her and her beau, a monster of a man with a balding head and a wedding ring and a loose smile that spelled trouble.

The last picture in the camera was of an open wallet. It showed a detective's badge and photo ID. It was the same man in the photo. Pete Longo.

Amin liked to wear his shirt out of his pants,

and he'd reached beneath it and drawn the .357 he'd purchased with Gerry Valentine's credit card that morning. Seeing it, Kris had nearly choked.

"Amin, I was only—"

"Joking?"

Kris smiled. "Yeah."

"I don't believe you."

She offered to have sex with him, as if fucking would lessen the betrayal. They'd gone into the bedroom, and he'd watched her undress and fold her clothes neatly and lay them in a pile. Then she lay on the water bed and motioned for Amin to join her.

She was easily the most beautiful woman he'd ever seen. The tiny brain that hung between his legs wanted to have sex with her, and he'd started to undo his pants.

Then he caught himself. He couldn't do it, not even in a moment of weakness. Screwing Kris would be the beginning of the end. She would destroy his resolve, and then he'd be lost. Lying on top of her, he'd pressed the .357 against her rib cage and pulled the trigger, killing her, as well as his desire to have her.

He snapped back to the present. The pit boss was standing behind the table, whispering to the dealer. The dealer nodded, then removed the cards from the shoe and added them to those in the discard tray.

"What are you doing?" Amin asked.

"Shuffling up," the dealer replied.

The dealer was starting the game over. It was called preferential shuffling, and a favorite method of casinos to thwart card-counters. It meant he'd been spotted by MGM surveillance. Rising, he scooped up his chips, and left the table.

The MGM had four exits. His rental was parked behind the casino, so he took the escalator down to a subterranean mall, and walked past the shops to the exit. The mall was filled with people, and he overheard someone say that a computer convention was in town. Reaching the exit, he spied a destroyer standing by the glass doors, and felt himself shudder.

Most of the big casinos employed destroyers. Their job was to guard the exits and thwart card-counters and cheaters from entering. They worked off hot tips and were financially rewarded when they nailed an undesirable.

The MGM's destroyer was black and built like an American football player. He had a tiny walkie-talkie headset and was talking rapidly. His eyes suspiciously brushed Amin's face. Then he stepped forward and tapped Amin's shoulder.

"Don't touch me," Amin said loudly.

The destroyer dropped his hand. "Let's see some ID."

"You don't have any right to ask for my ID," Amin said.

"Let's step outside."

Amin followed the destroyer through the glass doors. The destroyer stopped, and whipped out

116

his wallet from his back pocket. He was going to read from a card and inform Amin that he was trespassing. Then he would tell Amin never to step foot on MGM property again. Amin would agree and walk away. He'd done it many times, and saw tonight as nothing special.

Only the destroyer had a funny look in his eye as he read from the card. He cocked his head, as if trying to get a better look at Amin through the disguise.

"Don't I know you?"

Amin turned and began walking toward the garage. He knew his rights. He hadn't broken a single law. The MGM couldn't back-room him, like they could with a suspected cheater. *They can't touch me,* he told himself as he fled.

He heard the destroyer keeping pace behind him. This was unusual. He saw a couple walk past and cast him a suspicious look.

"I'm talking to you, brother," the destroyer said.

Amin knew that certain casinos routinely beat up counters. Bart had said it was what had driven him out of the business.

"Keep your hands where I can see them," the destroyer said.

He sounded like a cop. A lot of the casinos hired ex-cops to be destroyers. Still walking, Amin removed his hand from his pocket and let his car keys dangle from his fingertips. "Just my keys," he said.

He stopped at the garage's stairwell. He couldn't

remember on which level his rental was parked, and didn't want to go to the wrong floor.

The destroyer was right behind him. He came up, and pointed an accusing finger in Amin's face.

"I know you."

The third floor, Amin thought. He'd parked in the middle aisle on the third floor. He started up the stairs.

The destroyer grabbed him by the shoulder, and shoved him into the wall. Then he tore away Amin's beard and baseball cap. For a long moment, he stared.

"You."

Amin's keys were also a weapon. A little treasure he'd picked up during his travels. He squeezed the ring, and a stainless-steel three-inch blade popped out. In one swift downward motion, he sliced the destroyer's throat.

The destroyer staggered backward in the stairwell. The blood flowing down his neck shone brightly against his black skin. Amin's aim was good; he'd cut an artery. He raced up the stairs to the third floor and quickly found his car.

Climbing in behind the wheel, he felt his heart beating wildly and took several deep breaths. This was the closest he'd ever come to being caught. Hearing the engine turn over, he screeched backward out of the spot.

The car hit something solid. He threw the vehicle into park and jumped out. The destroyer lay face down on the asphalt behind the car, his legs quivering.

Amin's eyes found the long ribbon of blood running back to the stairwell. For a long moment, he wrestled with what that meant. *What type of man chases someone when he is dying?*

Amin thought he knew. Bending over the destroyer, he pulled his wallet from his pocket. No ID. That was odd. He searched his other pockets. In the destroyer's inner jacket pocket, he found a second wallet, designed to hold business cards. The ID was in there. Amin stared at it, felt himself shudder.

The destroyer was an FBI agent.

Amin backed over him a second time, then drove away.

CHAPTER 15

Valentine had killed his evening cruising the Strip in his rental, looking for Gerry.

It was like searching for a needle in a haystack, but sometimes that approach worked. As a kid, he'd read an O. Henry story about a boy who sees his father's murder, grows up to become a cop, and asks for the beat outside the New York Public Library, his reasoning being that the killer would someday walk past. The killer eventually did, and justice was served.

It was nine thirty when he walked into the Acropolis. Grabbing a house phone, he called upstairs to the surveillance control room and asked for Wily. Friday nights were when casinos made hay, and most security heads worked double shifts.

Wily came on a minute later. "What's up?"

"I want to get my room changed, just in case that guy I tangoed with earlier gets any more stupid ideas," Valentine said.

"No problemo."

"I also want to disappear from the hotel computer."

"You think someone in the hotel told that guy what room you were in?"

"That's exactly what I'm thinking," Valentine said.

He heard Wily's fingers tap a computer keyboard. "Done. I put you in the penthouse, Suite Four. Nick said you agreed to look at the tape of Lucy Price. Mind if I send it up?"

"Go ahead," Valentine said.

He got a key from the front desk and went upstairs. His new suite faced west and afforded a perfect view of the Strip. He called room service, ordered a cheeseburger and fries. His food arrived at the same time as the tape of Lucy Price.

He ate his dinner while sitting on the balcony. He'd left his cell phone on, and now the battery was running down. Every time it beeped, he thought it was his son calling. He stared down at the thousands of people milling on the sidewalks. Gerry was down there; he could feel it in his bones.

He finished his dinner, then went into the suite and popped the tape into the VCR. Going into the kitchen, he grabbed a Diet Coke from the mini fridge and drained half the bottle. He'd read somewhere that artificial sweetener was bad for you, and he imagined that after he died, a doctor was going to cut him open and discover that every artery in his body was clogged with the stuff.

Then he sat a foot away from the giant-screen TV and stared at Lucy Price.

★　　★　　★

121

The pang of recognition he'd felt on the balcony that morning returned. Like being stabbed with a beautiful memory. The tape was black and white, and showed Lucy and two men sitting at a table playing blackjack. Lucy was winning, and the look on her face was pure joy.

He took another swig of soda. Caffeine had a way of making him think clearly, and he watched the cards fly around the table. Lucy acted like she'd never played before, consulting a laminated Basic Strategy card each time she needed to make a decision. Valentine found himself smiling. She *really* was a beginner.

Basic Strategy for blackjack had been developed by a mathematician named Ed Thorp. It was the optimal way to play every hand, based upon the dealer's "up" card. Lucy would stare intently at the dealer's "up" card, then consult her Basic Strategy card.

It was comical to watch. Every time Lucy had to make a decision, the game came to a screeching halt. Casinos let players use Basic Strategy cards because the house still held a minimum 1.5 percent edge. It was enough to beat the daylights out of anyone.

Except Lucy.

After ten minutes, her pile of chips had grown by several thousand dollars. Only Lucy wasn't on a hot streak. She was just winning a few more hands than normal. Since she was betting five hundred dollars a hand, her winnings were adding up. Just a few hands was making a big difference.

What the hell, he thought.

Fifty minutes later, Lucy was up five grand.

Wily had said that Lucy had won a total of twenty-five grand, which meant she'd beaten them for five hours *straight*. Valentine found himself shaking his head. Somehow Lucy had changed the game's odds to be in her favor, and she was cleaning them out.

He killed the power on the VCR. Then he went onto the balcony and stared down on the neon city. The Strip had kicked into high gear, and he tried to guess how many people were down there. Five thousand? Ten? It was like trying to guess the number of ants in an anthill. Inside, he heard someone knocking on his door.

He crossed the suite and stuck his eye to the peephole. Wily stood outside, an empty cocktail glass in his hand. He looked three sheets to the wind.

Valentine hated drunks. His father had been one, and slapped him around when he was a kid. Then he'd grown up and paid his father back. In people who drank he saw weakness, and little else.

He let Wily in and offered him a chair. The head of security reeked of scotch, and he tried to keep the contempt out of his voice.

"What's up?"

"Look at the tape yet?" Wily asked, smothering a belch.

"Yeah. I'm surprised you let her play so long."

"You think she's cheating?"

Valentine thought back to the tape and chose his words carefully. "It's definitely not on the square. She always wins the big hands. Did you notice that?"

"What do you mean?"

"Whenever Lucy Price doubled down, she won. Whenever she split pairs, she won. That's why she beat you silly. She won the important hands."

A pained expression crossed Wily's face. "You tell Nick that?"

"I haven't told Nick anything. My guess is, you saw her reading the Basic Strategy card and pegged her a sucker. When she won a few grand, you credited it to beginner's luck. When she got *way* up, you figured she was on a hot streak and would eventually fall back to earth. Am I right?"

Wily stared into his glass. He seemed surprised that it was empty.

"You should have been a mind reader," he said.

Valentine found himself feeling sorry for him. Bad losses often cost security heads their jobs. He said, "Forty-nine out of fifty pit bosses would have done the same thing you did, and let Lucy Price continue to play."

Wily brightened. "Is that what you're going to tell Nick?"

"Yes. Tell me something. Did you interrogate the dealers who worked Lucy's table during her streak?"

"I did better than that," Wily said. "I had them polygraphed."

"And?"

"They came out clean."

Valentine leaned back and stared at the drunken head of security. Novice blackjack players did not win twenty-five grand placing five-hundred-dollar bets. The odds just weren't there for it to happen. He hated to be stumped, and this had him stumped.

"I need to talk to this woman," he said.

Wily gave him a scornful look. "How you going to do that?"

Valentine thought about the little dance on the balcony that morning. He couldn't deny the magnetism he'd felt when he'd held her in his arms. But that wasn't going to stop him from figuring out what she was doing. If Lucy was cheating, he would make her pay.

"Easy," he said. "I'll call her."

He had no trouble getting Lucy's phone number. She was a slot queen, and played in slot tournaments held by the large casinos. That meant her name, address, phone number, and preferences were stored in their databases. Calling around, he'd gotten a casino he did work for to give him Lucy's number. It had been easy.

She had three numbers: work, home, and cell. He nestled the cordless phone into the crook of his neck and debated which to call. There was a chance she was in a local hospital under psychiatric observation, but more than likely she'd been released and was home. Las Vegas was bad that way. It had the highest suicide rate in the country, yet the treatment that everyone subscribed to was to ignore the problem.

He decided to call her house. An answering machine picked up, her voice bright and cheery. "Well, hi there. You caught me at a bad time. Wait for the beep, and don't forget to leave your number. Bye."

The beep came a few seconds later. Clearing his throat, he said, "This is Tony Valentine calling for Lucy Price. We met this morning at the Acropolis. I was hoping—"

His words were interrupted by a piercing sound.

"This is Lucy Price," a woman's voice said.

"Hello," he said stiffly.

"Do you believe in kismet, Mister Valentine?"

"It's Tony. No, not really."

"I do. I'm sitting in front of my computer, staring at your Web site."

He didn't know what to say. Putting up a Web site had been Mabel's idea. Good for business, she'd assured him, and cheap. Only it made him uncomfortable as hell when he was on the phone with someone and she told him she was staring at his Web site. *Trying to trip me up?* he wanted to ask.

★   ★   ★

126

"So what do you think of my Web site?" he asked when they met for breakfast at ten o'clock the next morning.

"The graphics are cool. And the articles you wrote about casino cheating for *Gambling Times* were interesting, too," she said. "I never realized that there was so much cheating going on."

He was finding it hard to take his eyes off her. He'd woken up mad as hell that he hadn't heard from Gerry. But those feelings had disappeared when he'd set eyes on Lucy. She was a symphony in blue—a powder-blue pantsuit, a blue bow in her hair, and light blue eyeliner. Had the Web site mentioned blue was his favorite color? If not for the dark circles beneath her eyes, he would have found her beautiful.

He plunged a fork into his egg and watched the yolk burst. He had suggested breakfast, having remembered an advice column in a newspaper saying that it was a neutral meal. Lucy had agreed, and now they were sitting in the recently opened breakfast shop at Caesars Palace. She poured skim milk over a bowl of granola, then raised a spoon to her lips.

"How much is Nick paying you to check up on me?" she asked.

He blinked. Her voice hadn't changed, but her eyes had.

"Nothing. I'm doing it as a favor." Her eyes were burning a hole into his face, but she was still eating. He bit into his toast and said, "It's an interesting case. You believe Nick robbed you, and Nick thinks you cheated him. Nick's a square guy—I'll vouch for his honesty. So that would mean you're a cheater. Only I watched a surveillance tape of you playing blackjack, and I don't think you are. Which means both of you are wrong."

Lucy's spoon hit her bowl with a *plop*. "How's that possible?"

"Someone else is involved. What's the expression? Playing both sides for the middle? I think that's what is going on here."

"Which makes me a dopey dame who got suckered and didn't see it coming," she said, standing and throwing her napkin into her bowl. "Thanks a lot, Tony."

Embarrassed, he stood up. Only his pants didn't come with him. He grabbed them by the waist and tugged. She smirked inconsiderately.

"Airline lost my luggage," he said stupidly.

"So buy yourself another pair. It's called shopping. Ask your wife."

His mouth went dry. "Who told you I was married?"

"Your Web site has your name, and your son's."

"My wife died of a heart attack two years ago." He saw something in her face change. A chink in the armor. He said, "She used to buy my clothes, pick out the colors. I don't think I own anything that she didn't buy me."

"Except those pants," Lucy said. "You an odd size?" He nodded and she said, "So was my ex.

128

Look, Tony, I don't know where this conversation is headed, but all I really care about is getting my twenty-five thousand dollars back. If you can't help me, then shove off."

Her voice had turned harsh. This was Lucy the gambler, and he didn't like it.

"That's pretty inconsiderate," he said.

"Just because you talked me off that balcony doesn't mean I owe you anything."

"I wasn't helping Nick when I met you," he replied.

She had to think about what that meant. His breakfast was getting cold, and he sat back down, picked up his fork, and resumed eating. To his surprise, so did she.

The best thing about getting old was you appreciated how precious time was. They decided to start over. Lucy went first.

She'd grown up in Cincinnati. At seventeen, she drove to Las Vegas with her belongings tied to her car, became a dental hygienist, got hitched, had two kids, got divorced, and lost custody to her ex. She'd played slot machines for relaxation. She called her current financial situation "a setback."

Then it was his turn. His life was no movie—he'd been a doting husband, a good cop, and a so-so father, according to his son—and she stopped him when he'd said he was retired. "I know this is none of my business, but how old are you?"

"Sixty-three."

"I would have guessed fifty-three. I'm fifty-two."

He saw her smiling. It was starting to feel like a date, and he decided to put the conversation back on track. "After my wife died, I started consulting. Back when I was a cop in Atlantic City, I had this knack for catching cheaters. I could pick one off the floor, even if I didn't know what he was doing. Hustlers call it grift sense."

"How can you spot a cheater, if you don't know what he's doing?"

"Cheaters are actors. They know the outcome, so they have to fake their emotions. That's the hardest part of the scam."

"You can tell the difference between a realie and a phony?"

"That's right."

"So what am I?"

"A realie," he said.

He saw her smile again, and motioned to the waitress for their check.

They left the coffee shop. Of all the joints in Vegas, he had a soft spot for Caesars. There was live entertainment everywhere you looked, plus beautiful statues, Olympian wall art, and a staff that made visitors feel special.

They stopped at the Forum Shops. A sign for the TALKING ROMAN GOD SHOW said the next performance was in ten minutes. He'd seen the show before. Animatronic statues of Roman gods

130

narrated a wacky story to the accompaniment of lasers and booming sound effects. It was brainless, yet lots of fun.

They found an empty bench. Lucy sat sideways, her knee almost touching his. It was hard to believe she was the same woman he'd met yesterday. She'd bounced back quickly from the edge of despair.

"How can you tell I'm a realie?"

"I don't think Sharon Stone could fake the emotion I saw on the tape of you winning at blackjack," he replied.

For some reason, this made her laugh. "Okay. If you could tell by the tape that I'm not a cheater, then why did you want to talk to me?"

She was grinning like a cat, and he wondered if she was trying to trap him into admitting there was an ulterior motive in him inviting her to breakfast. There wasn't, so he answered her honestly.

"Because there are two things bothering me."

Her smile faded. "Oh. What are they?"

"The first is the simple fact that you started with ten thousand dollars, and you ended up with twenty-five thousand of the casino's money."

"So? Aren't people allowed to win sometimes?"

"They are, but not like that."

"What do you mean?"

He hesitated. Lucy was a gambler. Most gamblers thought they understood the games. They did, when it came to the rules and strategy. But few understood the math, especially when it came to winning and losing. In that department, just about everyone who gambled was a sucker. He stood up. "I'll be right back."

He bought stationery in the gift shop. When he returned to the bench, a guy with a bad dye job and lots of gold chains was putting the moves on Lucy. Seeing him approach, the guy shrugged and left. Valentine sat down and tore the plastic off the paper.

"All right," Lucy said, "show me why I'm not supposed to win."

He drew a chart on a piece of paper. It was the same chart he used when he gave talks at Gamblers Anonymous. Finished, he turned the paper upside down. Her eyes locked onto the page.

THE REAL ODDS

Objective: Double your money before going broke. Player starts with $200 and makes single-dollar bets. Game is blackjack, with house holding 1.4% advantage.

# of Hands Played	The House Edge
1x	50.7%
5x	53.5%
10x	57%
20x	63.8%
50x	80%
100x	94%
200x	99.7%

She lifted her eyes from the page. "Is this for real?"

"Afraid so," he said.

"But how can the casino's edge increase? Doesn't it always stay the same?"

"For each hand, yes."

"So the edge doesn't change."

"No, but it eats into your bankroll. The edge gives the casino one-point-four cents of every bet you make. You lose gradually, which makes your objective of doubling your bankroll impossible. The more bets you make, the worse it gets. It's what pays for this place, and every other place in town."

"The edge," she said.

"That's right. Over the long haul, you can't beat it."

"Only I did. Did I get lucky?"

He pointed at the top of the chart with his pen. "Luck is betting all your money on a single hand. The first bet, you're playing nearly even with the house. If you win, that's luck. You played for five hours, and won over fifty percent of your hands. Luck had nothing to do with it."

She drew back into herself, not sure where the conversation was headed. "You said there were two things bothering you. What's the second?"

He hesitated. Lucy caught it, put her hand on his knee and dug in her nails hard. Grimacing, he said, "Your story sounds like a fairy tale. You never played blackjack before. Well, why did you play? My guess is, someone talked you into it."

133

A startled look spread across her face.

"I also think this same person staked you ten grand. He talked you into playing blackjack at the Acropolis. You had a deal with him."

"Why do you think someone staked me?" she asked, growing angry. "Why couldn't it have been with my money?"

Because you owe money all over town he would have said to anyone else sitting on that bench. Only he didn't want to hurt this woman. She'd been through enough.

Her hand was still on his knee. He rested his hand on hers.

"Greasy guys with diamond pinkie rings bet five hundred a hand," he said. "Or oil tycoons wearing Stetsons. But a novice playing her first time? A hundred a hand I could live with. Not five hundred. Someone told you to do that."

He saw the flicker of understanding register on her face. He was on to her, and she knew it. "Lucy, please, level with me. Who staked you? What's going on?"

"I . . . can't tell you that."

"Please."

She shook her head. "I have to go." She jerked her hand free of his grasp and abruptly stood up. She walked away quickly, purse clutched to her chest, eyes scared.

"Lucy—"

"No!"

He saw the guy who'd been hitting on her

emerge from one of the Forum Shops. Walking over, he tried to start up a conversation. Mister-Never-Give-Up. Lucy stopped long enough to slap him in the face, the harsh sound reverberating across the Forum's domed ceiling like a gunshot.

CHAPTER 16

Taking cabs in Las Vegas was a waste of time, so Valentine hiked back to the Acropolis. It was only three blocks, plus the long walk down Caesars entranceway. The casino had moving sidewalks to bring people in, but not out.

The air was brisk and clean, the sun a metallic sliver in the vivid sky. He walked quickly, wanting to burn off the bad feelings weighing him down. Lucy was somehow involved in this scam, and he didn't want her to end up getting hurt. He normally didn't feel that way about cheaters, and found himself trying to rationalize his feelings. She didn't seem to be a part of a gang, and was probably just a patsy. She was being taken advantage of, he decided.

He strode past the entrance, the sun's harsh rays showing every crack and paint chip. Behind the dreams there was always a harsh reality. Lucy's reality was that someone had staked her to play blackjack and pointed to a specific table. That same someone gave her a Basic Strategy card and told her to follow it. Wily had polygraphed the dealers who'd worked Lucy's table. But that didn't mean someone else wasn't involved in the scam. Perhaps it was one of the other players. Or someone standing behind the table, out of the surveillance camera's range. That person had engineered the scam and later stolen Lucy's winnings from the safe in her room. It was the only possible explanation for what had happened.

He walked up the Acropolis's winding entrance. A workman was scrubbing Nick's ex-wives with a soggy mop, the soapsuds clinging to all the wrong places. *Nowhere else in America could someone get away with this,* he thought.

Going inside, Big Joe Smith pulled him into One-Armed Billy's alcove, and he got his picture taken with a gang of tourists, autographed their visors and T-shirts, then left.

"Hey, Mister Celebrity," Wily said when he entered the surveillance control room a minute later. He'd been watching on the monitors, and was laughing.

"I need to ask you some questions," Valentine said.

"Your wish is my command."

"The night you taped Lucy Price, did you film her from any other angles?"

"We filmed her from every angle but up her skirt," Wily said.

"Was anyone standing around the table, watching her play?"

"There were a couple of people watching her, now that you mention it," Wily said. "Think they might be involved?"

Valentine wanted to smack Wily in the head. Fifteen years working for Nick, and Wily was lucky he found his way to work every day. Lucy Price was an *amateur*. Other players never watched amateurs play.

"Yeah, I think they're involved. Let me see the tapes."

"No problem, Kemosabe."

Wily went to the raised console that sat in the room's center. The console was the casino's version of central command. Sitting in front of a computer, he pecked a command into the console's keyboard, then leaned back in his chair and waited for a response.

Since nearly being ripped off by Frank Fontaine, Nick had bought an advanced surveillance system called Loronix. Loronix recorded digitally and could hold seven days' worth of film. The picture had a special watermark that showed any foul play or image altering after the fact. That way, the tapes would always stand up in court.

Wily pointed at the wall of video monitors. "Lucy's on monitors one through four."

Valentine crossed the room and stared. On the monitors, he saw two spectators watching Lucy play. A plump woman clutching a plastic coin bucket, and a skinny guy wearing a baseball cap and cheap shades. Wily edged up beside him.

"Recognize either of them?" Valentine asked.

"The woman's a local," Wily said. "She comes in and blows her Social Security check playing video poker."

"Ever have any problems with her?"

"Naw. Wait. There was one time . . . she found a gold coin on the casino floor, thought it was Nick's lost treasure. Got real upset when she discovered it was a piece of candy wrapped in tinfoil."

Nick's lost treasure was a part of Vegas lore. During one of his divorces, Nick had told a trusted employee to hide a cache of gold coins he'd bought from a treasure hunter. The coins were from a sunken Spanish ship called the *Atocha*, and worth a fortune. Nick's employee had hidden the coins, then dropped dead from a heart attack. No map had been left, nor any clues leading to the coins' whereabouts.

Valentine resumed staring at the monitors. The woman with the coin bucket left, leaving the man with the baseball cap. He was scruffy and hadn't shaved in several days.

"Recognize him?"

Wily brought his face next to the screen. "No. Hard to see his face beneath the cap and the whiskers and the shades."

"No kidding."

"Think he has something to do with it?"

"Yes."

They watched the scruffy guy for ten minutes.

The man shifted his position and once walked away, but then came back. He was definitely watching Lucy play.

"See anything that doesn't look right?" Valentine asked.

Wily was smart enough to know when he was being baited. He stared for another minute, then said, "I give up."

"Take a look at his shoes."

Wily did, and spotted the discrepancy immediately. "Cowboy boots made out of alligator or snake. Doesn't go with the cheap sunglasses, does it?"

"No, sir."

Wily trotted over to the master console and began typing. The picture on the monitor froze, and the man's reptilian cowboy boots became enlarged. Valentine walked behind Wily, trying to figure out what the head of security was doing.

"What are you doing?" Valentine asked him.

A surprised look crossed Wily's face. In a loud voice, he said, "Ladies and gentlemen, can I have your attention, please. Something historic has just happened." Ten technicians in the room collectively lifted their heads. "I just did something that Tony Valentine—*the* Tony Valentine—hasn't seen before. Please mark down the date and time for future reference. Thank you." Turning to his guest, he said, "Hope I didn't embarrass you."

"Just answer the question."

"Loronix has this great feature. I can freeze an

image—like this guy's cowboy boots—and compare it to the last seven days' worth of film on the computer's hard drive. Loronix will find all the matches and pull them up. It's a great way to gather evidence on someone."

Valentine was stunned. He'd been given a demonstration of Loronix, and this feature had never been mentioned. He patted Wily on the shoulder and saw him smile.

"Good work," he said.

A yellow light on the console began to flash. Wily punched in a command. The console had a small screen, and a bunch of gibberish appeared. Wily spent a moment deciphering it, then said, "Looks like our friend with the cowboy boots was in the casino twelve times in the last week. Want to look at him some more?"

"I sure do."

Valentine returned to the wall of monitors. The retrieved films of the guy with the cowboy boots appeared on twelve separate screens. The guy was a stroller, and the films showed him walking around the casino, pausing occasionally to watch the action at roulette, blackjack, the craps table, and the Asian domino game called Pai Gow. Not once did he stop and actually play.

On one screen, he was standing at a pay phone. As he brought the receiver to his mouth, he lifted his face. The surveillance camera caught his profile, and Valentine felt a knot tighten in his stomach.

"For the love of Christ," he said under his breath.

He stared across the room at Wily. Wily had been there the night the Acropolis had nearly gone down. "It's Frank Fontaine," he said.

"Fontaine's in the slammer, doing thirty," Wily replied.

"Look at him."

Wily came over and put his face up to the monitor. "There's a resemblance, but that's it. Besides, this guy has a scar on his face."

Frank Fontaine was the greatest casino cheater of the past twenty-five years. His scams were works of art, and always involved employee collusion. There was no doubt in Valentine's mind it was him.

"You think I'm wrong?" Wily said.

"Yes."

"Tony, you're getting old."

"You think so?"

"Yeah."

"I'm going to tell Nick."

A look of apprehension crossed Wily's face. "You *really* think it's him?"

"Yes."

Wily went to the console, punched in a command, then crossed the room to the laser printer in the corner. A printed sheet came out. He held it up so Valentine could see it. It was the photograph of Fontaine talking on the phone.

Walking over to a technician, Wily handed him

the photograph and said, "Make a few hundred copies and distribute them to every employee. If anyone sees this guy, tell them to send up a flare."

Valentine watched the technician leave. Then he looked at Wily. He hadn't liked the crack about getting old. That was the thing he hated the most about Las Vegas. People didn't stay your friend for very long.

Walking over to the printer, he removed Fontaine's photograph and left without saying a word.

CHAPTER 17

Mabel got up Saturday morning, fixed herself a fruit smoothie, and walked down the street to Tony's house. She drank her breakfast while sitting at Tony's desk, fielding e-mails and phone calls from panicked casino bosses that had come in the night before. In a business that never went to sleep, Friday nights were particularly hectic, and she spent an hour going through Tony's messages. At ten o'clock the phone rang. It was Tony's private line, and she snatched it up. It was Yolanda.

"Can you come over here?"

"Of course. Are you all right?"

"I'm fine," Yolanda said. "It's about Gerry."

"Be there in five," Mabel said. She exited Tony's e-mail, then shut his computer down. They lived in the lightning capital of the country, and leaving the computer on was an invitation for disaster. As she rose from her chair, the business line rang. She stared at the caller ID, then brought her hand to her mouth.

"Oh, no," she said.

The caller was Richard Beamer, manager of the

exclusive Liar's Club in Beverly Hills. He had overnighted a certified check two days ago and been calling ever since. *And she'd forgotten to tell Tony.*

Beamer's check lay on the desk. It was for three grand, Tony's usual fee. She'd grown up during the tail end of the Depression and could remember eating three-day-old bread, and standing on line with a wooden bucket to scoop sauerkraut and pigs' feet from a barrel. She answered the call.

"Grift Sense. Can I help you?"

"This is Richard Beamer. Did you speak to your boss?"

"He's on a job in Las Vegas," she said truthfully. "He asked me to take the information. Once he figures out what these cheaters are doing, he'll call you."

"They were here last night," Beamer said. "The other members want them thrown out. My job is at stake."

"Then why don't you?"

"I can't expel them without proof. They'll sue the club."

"What game are they playing?"

"Poker."

Mabel had an idea and put him on hold. From the bookshelf, she removed one of Tony's favorites: Poker to Win, by Al Smith. Tony said that 99 percent of the guys who cheated at poker used three scams described in the book: Top Hand, the Cold Deck, and Locating. She opened the book to the table of contents and picked up Beamer's line.

"I'm back. Let me ask you some questions."

"Is Mister Valentine going to call—"

"Do your cheaters sit beside each other when they play?"

"Why yes, they do," Beamer said. He sounded like someone who'd had acting lessons, his voice animated. "How did you know that?"

"It's common among cheaters. Now, does one of your cheaters always drop out of the game, and the other wins?"

Beamer gave it some thought. "No. Sometimes they both stay in."

Mabel smiled. That ruled out playing Top Hand, which was the signaling between players of who had the strongest hand, with the weaker dropping out. "Next question. Have you seen either player spill a drink on his cards, and replace them with a new deck?"

Another pause. "Not that I can recall. Let me guess. The new deck is stacked so they'll win."

"Yes. It's called a Cold Deck," she said, reading from the book. "The cards are usually false-shuffled when they're introduced into the game."

"I would have noticed that," Beamer said. "I'm a card player myself."

"Last question. Have you noticed the cheaters comparing hands after they've both dropped out?"

Beamer didn't hesitate this time. "Yes. They do that a lot. They'll drop out of a hand and then compare the cards they had. I thought it was harmless."

"They're memorizing them," Mabel said, having flipped to the section on Locating. "The next round, the cards are passed to one of the cheaters. He shuffles but doesn't disturb the memorized cards. On the last shuffle, he adds twenty cards to the bottom, then offers them to his partner to be cut.

"His partner cuts at the memorized stack and brings the cards to the top. The cheater then deals. He plays a game like Seven Card Stud, where the first two rounds are dealt facedown."

"The hole cards," Beamer said.

"That's right. By looking at their own hole cards, the cheaters work backward in their memorized stack and know the other players' cards."

"That's it!" he exclaimed.

"It is?" Mabel said.

"That's *exactly* what they're doing," Beamer said triumphantly. "They always play Seven Card Stud, where each player gets two facedown cards. You nailed it, Miz . . ."

"Call me Mabel," she said.

"You nailed it Mabel," he said. "Much obliged."

The line went dead, and Mabel placed the receiver in its cradle. She picked up the Liar's Club check and gave it a kiss, then remembered that Yolanda was waiting for her.

Mabel locked the door to Tony's house and walked down the front path. It was a beautiful morning, the air crisp and infused with ocean spirits, and she crossed the street with a smile on her face.

Yolanda and Gerry lived across the street in a 1950s clapboard house. The house had a screened front porch and all the original fixtures and appliances. Having them in spitting distance—Tony's words—wasn't easy, but Mabel had come to the conclusion that family relationships rarely were. She pressed the buzzer, and the door opened.

"Hey," Yolanda said. She wore a pink maternity dress, no makeup, her hair tied in a ponytail. Her brown eyes looked very sad.

"Sorry it took me so long," Mabel said.

Yolanda ushered her inside, then padded noiselessly down the hallway to the back of the house. Mabel followed, glancing at the silent TV in the living room. It had a cartoon on, and there was a yellow legal pad in front of it. Yolanda had started watching the popular kids' shows, and was rating them based on the level of violence and the content. She had decided that she was going to determine what her child watched on the boob tube.

Mabel stepped into the kitchen. It was small, with barely room for a breakfast table. She saw Yolanda moving a pile of medical books from the kitchen table.

"Let me help you with those."

Mabel helped her put the books on the stove. Yolanda had been interning at Tampa General Hospital across the bay until she'd gone out on maternity leave. The hours were long, the pay lousy, and she was loving every minute of it. She pulled out a chair for Mabel, then took the one beside it.

"What did Gerry do now?" Mabel asked, sitting.

Yolanda let out an exasperated sigh while looking at the picture of Gerry on the table. He was dark and handsome, with a smile that could light up a room.

"He sent me an overnight package."

"Is that bad?"

Yolanda rose from her chair and took a cardboard box off the counter. It had an OVERNIGHT label plastered on its side. She handed it to her.

Mabel peeked inside and felt her heartbeat quicken. She looked at Yolanda, and the younger woman nodded. Mabel removed a stack of bills and held them in her hand. Twenties and fifties, most of them wrinkled. She took out the other stacks. It looked like more than it was, but it was still a lot.

"Did you count it?"

Yolanda nodded. "There's sixty-five hundred dollars in that box. I may have had a sheltered upbringing in San Juan, but I'm not dumb. Why didn't Gerry send a check, or wire the money?"

Mabel knew the answer, but refused to say it.

"Because he stole the money, that's why."

"You don't know that for sure," Mabel said. "You should give him the benefit of the doubt."

Yolanda stared into her guest's face. "Tony sent

Gerry to Las Vegas to learn how to card-count. I think it was a test. I think Tony wanted to see if Gerry could resist the temptation. And Gerry failed. He's stealing from the casinos."

"Card-counting isn't stealing," Mabel said.

"Call it what you want, it's still wrong, and Gerry's doing it."

"But he's only been in Las Vegas for five days," Mabel reminded her. "He couldn't have learned how to card-count that quickly. It's more difficult than that."

Yolanda considered it while staring at the stacks of money in Mabel's lap. Lifting her eyes, she said, "Okay. If my husband isn't card-counting, then what *is* he doing?"

It was a good question, and Mabel racked her brain for an intelligent answer.

"Let me know when you think of something," Yolanda said, and walked out of the kitchen.

CHAPTER 18

Valentine was still smarting over Wily's crack when he walked into his suite a few minutes later. What did getting old have to do with his vision? He knew a crook when he saw one, and the man on the surveillance tape was the biggest crook of all.

An envelope with his initials was propped on the coffee table. He tore it open and saw it was from Nick.

Hey Jersey Boy,
   Bart Calhoun is the invisible man. All my spies could dig up was his cell #. Sorry.

NN

Bart's cell number was at the bottom of the page. Valentine got a soda and went onto the balcony, his mind wrestling with how to handle this.

He and Bart had a history. In 1980, the New Jersey Casino Control Commission had decided to try an experiment and let card-counters play blackjack at Atlantic City's casinos. The result had been the immediate loss of millions of dollars.

The experiment was halted, and the counters left town.

Except for Bart. Bart liked the little city by the shore, and devised a unique way to keep playing. He sent teams of counters into the casinos and had them sit at different blackjack tables. When a counter determined a table was "ripe," a signal was given—usually the lighting of a cigarette. Bart would descend, bet heavily, and clean up.

Stopping Bart hadn't been easy. Technically, he wasn't counting, so barring him wasn't an option. Valentine had solved the problem by contacting the IRS and making them aware of the gigantic sums Bart was winning. They had swooped down like vultures, and Bart had run.

Most counters had phenomenal memories, and he was sure Bart remembered him. The question was, was he holding a grudge? There was only one way to find out. Going inside, he found the cordless phone and dialed the number on Nick's note.

"Who's this?" a husky voice answered.

"Hi. My son is enrolled at your school, and I need to speak to him."

"How'd you get this number?"

"A friend gave it to me."

"Who's that?"

Valentine had learned that when you were bull-shitting someone, it was best to tell as few lies as possible. "Nick Nicocropolis."

There was a long pause. "What's your son's name?"

"Gerry."

The sound of a match being struck against a flint crackled across the phone line.

"What's this about?"

"His wife is going to have a baby."

Calhoun snorted. "Figures. She's been calling him every ten minutes. Hold on." He put him on hold, then returned a few moments later. "Most of my students stay at the Red Roost Inn while they're here. It's in Henderson. 702-691-4852."

Valentine thanked him and started to write the number down.

"Mind answering a question, mister?" Calhoun asked.

"Not at all."

"Is this Tony Valentine I'm speaking with?"

Valentine stopped writing. He hated it when people he'd once chased got the goods on him. "Yeah. What did Gerry do? Use his real name when he registered?"

"Naw, he used a phony," Calhoun said. "He just looks like you. It's a funny world. You ran me out of Atlantic City, and now your son is learning to be a crook."

"Hysterical," Valentine replied.

Calhoun hung up on him. Valentine smiled, happy he'd gotten in the last jab. He punched in the number for the Red Roost Inn.

Gerry was lying in bed in his motel room when the phone rang. He tried to imagine who it was.

Yolanda? Or his father? He didn't want to speak to either one, fearful of the tongue-lashing he knew was coming. Better to let his caller leave a message.

The ringing stopped. He waited a minute, then went into voice mail and found a message. His father, sounding pissed off.

"Your wife is worried sick, and so am I," his father said. "I'm staying at the Acropolis. 611-4571. Suite Four. Call me when you get this. You hear me?"

Gerry realized he was grinding his teeth. Leave it to his old man to track him down. He'd call his father back, but not right away. He erased the message and climbed out of bed.

He took his time dressing. He hadn't slept much, too worried by what had happened at the MGM Grand. There was no doubt in his mind that he'd gotten photographed, and that his face was now in a computer. His days of rat-holing chips for Amin and Pash were over.

But that didn't mean they couldn't make money together. He had an idea, a really good idea. But he needed to run it by Pash first. He went to the door that separated their rooms and knocked. Pash appeared, holding a toothbrush.

"Want to take a road trip?" Gerry asked.

"What do you have in mind?"

"A whorehouse."

Pash smiled, the toothpaste making him look like he was foaming at the mouth.

"A *wonderful* idea," he gushed. "Let me tell Amin."

Gerry stared through the open door. Amin lay naked in bed, staring at the mute TV. He watched Pash tell him he was going out. Amin cast him a disapproving stare. Pash shrugged and went into the bathroom. A minute later he emerged with his hair freshly parted and smelling of aftershave.

Great, Gerry thought.

Pash pulled out his cell phone when they were on the road, and called a brothel. They were legal in every county in the state with less than four hundred thousand residents. Gerry pulled into a convenience mart and went inside.

When he came out, Pash was in the middle of a heated negotiation. Pash's taste was for dark-skinned girls, and he knew to call ahead to avoid being disappointed. He also knew it was best to hammer out a rate before stepping foot in a place.

"Hey," Pash said, cupping his hand over the mouthpiece. "The madam said she'll give us a deal for two. What kind of girl you want?"

Gerry sucked on his Slurpee. He'd planned to take Pash to the brothel and pretend none of the ladies were to his liking. "I'll decide when I get there," he said.

"Come on, what do you want?"

"Do your own deal," Gerry said.

"But—"

"I'm doing this for you, buddy."

The words were slow to sink in. Pash's face brightened. "You are?"

"Yeah," Gerry said. "You need to get laid."

Nevada had thirty licensed brothels, or ranches as everyone liked to call them. Pash had decided that he wanted to try the Chicken Ranch.

"Everyone says it's the best," he explained to Gerry.

It was in a burg called Pahrump, the town a shining example of what would happen if the nation's gun laws were repealed. In Pahrump, rifles and shotguns were displayed in gun racks of every pickup, the locals proud of their Wild West heritage.

"There's the sign," Pash said excitedly.

A billboard loomed ahead. HIT THE GAS! THE WORLD-FAMOUS CHICKEN RANCH, FIVE MILES. They pulled into the gravel lot a few minutes later.

It resembled an oversized motel, with rocking chairs on the front porch and smoke pouring out of a stone chimney. As they got out, Gerry spied a surveillance camera perched beneath the corner of the building.

A plump, grayish woman greeted them at the door. She reminded Gerry of his Cub Scout den mother. It was a bad image to be carrying around inside a whorehouse, and he tried to erase it from his mind.

"You must be the fellow I spoke to earlier," she said to Pash.

"That's me," Pash said brightly.

"You like dark."

"That's right."

"Very dark?"

She made it sound like he was ordering chicken. Pash nodded vigorously.

"You came to the right place, young man. The Chicken Ranch was voted best brothel in Nevada last year. Best accommodations, best food, best bar, and best of all—"

"The best women," Pash jumped in.

"You saw our ad."

"Yes. Your Web site is very good, too."

She slung her arm through Pash's and escorted him inside. Gerry stayed two steps behind, grateful she hadn't latched onto him. Maybe she'd spied the hesitation in his face, or the cowardice in his eyes. He and Yolanda had stopped having sex months ago, and he'd sworn he wouldn't touch another woman.

Crossing himself, Gerry went inside.

Thirty minutes later, Pash was wearing a FRESHLY PLUCKED AT THE CHICKEN RANCH T-shirt while eating pancakes at a diner down the road.

"Why did we have to leave so fast?" he asked.

Gerry blew the steam off his coffee. "You see all those cameras?"

"What about them?"

"Brothels are like casinos. The state *makes* them have surveillance cameras. I didn't want to stay in there any longer than we had to."

Pash shoved a forkful of dripping blueberry pancake into his mouth. "You think the state is looking for us?"

"After that stunt last night at the MGM Grand? You bet they are."

"This is not good."

"You need to start playing in casinos that aren't slick with their surveillance. Like up in Reno, and those dives in Mississippi."

"How do you know which casinos are slick, and which aren't?" Pash asked when he was finished eating. "Isn't that information secret?"

Gerry pulled out a business card and slid it across the table. "It is secret. But he has access to it."

Pash stared at the card. "Grift Sense? Who is Tony Valentine?"

"My father. It's his business. He helps casinos catch cheaters."

"Your father is a policeman?"

"Retired."

"Do you work with him?"

"I'm his partner. I'm getting my cards next week."

Pash tore away the paper napkin tucked in his collar. He suddenly looked scared. "Why are you telling me this? What do you want?"

Gerry smiled at him. "My father sent me to Bart's school to learn card-counting. What I learned was, it's a good business, and it isn't illegal. There's only one drawback, and that's if you get photographed. Then you're screwed.

"My father does consulting work for casinos all over the country. He knows which casinos have sophisticated surveillance equipment, and which don't. Did you know that the Mississippi riverboats have the least amount of surveillance equipment?"

"Why is that?"

"The riverboats are made of wood and have certain weight restrictions. They cut down on the cameras and recording equipment so they can carry more passengers."

"This is very valuable information."

Gerry had gotten his attention, and leaned forward. "You and Amin have worn out your welcome here. You need to move to greener pastures, and I can help you."

Pash fingered the business card and said, "How much do you want?"

"One-third, same as now."

"Will you still rat-hole chips for us?"

"On weekends, sure. It will be a breeze."

"A breeze?"

"Easy as pie. Your risk of getting caught will drop to zero."

"You think so?"

Gerry nodded. He'd thought it out and saw no flaws in his plan. "There's a brand-new casino opening every week. Most don't know their ass from third base when it comes to spotting counters. I'll tell you and Amin where those casinos are." He smiled, saw Pash smile along with him. "You'll be in fat city."

"Fat city? Where is that?"

Gerry took out his wallet and paid for the meal. "It's right next door to heaven," he said.

CHAPTER 19

Valentine spent the morning on the balcony of his suite, enjoying the beautiful weather while waiting for Gerry to call him back. By noon, his patience had run out, and he called the Red Roost Inn. The manager answered sounding all out of breath.

"I hate to cause you work, but would you mind going to my son's room and knocking on his door? I haven't spoken to him in days. Save an old man from worry."

The manager said sure and dropped the phone on the desk. Valentine found himself grinning. He'd never used the senior citizen angle before and was surprised at how well it worked. Maybe getting old wasn't so bad.

"Room's empty," the manager said when he returned. "Your son came by earlier, asked if I had a road map he could look at. I think he was going to Pahrump."

"Is that an animal, mineral, or vegetable?"

"It's a little town up in the mountains, about an hour's drive."

"What's the attraction?"

"Beats me," the manager said.

Valentine thanked him, and hung up feeling mad as hell. There was no doubt in his mind that Gerry was avoiding him. Some days, he wondered why he wasted his time trying to help his son. Going back inside, he slammed the slider closed.

The surveillance photograph of Frank Fontaine lay on the dining room table, beside it the cordless phone. He'd been weighing calling Bill Higgins for several hours. Fontaine had cost Las Vegas's casinos millions over the years, and Bill would start an investigation once he'd heard that Fontaine had ripped the Acropolis off.

What had stopped him from calling was Lucy Price. He'd left breakfast this morning convinced Fontaine had tricked her into participating in his scam. The sixty-four-thousand-dollar question was, how had he done it? If he could find out, he might be able to save Lucy from getting hauled off to jail.

He removed the card with her phone numbers from his wallet, then picked up the phone. She'd left breakfast pretty angry, and he wondered if she'd take his call. There was only one way to find out, and he called her at home. She answered on the first ring.

"I need to talk to you," he said.

Lucy lived in a modest condo in the community of Garden Terrace in Summerlin, ten minutes from the Strip. He arrived at her front door at twelve-thirty, expecting to take her to lunch. She was wearing jeans and a faded red polo shirt. It was a great color on her.

"My turn, this time," she said, ushering him inside.

The place wasn't much to look at—a sagging couch, an ancient TV with rabbit ears, a few mismatched chairs, some art show prints on the walls—but she'd somehow made it feel like home. As he followed her into the dining room, he noticed an abundance of flowers and potted plants that tied it all together. She had a green thumb; something was blooming wherever he looked.

She'd set the dining room table for two. On it was a basket of toasted bread, a bowl of tuna fish, another of egg salad, a basket of potato chips, and two glasses of lemonade. It reminded him of the picnic lunches he and Lois had shared when they'd first dated. He pulled out Lucy's chair.

"Such a gentleman," she said, taking her seat.

He sat across from her. Staring into her eyes, he saw a slight puffiness. Had he made her cry earlier? He nearly asked her, then bit his tongue.

"How was your morning?" she asked.

He took two slices of toast when she offered him the basket, and made a tuna fish sandwich under her watchful gaze. "I watched some surveillance tapes."

"Learn anything?"

She wasn't touching the food, preferring to watch him. He always got hungry when he was

working, and he nodded and bit into his sandwich. The tuna fish was spicy, just the way he liked
it. He finished the sandwich, then helped himself
to the potato chips. Her eyes never wavered, and
once he saw her start to grin, only to see it fade.

"That was good," he said. "You shouldn't have
gone to so much trouble."

"I wanted to see you again," she said.

The words had a more powerful effect on him
than he would have liked. Being married forty
years, he'd taken for granted that there was a
woman in his life who wanted to see him again.
Losing that had been one of the hardest things
he'd ever endured.

"Oh," he said.

"I have something for you," Lucy said.

He followed her into one of the bedrooms. It
was as Spartan as the rest of the house, with none
of the furniture matching. On the bed lay three
pairs of men's pants, one tan, one black, one
brown. She said, "My ex's. Don't know why he
left them behind, maybe to remind me of something."

Valentine checked the labels. Waist 35, leg 34.
His size. Lucy said, "If any of them fit, they're
yours," and walked out of the room, shutting the
door behind her. For a long moment he stood
there, not knowing what to make of the offer, and
then realized she was just trying to be nice. Taking
off his pants, he began trying the clothes on.

★   ★   ★

The black pair fit just right.

He appraised his reflection in the vanity. Black had always been his best color. A strange thought occurred to him. Lucy resembled his late wife in many ways. Did he bear any resemblance to her ex-husband?

He looked around the room for a picture. On the dresser he spied a plastic frame, turned face-down. He picked it up. It was of Lucy, taken several years ago. Her hair was frosted, but otherwise she looked the same. She was holding a giant check and smiling. The check was from the Flamingo casino, and made out to her for $250,000.

He stared at the picture for a long moment. In his mind's eye, he saw her at the Flamingo, sitting in front of a slot machine, the reels showing JACKPOT and the machine going bonkers. Saw her jump up and down and scream. Felt all her joy.

It answered all the questions he'd had about her. He put the picture back the way he'd found it and walked out of the bedroom. He found her on the couch in the living room, leafing through a glossy magazine. Before he could sit down, she made him walk in front of her, and nodded her head approvingly. "That's much better. Those other pants made you look—"

"Like an old geezer?"

"Frumpy," she corrected. "These make you look sexy. Wish they'd made my husband look that way."

Sexy. He couldn't remember anyone ever describing him that way before, and he wasn't sure he believed her. The couch sagged as he sat down. She threw the magazine to the floor and turned sideways. He tried to think of a tactful way to say what he wanted to say, only he'd never been good in that department, so he just spit it out.

"I just had an epiphany," he said.

"I thought only Joan of Arc had those."

"I've had them since I was a kid," he explained. "I'll look at something that doesn't make sense, and my brain will turn it upside down, and then it does make sense."

"Are they accompanied by bolts of lightning and clashes of thunder?"

He shook his head. "Nothing that dramatic."

"Are you going to share yours?"

"It's about you."

Her jaw tightened. "Well, then I guess I'm entitled to hear it."

He put his hands into his lap, suddenly feeling uncomfortable as hell. Taking a deep breath, he said, "In the bedroom I saw a picture of you winning a quarter million bucks. Can I ask you a question?"

"Sure."

"Was it your first time playing the slots when you won that jackpot?"

She drew back in surprise. "How did you know that?"

"It's a common denominator among people who play a lot."

"You mean among slot queens?"

He nodded, glad she'd used the expression first.

"Is that what makes us addicts?" Lucy asked, her voice serious. "We won big the first time and thought we had the magic touch?"

He nodded, and added, "Winning changes people."

"I can buy that. Is that your epiphany?"

"There's more."

"Fire away."

He took another deep breath, then said, "I need to explain something. Have you ever heard the expression *takeoff agent*?"

"No."

"Cheaters use takeoff agents to win money at rigged games. Usually, they're guys between thirty-five and fifty who like to gamble and resent the casinos for taking their money. Cheaters usually find them in casino bars crying in their beers.

"The cheater takes the guy to a poker game and deals him several winning hands. The guy's behavior is scrutinized. If he passes muster, he finds out the game is rigged and the other players are part of the team. Then his role in the scam is explained to him."

"What does this have to do with me?"

"Not long ago, you were playing slots at the Acropolis, and you met a guy. He's a smooth talker and a real charmer. So smooth, you stopped wondering where he got the scar on his face."

Lucy swallowed very hard.

"He's a crossroader—he rips off casinos for a living. Somehow he knew you had the magic touch. He got talking to you, and asked you if you'd ever played blackjack."

Valentine hesitated. He was guessing now, and waited for her to respond.

"Go on," she said.

"You said no, you hadn't. He told you about virgin luck—how people who play for the first time often win. You knew what he was talking about, because you'd won a quarter million at slots the first time."

Lucy's face had turned stone cold. He could no longer read her expressions or her feelings. He said, "He took out a Basic Strategy card and taught you how to play. Then he took out a deck of cards and dealt you several hands. And an amazing thing happened. You won every hand. He was so impressed, he offered to stake you. He gave you ten grand, and pointed at a blackjack table. If you won, you'd split the winnings. If you lost, you wouldn't owe him a thing."

He stopped because Lucy's eyes told him to stop. She said, "How the hell do you know that? Were you spying on me the whole time?"

Valentine shook his head.

"Then explain yourself. And don't give me any more cock and bull about having an epiphany. I stopped believing in that nonsense when I quit reading romance novels."

He stared at the worn patch of carpet between his feet. He'd never been good at sugarcoating things, and he knew that he'd hurt her.

"He set you up. He turned you into his takeoff agent, only you didn't know it."

"How did he do that?"

"He's a mechanic. When you first played, he dealt you winning hands. There was no luck involved."

"But I *saw* him shuffle the cards."

"Half the deck was stacked. He shuffled the half that wasn't. You couldn't lose, trust me."

"Which makes me what? An unwitting shill?"

Valentine said "yes" in a soft voice.

"The blackjack table he told me to play at," Lucy said. "He was real specific about which one. Was that game rigged as well?"

"Yes."

"Someone else involved?"

He nodded.

"But you don't know who?"

"No, but I plan to find out," he said. He lifted his eyes. Lucy was seething, her face hard and unforgiving.

"I get it," she said. "You're like the Royal Canadian Mounties; you always get your man. That's what drove you to call me. You wanted to nail him. You didn't care about the money I lost." She spread her arms and said, "See the Taj Mahal I live in? I barely scrape by. That money was going to get me back on track. It was my salvation."

He didn't know what to tell her. The money had never been hers. Only Lucy wasn't willing to accept that. He felt bad for her even if she was a sucker, and said, "Can I ask you something? Why did you go along with him?"

"Because he said Nick was a bastard, and he had it coming," she said.

Valentine blinked. It *was* Fontaine. He saw her rise from the couch.

"Get up," she said.

He rose slowly, his hands unconsciously making a conciliatory gesture. She pointed at the front door. "Leave. And don't ever call me again."

"Lucy, I'm trying to help you."

"Sure you are. The next thing I know, the cops will be banging on my door."

At the door he turned, his mind struggling for something to say. "Thanks for the pants," he blurted out.

The words hadn't come out right, and he made it out of the house before she threw an ashtray at him.

CHAPTER 20

Talking to women had never been his strong suit. He went back to the Acropolis and found the lobby jammed with gawking tourists. There was a photo shoot going on, and he elbowed his way through the crowd.

In the center of it all, Nick lay on the floor in a garish purple suit, surrounded by a sea of gold coins. Wanda stood behind him in a mermaid's outfit, her breasts practically exploding over the top of the shimmering costume. Nick was getting in touch with his inner child, and waved gleefully at him.

"We need to talk," Valentine said over the noise.

"Can't you see I'm working?" Nick said. "These guys are from the Discovery Channel. They're filming a show about lost treasures. They're going to do a segment about my losing the gold coins from the *Atocha.* Wanda set it up."

Valentine glanced at Wanda and saw her flash a smile. Was Nick implying that he'd actually married a woman with a brain? That would be a first.

"It's about Frank Fontaine," Valentine said.

"Let me guess," Nick said. "He died in the joint, and you just had to tell me."

"I saw him in your casino."

To the anger of the Discovery Channel crew, Nick jumped off the floor, kicking the fake gold coins in every direction. Grabbing Valentine by the wrist, he dragged him into One-Armed Billy's alcove and threw the chain up so no one could enter. Big Joe Smith remained passively on his stool.

"You saw Frank Fontaine in *my* casino," Nick said, just to be sure.

"That's right."

"Is he involved with Lucy Price?"

"He set her up."

"So what do I do?" Nick said anxiously.

"First, I need to figure out exactly how Fontaine ripped you off, and who on your staff is involved. Once I have evidence, I'll call Bill Higgins and get the Gaming Control Board to make the arrests. You need to make a statement; otherwise, cheaters are going to think this place is a candy store.

"In the meantime, you personally need to start watching things. Start with the cage. If a customer tries to make a large withdrawal, you may want to hold things up and have a look."

"Am I that vulnerable?" Nick asked worriedly.

Valentine nodded. Frank Fontaine didn't scam casinos; he shut them down. A lot more money than Lucy Price's twenty-five grand was at stake here.

Nick kicked the carpet in anger. "Turn your head for a second in this business, and somebody will pick your pocket."

A woman wearing a DISCOVERY CHANNEL shirt appeared in the alcove's doorway. She carried a clipboard and appeared to be in charge. "Nick, we need to wrap up the segment. Your customers are stealing the fake coins."

She left, and Nick suddenly punched the air. "Fontaine wants a fight, he's going to get one." He looked at Valentine. "Just tell me what you want me to do."

"Meet me in the surveillance control room in ten minutes."

"Done," Nick said.

Valentine went to the surveillance control room on the third floor and found Wily in front of the wall of video monitors. Wily had seen them talking on a monitor and knew there was a storm brewing. Valentine got him into his office, then shut the door so none of the other surveillance technicians could hear.

"Am I in trouble?" Wily asked.

"No, I left you out of it."

The head of security smiled. "Thanks for the save."

"That's the good news. The bad news is, the guy I saw on the tape this morning *is* Frank Fontaine." He let the news sink in, then continued. "Lucy Price is involved, although she didn't know it up front. My guess is, Fontaine's working a much bigger operation downstairs, and we're only seeing a slice of it. How many times did the computer say Fontaine visited the casino in the past week?"

"Twelve," Wily said.

"What games did he visit?"

"All of them."

Valentine leaned on the edge of the desk. If Fontaine was working scams on every game, it meant he was using a small army of accomplices. To do that, he needed someone working with him in the surveillance control room.

"How many people you have working the monitors?" Valentine asked.

"Right now? Fourteen."

"How many can you trust?"

Wily went into the next room and got a log sheet that showed who was working that shift. His eyes scanned the list of names. "Nine of these people I'd vouch for. The other five are new."

"How new?"

"A month."

"Send them home."

"Right now?"

"Right now. And get their personnel folders while you're at it."

Wily went into the next room and sent the five employees home. He left the door ajar, and Valentine saw Nick enter the surveillance control room. The purple suit was gone, replaced by a black silk shirt, black silk trousers, and layers of thick gold chains. Nick was a retro man and proud of it. He found Valentine in the office.

"Let's kick some ass," the little Greek said.

Wily got his nine trusted employees to leave their stations and assemble in front of the video wall. All had been in Nick's employ for ten years or more and had gray or white hair. At one time or another, Valentine had spoken with each of them. Their jobs didn't pay great, but Nick gave them health insurance and a pension plan, so they hung around and kept things honest downstairs.

"I've been doing work for this casino for a while," Valentine said. "I've made good money off Nick, so I think it's time I give something back. I'm going to teach you how I catch crossroaders. It's based on a system I developed in Atlantic City. I call it Logical Backward Progression, or LBP. It uses memory, and common sense. Everybody ready?"

Several faces in the group lit up. Others simply nodded.

"A few days ago, a blackjack player named Lucy Price won twenty-five grand at one of your tables. Based upon the astronomical odds against what happened, I'm convinced it was a scam. However, I don't know how the scam worked. So I'm going to use LBP and examine what I do know."

He picked up a legal pad from a desk, and a Sharpie, and began to write.

1. *Lucy Price/beginner*
2. *Bets $500 a hand*
3. *Plays with a Basic Strategy card*
4. *Plays 5 hours straight*
5. *One other player at table*
6. *Also played 5 hours*
7. *Lost*
8. *Didn't play Basic Strategy*

Valentine put his pen down and handed the legal pad to the technician to his right. She read the page, then passed it to the next person. He waited until everyone was done, then said, "Based on these facts, what do we know?"

A technician named Nadine cleared her throat. She was from a former Soviet bloc country and had come to Las Vegas right after the Berlin Wall had fallen. Nadine had a knack for spotting improprieties in players. Not grift sense, but damn close.

"Her play is entirely predictable," Nadine said.

"Because she's playing Basic Strategy?"

"That's right. In fact, Lucy Price really wasn't playing her hands at all. The Basic Strategy card was playing her hands. She was just doing what the card told her to."

"Why is this important?"

Nadine smiled. "The other player knew exactly what she was doing."

Valentine wanted to hug her. It was so simple that it had flown right by him. The information was letting the other player at the table play Lucy's

176

hand. Cheaters called it playing early anchor. Valentine explained, and everyone smiled. Except Nick.

"What do you mean, the other guy's playing her hand?" Nick said.

"I'll show you, " Valentine said.

The nine technicians crowded around the wall of video monitors. Wily brought up the tape of Lucy on the master console and beamed it onto every screen.

The tape showed the end of Lucy's streak. Valentine watched the other man at the table. He sat to Lucy's right and drew his cards before Lucy did. He was controlling the play.

Valentine waited for someone else to pick it up. Nadine again came to the rescue. She pointed at the same player.

"He's playing Lucy's hand," she declared. "He knows which cards are coming out of the shoe. If Lucy has eleven, and the next card in the shoe is a ten, he won't take it, giving Lucy the card so she wins her hand. Conversely, if he sees a scare card on top, say a four or a five, he'll draw it, so Lucy *won't* get it. He's either helping her, or he's protecting her. It gives Lucy an unbeatable edge."

Nick was acting like his pants were on fire. "What the hell are you talking about? How the hell does he know which cards are coming out of the shoe?"

Nadine glanced at Valentine. She had an understated way about her that he'd always admired. Smart, but not a show-off.

"Be my guest," Valentine said.

"The cards are marked," Nadine explained. "The player sitting to Lucy's right is controlling Lucy's hand by drawing cards that will hurt Lucy, or standing pat when there's a card that will help Lucy."

Nick looked at Valentine. "How does Fontaine play into this?"

"He's standing behind the table out of the camera's range, directing the action."

Nick looked at Wily. "Read my mind."

Wily scratched his chin. "You want to know who delivers the cards to the table."

"Boy, are you smart," Nick said.

Going to the master console, Wily accessed the casino's database, bringing the man's name up within a matter of seconds. He whistled through his teeth. For a clue to jump out and bite Wily meant it was the size of an elephant, and everyone in the room waited expectantly.

"The guy's new, too," Wily said.

Within a matter of seconds, Wily pulled up the name of every new hire the Acropolis had made in the past three months. There were thirty names.

"Is that a lot?" Valentine asked Nick.

"Yeah, it's a lot," Nick said. "I should have seen it sooner."

"Seen what?"

Nick was scanning the new hires' employment profiles on the computer, and he pointed at the screen. "Everyone of them used to work at Sin. The place has only been open six months. Why are they leaving to come to work for me?"

Nick paused, as if expecting one of the technicians to suggest what a swell boss he was. When no one volunteered, he said, "It's an invasion, that's why. Chance Newman and Shelly Michael and Rags Richardson want to tear the Acropolis down and build a moving walkway that will connect their casinos to each other. My spies have told me. I know." He shifted his gaze to Valentine. "So they hired Fontaine to put me out of business. I just don't understand one thing."

"What's that?" Valentine asked.

"How the hell did they spring Fontaine out of the federal pen?"

The same question had been bothering Valentine. Chance and Rags and Shelly were powerful men, but that power didn't extend to freeing murderers from prison. There was something else going on here, and he was determined to find out what.

"Let me see the files of those thirty new hires," he said.

CHAPTER 21

Mabel had always believed that the majority of the world's problems could be solved with a good meal. So she took Yolanda to the Bon Appétit restaurant in nearby Dunedin, and they spent the afternoon watching the sailboats in Clearwater Harbor while sampling wonderful seafood appetizers. By the time the waiter brought the check, Yolanda was acting like her old self, and smiling again.

"I'm sure there's an explanation for everything that's happened," Mabel said during the drive back to Palm Harbor. She saw Yolanda shift uncomfortably and couldn't tell if it was the baby, or her fears about Gerry. "By the way, how would you like to sample the world's best pound cake?"

"Only if you made it," Yolanda said.

A few minutes later, Mabel pulled into Tony's driveway. She baked several pound cakes every month, and always put one in Tony's refrigerator. They were good warm, better cold, and Yolanda was smiling again when they sat down in Tony's kitchen.

"I love eating for two," she said, cutting herself a thick piece.

"Enjoy it while you can," Mabel said.

The doorbell rang. Mabel found her shoes and walked through the house to the front door. The door had a glass cutout, and she spied an attractive male in a suit and tie on the stoop. Most of their visitors were delivery people who resembled rejects from a hostile alien planet. She unchained the door and pulled it open.

"Good afternoon. Can I help you?"

"Special Agent Timothy Reynolds of the FBI," he said, holding up a laminated ID. He was about six-one and athletically built, with a cleft in his chin and eyes too small for his face. Mabel squinted at the ID, and he flipped his wallet shut.

"I'm looking for Tony Valentine. May I come in?"

The two statements did not go together, and Mabel felt herself stiffen.

"Tony is out of town, and no, you cannot come in."

"I was being polite, ma'am," he said.

He opened the screen door and put his foot deliberately inside the house. Mabel didn't budge. Two months ago, a man from the swamps had entered the house and abducted her. She'd made it easy for him by turning her back. Never again.

"No," she said firmly.

"Ma'am, by the powers vested in me—"

"My name is Mabel. Mabel Struck."

"Ms. Struck, by the powers vested in me by the United States government, I'm asking you to please stand aside so that I may enter this house."

"Where's your subpoena?"

Reynolds paused, studying her. "Homeland Security Act. I'm sure you've heard of it?"

"Yes," she said coolly. "I didn't know that it meant that you could come to a private residence and, without stating what you wanted, barge unannounced into someone's home. There happen to be other people here."

"I told you what I wanted," Reynolds said.

"And I told you, Tony isn't here. Do you want to search the place?"

"I want you to step aside so that I may enter the house. Otherwise . . ."

Reynolds didn't want to say it. Otherwise, he'd have to cite her for obstructing justice. Up close, he wasn't a bad-looking young fellow. Nice teeth, strong jawline. His breath smelled like a mint, and she guessed he'd popped one into his mouth in the driveway. Not a beast, she decided.

She let him enter, then locked the door behind him. "I thought the FBI always worked in pairs," she said.

"We do," Reynolds replied.

Reynolds's partner had come in through the back door. As Mabel entered the kitchen he introduced himself. Special Agent Scott Fisher. Another handsome, clean-shaven fellow in a suit and tie.

Reynolds pulled a chair out from the kitchen

table. "Please, make yourself comfortable, Ms. Struck."

Mabel remained standing. She glanced at Yolanda, who still sat at the table, and saw the frightened look on her face. Yolanda was equating the FBI's appearance with something Gerry had done.

"These men are looking for Tony," Mabel explained.

"Oh," Yolanda said.

"Please sit down," Reynolds said.

Mabel felt herself growing angry. Two men imposing themselves on two women, that's what was going on here. Her rear end made a loud *rhump!* as she hit the chair.

Reynolds crossed the kitchen so he was standing beside his partner. He pulled a spiral-bound notebook out of his back pocket, flipped it open, and stared at his notes. "Here's the deal, ladies. We need to talk to Tony Valentine, and we need to talk to him right now."

"Good luck," Mabel said.

When neither man said a word, she explained. "Tony considers cell phones one of life's great nuisances. He rarely leaves his on, even when someone says they'll call him."

"Have you spoken to him recently?"

"Yes. A few hours ago."

"Where was he calling from?"

"Las Vegas."

"We know that. Where in Las Vegas? The FBI

183

has been looking for him since yesterday. He's not registered in any hotel."

Mabel stiffened again. *How* did they know that? "He's on a job. If you want to talk to him, leave a message on his cell phone. I'm sure he'll get right back to you."

Reynolds flipped his notebook shut. The nice-guy look had vanished from his face. "Are you his wife?"

"Office manager," she replied.

"Are you aware that Tony Valentine wrote a letter right after 9/11, claiming the FBI was harassing Arab Americans living in the United States?"

Mabel nearly choked. *"What?"*

"And that he's a suspect in the murder of a woman suspected of laundering casino chips for an Arab gambler, who's also wanted by the FBI?"

Mabel shook her head, stunned.

"My partner and I are going to search the house," Reynolds said. "We are looking for any correspondence between your boss and any Arab gamblers. We're also looking for these." From his pocket, he removed a casino chip and held it in front of Mabel's face. It was brown, or what gamblers called a chocolate chip. "If you can help us in any way, please do so right now. Otherwise, I advise you to remain seated."

"And if we don't," Mabel said.

"Then we'll be forced to arrest you."

He stared at Mabel with murderous intensity, then shifted his gaze to Yolanda. The younger woman looked petrified, and an alarm went off in Mabel's head. Yolanda was as big as a house, yet neither man had mentioned it. Men *always* said something around a pregnant woman. Tony was always telling her to look for the little incongruities, and Mabel realized this was one. These men weren't FBI agents. They were imposters.

"Do you understand?" Reynolds asked them.

The two women nodded their heads.

"Good," he said.

Mabel knew who they were. They worked for a competitor of Grift Sense. The same competitor who'd tried to hack Creep File from Tony's computer a month ago. Tony's firewall had stopped them, so the competitor had sent these thugs.

"I'd like to see your credentials again," Mabel said.

Reynolds glared at her.

"I didn't have my glasses when you came to the door." She picked them up off the kitchen table and put them on. "If you don't mind."

Reynolds shook his head. "No," he added for emphasis.

"A real FBI agent wouldn't refuse my request," she said.

"Don't push it," Reynolds said.

It was all the proof Mabel needed. To Yolanda, she said, "I don't know about you, but I'm parched. Want a cold drink?"

Yolanda said "sure" under her breath, her eyes

glued to Reynolds's face. Mabel thought of the burden of carrying the unborn, and what had to be going through her head. She rose from the table, looked casually at Reynolds and Fisher and repeated the question. She touched the refrigerator door, waited.

"Nothing for me," Fisher said.

Reynolds grunted, "No thank you."

Opening the refrigerator, Mabel removed the loaded Sig Sauer keeping the cottage cheese company. It had been Tony's idea to put the gun there, instead of the hollow book in his study. It was the same gun she'd used two months ago to shoot her abductor through the heart. The therapist she'd gone to see had asked her if she felt revulsion toward the weapon. On the contrary, she'd told him. She kissed its barrel every day.

Pivoting on the balls of her feet, she aimed the gun at the two men and saw the life drain from their faces.

CHAPTER 22

Valentine sat behind the desk in Wily's office in the surveillance control room. The office was windowless and as dreary as a cave. Wily materialized in the doorway, clutching a stack of file folders to his chest.

"These are the personnel files of the new hires," he said, placing the folders on the desk. "Nick's right. It is as suspicious as hell they all flocked over here at once. I should have suspected something."

Valentine started examining the files and saw that Wily had done a smart thing. He'd separated the employees by the games they worked. Of the new hires, four dealt blackjack, one was a pit boss, six dealt craps, six worked roulette, four dealt poker, six emptied slot and video poker machines, two worked the cage, and one was in finance.

Valentine closed his eyes. He was working with a big puzzle, and there were a lot of pieces here. He spent a minute sorting through them in his head. Then he opened his eyes. Wily was standing in front of the desk, waiting expectantly.

"What you got?" he asked.

"Nick said something interesting before,"

Valentine said. "He said he knew that Chance Newman wanted to tear down the Acropolis and run a road through the property. That's why Fontaine was brought in."

"So?" Wily said.

"The Acropolis makes money, right?"

Wily smiled brightly. "Nick cleared six million last year."

"Okay. Fontaine isn't going to close Nick down by stealing twenty-five grand at blackjack. That's just the tip of the iceberg."

Wily cast his eyes downward. Then, like a comic strip character, the proverbial lightbulb went off above his head, and he said, "What you're saying is, we're getting scammed at *all* our games."

"That would be my guess."

"But that would be obvious, wouldn't it?"

"Not if it's being hidden."

Wily took a deep breath. The look of a man about to lose his job was no longer on his face. Now it was one of anger. He drew a file from the pile and held it beneath Valentine's nose. It was the file for their new guy in finance.

"This joker's hiding all the losses, isn't he?"

"I think so," Valentine said.

"So we're getting bled to death."

"Yes."

Wily bit his lower lip. There was no way of knowing how bad the damages were until they started digging. Judging by the amount of time the thirty new hires had been employed by Nick, the chances were the losses were heavy. Nick might very well be ruined, and Wily knew it.

Valentine got up and patted the head of security on the shoulder. He saw the life come back to Wily's face, but not much of it, and said, "Where is Nick, anyway?"

"Upstairs with Wanda."

"You're kidding."

"Nick's a creature of habit. Time for his afternoon screw."

Valentine had to give Nick credit. He knew things were bad, but he didn't let it spoil his day. Pointing at the files, he said, "How many of these folks are working right now?"

Wily looked through the stack. "Sixteen."

"Let's figure out what they're doing before we start pointing fingers. Don't want Nick to get sued on top of everything."

"Wouldn't that be swell," Wily said without humor. "Where do you want to start?"

"The catwalk," Valentine said.

The Acropolis was one of the last joints in Las Vegas to have a catwalk. Back before computers dominated the world, every casino had a catwalk. Usually, they were cavernous spaces in the ceiling with a narrow walkway and a railing. Through two-way mirrors, security people had watched for cheaters. Valentine had made his chops on a catwalk, and still considered them the best thing going.

"Ready when you are," he said to Wily.

"What game you want?"

"Craps."

Wily had spread the personnel files across the catwalk. He pulled the files of three employees dealing craps, and Valentine thumbed them open. Each had a snapshot of the employee. All guys. One redhead, one bald, and a blonde who spent too much time sunbathing. Staring down, he quickly found them at the table.

Craps was a furious game. The three new hires were working different sides of the table. They seemed to be working the table hard. Too hard, he decided.

He scouted the faces of the other players. A flashy kid in an Armani suit was shooting the dice. On his coming-out roll, he shot a six. That made the point six. He needed to throw a six again before shooting a seven or eleven, and losing.

The flashy kid picked up the dice and shook them. A hot girl in a leather mini skirt was draped on his arm. The kid raised the dice to her lips, and had her kiss them for luck.

The kid lowered his arm. His hand hung over the girl's pocketbook for a split second, and Valentine envisioned the dice secretly being dropped, and the loaded pair in his palm, called tops, invisibly replacing them. Tops had only three numbers on each die—in this case, the two, four, and six. With tops, the flashy kid would never roll a seven or eleven and crap out, and eventually roll a six. Because the human eye could only see three sides of a die at any single time, the gaff was undetectable.

Three rolls later, the kid won. Using a purse to switch dice wasn't new. What Valentine didn't understand was the three employees' role in the scam. He decided to watch them closely. Wily did the same.

To his credit, Wily made the scam.

"They're screwing the other players at the table," the head of security said. Pointing at the redhead, he said, "He's talking players out of making smart bets, where the odds are good, and steering them to making proposition bets, where the odds are terrible."

"What's the blonde's angle?"

"He's shorting the legitimate winners on the payoff," Wily said. "He's the banker. When he pays out, he cuts the chips on the table, then makes a giant stack out of the winnings and pushes them toward the winner, palming one in his hand."

"And adding them back to the tray," Valentine said.

Wily nodded. "He's making the losses look less than they are."

"Which is why no one up in the surveillance control room caught on," Valentine said.

"Guys upstairs are trained to watch the stacks. If they get short, they get tense."

"How about the bald guy?"

"The stick man? He's getting the crooked dice

off the table and switching them with a regular pair in his apron. If a floor manager strolls by and wants to look at the dice, they'll be clean."

Valentine pushed himself off the railing. He was positive similar scams were taking place at the other tables where the new hires were working, scams that required gangs of hustlers schooled in the art of subterfuge. It was a Frank Fontaine trademark, with Oscar nominations going to everyone involved.

"Give me the file on the finance guy," he said.

Wily handed the file over. Valentine opened it and stared at the new hire's picture. Albert Moss, age thirty-five, a curly-haired guy with a loose smile. Moss's job was to check the daily financials and keep Nick appraised of the casino's win–loss ratios. Only Moss wasn't doing that. He was cooking the books and telling Nick that there was money coming in the door, when the money was really going out the door. He was painting a picture of financial stability, letting Nick spend his afternoons in the arms of his nubile young bride without a worry in the world.

"I'm going to go see Nick, tell him what's going on," Valentine said.

Wily hesitated. "You going to tell him I screwed up?"

Valentine whacked him on the shoulder with Moss's file. "You didn't screw up. So I won't say that."

Wily grinned. "Thanks, man."

★   ★   ★

Nick's office in the Acropolis was like his house: a testimonial to bad taste that had been converted into a Laura Ashley showroom. Nick's secretary didn't work on weekends, and Valentine walked unannounced into the great one's office. It was empty.

He went to the door that led to Nick's private bedroom. A DO NOT DISTURB sign hung from the knob. Screwing was to Nick what eating was to the rest of the world. If he didn't get enough, there was no worse person to be around. Valentine tapped lightly on the door.

"Come on," Nick called out.

He cracked the door open. The room was huge. Nick sat on a bed in his jockeys, clapping like a kid at his first baseball game. Wanda, who was stark naked, was standing on her head on a metal contraption that let her spin with her legs stuck out in opposite directions. Blaring disco music played in the background.

"Come on . . . baby!" Nick exclaimed.

Valentine immediately shut the door. Then it registered in his brain what he'd just seen. It was Wanda's act from the talent portion of the Miss Nude World competition, the act that had captured Nick's eye, and stolen his heart.

He made it into the hallway before peals of laughter seeped out of him. It was laughter to make you hurt, and he leaned against a potted plant and held his sides until it subsided.

★   ★   ★

Valentine waited ten minutes before rapping on the bedroom door again.

"We're all friends here," Nick called out.

He opened the door and stuck his head in. Nick lay beneath satin sheets, staring dreamily at his reflection in the mirrored ceiling. The bathroom door on the other side of the room was closed. Behind it, Valentine could hear water running. Nick lifted his head, then sat bolt upright.

"No offense, Tony, but can't this wait?"

"No. Can I come in?"

"Sure. Make yourself at home. We're only screwing."

Nick slipped naked out of bed. His body was covered with black hair and looked like something that had just washed up on the beach. Putting on a monogrammed bathrobe, he met Valentine in the room's sitting area. Valentine handed him Albert Moss's file. Nick read through it.

"So, what's Curly doing?" he asked.

Valentine explained how Nick was being systematically bled by Fontaine's gang, then said, "The reason you're not seeing it on your books is because Albert Moss is hiding it from you. Moss has been cooking the books for three to four weeks, which means you're out a whole bunch of money."

"How much?"

Valentine had thought about it while waiting in the hallway. He'd done enough work for Nick to know how much money flowed through the

Acropolis each day. He also knew there was a limit on how much cheaters could steal before it became obvious.

"Seven to eight million bucks. That might be on the low side."

Nick shut his eyes. "What's the high side?"

"Ten to twelve million."

Nick whistled through his teeth. "Does that put me in the *Guinness Book of World Records*?"

"It might." Valentine hesitated, then asked him the question that had been bothering him since he'd done the math. "Can you cover it?"

Nick opened his eyes, and shook his head.

"No way," he said.

CHAPTER 23

Mabel wanted to talk to Tony before calling the police. Only Tony's cell phone wasn't on. *Damn him!*

Hanging up, she stared across the kitchen at Reynolds and Fisher. They were handcuffed together, hanging from a chin-up bar in the kitchen doorway. They looked madder than hell. Yolanda had cuffed them and gone through their pockets while Mabel held the Sig Sauer on them. Their IDs said they were FBI agents, but Mabel wasn't buying it. There was no reason for them to come barging in the way they had and accuse Tony of being unpatriotic and anti-American. The FBI had worked with Tony on many cases; they *knew* him.

"Shit," Mabel swore under her breath. What if they *were* FBI agents? Then she and Yolanda would be in more trouble than an army of lawyers could handle. If only she hadn't pulled the gun on them. But Reynolds and Fisher had acted like gestapo, and something inside her had snapped.

"Call him back," Yolanda said. She'd taken a yogurt out of the refrigerator and was eating it with a spoon. It somehow added normalcy to a picture that had none.

"Okay." Mabel hit REDIAL, and was immediately put into Tony's voice mail. "Damn."

"What's the matter?"

"His cell phone's still turned off."

She hung up and saw Reynolds staring help-lessly at her from across the kitchen. He had an embarrassed look on his face. Tony had said that having a gun pointed at you disrupted your bowels, and she wondered if he'd wet his pants.

Yolanda put her spoon in the sink. "I think we'd better call the police. It's what Tony will tell us to do anyway."

Yolanda was right. The local cops needed to get involved. Mabel glanced at her watch. Several minutes had passed since she'd pulled the gun from the fridge. The police were going to ask her why she'd waited to call them. She didn't have a good answer, but figured she'd come up with something by the time they arrived.

She picked up the phone and, while punching in 911, heard the dial tone go flat, then fade away and disappear. She clicked the receiver several times with her finger, but got nothing. Hanging up, she said, "That's strange."

Yolanda plucked an apple from the fruit bowl sitting on the counter. "What is?"

"The phone just went dead."

The kitchen wasn't terribly big, and from where Mabel stood, she had a clear view of the backyard through the window above the sink. Tony said fences made good neighbors, and a three-board one lined his property. Butting up to it was a phone pole, and Mabel saw a man scurry down it. *He cut the line,* she thought. She shot a glance at Reynolds and saw him shake his head.

"Is he with you?"

Reynolds licked his lips, hesitated.

"Go ahead and say it," she told him.

"Yes, he's with us. Ma'am, you are in so much trouble," he said.

Mabel felt an icy finger run down her spine. That wasn't the kind of threat that thieves made. She edged up to the window and watched the man jump off the phone pole, then go running down the narrow alley behind the house. Across the alley was another New England clapboard house constructed by the same builder who had built Tony's house. On its shingle roof she saw a man hiding behind the chimney. Yolanda bumped into her, munching on her apple and sharing her view.

"What's that guy doing up there?" she asked.

"I was wondering that myself," Mabel said. Leaning over the sink, she brought her nose up an inch from the glass and stared. "It looks like he's holding something."

Yolanda dropped her half-eaten apple into the sink.

"Oh, my God," she said.

Mabel kept staring. "What is it? It looks like a shovel . . ."

"Oh, my God," Yolanda said again.

Mabel pulled away from the window. Yolanda had her hand over her mouth, and the expectant-mother glow had drained from her face. Mabel grabbed her by the wrists.

"What is it? Tell me."

"He's holding a rifle," Yolanda said fearfully.

Nick had owned the Acropolis for more than thirty years, and had experienced a lot of bad times and misfortune along with every other casino owner. What he hadn't experienced was the widespread looting that Valentine had described to him. Few casino owners had.

"Ohhh, Nicky," Wanda called from the bathroom.

Nick raised his head. "I'm busy, honey. We've got company."

"But I have something to tell you. Something wonderful."

"Can't it wait?"

His bride emerged from the bathroom wearing six-inch heels and a bathing suit made from pink dental floss.

"But Nicky . . . ," she pouted, standing expectantly in the room's center.

Nick stared through her, too immersed in his casino's demise to realize Wanda might have something important to say. Stung, she grabbed a robe from the closet and marched out of the bedroom, slamming the door behind her. Shaking his head,

Nick said, "The other day, Wanda tells me it's my duty to make the coffee every morning. *My duty.* I say, baby, why is it my duty? And she goes and gets her Bible, and opens it up to a page, and points. Guess what it said."

"I haven't a clue."

"Hebrew."

A few moments passed, then Nick said, "So what do I do?"

Valentine had given Nick's options some serious thought. If he could prove to the Gaming Control Board that the Acropolis had been cheated, Bill Higgins would throw the thirty employees in jail, seize their bank accounts, plus their homes, cars, and everything of value they owned. They would be stripped clean. It wouldn't cover Nick's losses, but it was a start.

"Call an emergency meeting of your new hires," Valentine said. "We'll back-room them, and I'll interrogate them. I'll turn them against each other. I'll promise to cut deals with the guys I have by the balls in return for the information I don't have."

"You think it will work?"

He nodded. "Cheaters always squeal. It's their nature."

Nick called Wily and had him set the meeting for four o'clock in the casino's basement. "No, I'm not going to fire you," he told his head of security. Hanging up, he said, "Give me five minutes to get dressed. We can go downstairs together."

200

Valentine went into Nick's office to wait. He remembered his earlier promise to Mabel and powered up his cell phone. She'd asked him many times to leave it on, but he'd never seen the value in it. Too damn intrusive.

He had a message. He retrieved it and heard his neighbor's voice.

Mabel was screaming at him.

CHAPTER 24

Valentine's heart jumped into his throat. Hysterical women did that to him. From what he could make out from his neighbor's message, there were two men inside his house who may or may not be FBI agents and were handcuffed to his chin-up bar, while a third man was on the neighbor's roof with a rifle. The phone lines had been cut, and Mabel was calling him from Yolanda's cell phone.

"Call me back on Yolanda's cell!" she told him.

He punched in Yolanda's number. A frantic busy signal filled his ear. The call wasn't going through. Going to the bedroom door, he rapped loudly. Nick bid him entrance, and he stuck his head in. "I need to use a phone. It's an emergency. My cell phone isn't cooperating."

Nick emerged still dressed in his robe. He escorted Valentine across the room to his desk. It was as big as a sports car and covered with photographs. He pointed at the phone. "Use line two. It's my private line."

Nick went back to the bedroom. Valentine picked up line two and dialed Yolanda's cell number while staring at the photographs. Groups of smiling Greek fishermen stared back at him. In the photos, the men were standing on fishing docks and holding up their catches.

He heard the connection ring through. Mabel answered on the first ring.

"Hey," he said.

"Oh, Tony," his neighbor replied. "I've done something truly awful."

He listened to Mabel explain what had happened. She and Yolanda were staying away from the kitchen window, fearful of the sniper on the roof next door. And there was a strange car parked in his driveway, and she had heard scratching sounds around the house.

"Why did you pull the gun on them?" he asked when she was done.

"Because they barged in here and practically called you a traitor," she hissed. "You always told me you had a good relationship with the FBI, and these men acted like they'd never heard of you."

"They called me a what?"

"Well, they said you were unpatriotic."

Valentine felt his face burn. He hung his flag out on Veterans Day, paid his taxes, and believed in truth, justice, and the American Way.

"Are they within earshot?"

"You bet they are," his neighbor seethed.

"Put one of them on."

He heard Mabel cross his kitchen, and the sound of the cell phone being placed beneath someone's mouth. Mabel had said she'd handcuffed the agents to his chin-up bar, and he wondered how they felt about being outwitted by a sixty-five-year-old woman. He said, "This is Tony Valentine. Who is this?"

"FBI Special Agent Reynolds," a man's voice replied.

"Sounds like you and your partner are in a pickle," Valentine said.

There was a long pause. Reynolds cleared his throat. "Your friend Mabel is in a lot of trouble, if you hadn't already figured that out."

"So are you," Valentine replied. "I want you to call off your dogs."

"Excuse me?"

"The guys who've surrounded my house, and the guy on the roof with the rifle. I want you to call them off."

"What are you offering in return?"

"The opportunity to end this peacefully, without anyone getting hurt."

Another pause. Reynolds said something to his hanging partner. Valentine made out the words *It's worth a shot* and heard Reynolds agree.

"Mind telling me how?" Reynolds asked him.

"Easy," Valentine replied. "I'm going to have a chat with Peter Fuller, your boss. You wouldn't have a number where I might reach him, would you?"

Reynolds gave him Peter Fuller's private number, then promised to keep the agents surrounding the house at bay. Valentine hung up and walked out of Nick's office.

He took the elevator to the penthouse floor, which was one floor below. From his suite he got the laptop computer he'd bought when he'd opened Grift Sense and went back upstairs.

Sitting at Nick's desk, he ran a wire from the laptop to the phone jack in the wall, and within a minute was connected to the Internet. He picked up the phone and punched in Peter Fuller's number at the FBI. A woman answered with a curt, "May I help you?"

"This is Tony Valentine for Director Fuller."

"Director Fuller is unavailable. May I help you?"

"Get him anyway. And while you're at it, give me his e-mail address."

"That's out of the question."

"Tell him I have the pictures."

"Excuse me?"

"The pictures. Tell him I still have the pictures from Atlantic City."

The woman hesitated. How much did she know about Fuller? Plenty, he guessed; most personal secretaries knew more about their bosses' habits than their wives.

"Please hold," she said.

While Valentine waited, he entered his e-mail account and went into the SAVED MESSAGES folder. Retrieving a message titled FULLER, he opened it. On the laptop's blue screen appeared ten pictures of Fuller screwing a hooker in Atlantic City in

1979. The hooker was tied to the headboard of a bed, and did not look happy with the arrangement. Valentine had gotten the pictures from a serial killer who'd blackmailed Fuller into leaving Atlantic City with his partner. By leaving, Fuller had allowed the serial killer to claim one final victim, an injustice that Valentine had never forgiven him for.

Fuller was a bad apple. Law enforcement had its share of bad apples. The system was supposed to weed them out the higher you rose, but occasionally one slipped through the cracks like Fuller had.

He and Fuller spoke a couple of times a year, usually when Fuller needed help on a gambling-related case that had the bureau stumped. Fuller was always quick to remind him that he'd patched things up with his wife, whom he'd abused, and his partner, whom he'd lied to. He liked to say that he'd found the good life. When he wasn't working, he was driving his daughter to soccer practice, or leading his son's Boy Scout troop.

Valentine didn't believe a word of it.

Fuller liked sex, and he liked it rough. To get it, he hired prostitutes to service him. The patterns he'd shown in Atlantic City were of a man who lived in two worlds—the real one, and the one behind the curtain of his conscience. Hurting women during sex turned him on. It was what psychologists called his erotic mold, something he *couldn't* change.

"Valentine?" a man's voice said.

"That you, Fuller?" he said.

"Yes. Go ahead."

"I'm calling about a situation at my house. Two of your agents are being held at gunpoint by my office manager. You aware of this?"

"What did you tell my secretary about the pictures?"

"What pictures?"

"Don't pull that horseshit with me," Fuller thundered at him. "What did you say to her?"

"I said I still had the pictures from Atlantic City."

"You told me you destroyed them."

"I did. But first, I burned them onto the hard drive on my computer. I'm looking at them on my laptop. You know, you've hardly aged."

Fuller cursed like he'd hit his thumb with a hammer.

"What do you want," he seethed.

"An explanation," Valentine said. "I don't deserve to have my house searched without the decency of a phone call. Your agents inferred that I was some kind of traitor. I resent that."

"Your name came up in conjunction with a case involving national security. It was decided that your house should be searched."

"Decided by who?"

"By me," Fuller said.

"You couldn't call me? You didn't think I'd help you?"

"I couldn't call you because you're a suspect in

207

a murder investigation. Your business card, and a Nike gym bag identical to one you purchased six months ago, were found at the crime scene."

"I got here yesterday," Valentine said. "You want to hear my itinerary? I didn't have time to kill anybody, for Christ's sake."

"Your flight landed the day *before* yesterday," Fuller corrected him, "a few hours before the victim was killed. Your things were found at the scene."

"My flight was delayed in Dallas," Valentine replied. "I arrived yesterday morning at one A.M. The airline lost my bag, and I killed two hours at the airport, filling out a claim sheet. If you don't believe me, call Delta."

"How do you explain your card and gym bag," Fuller said.

"I've given out plenty of business cards in Las Vegas," he replied. "And the Nike gym bag is back in my closet at home. I don't travel with it."

"You landed when?"

"One A.M. I checked into Sin at three. There's records of all this stuff. And plenty of eyewitnesses."

There was silence. Then Fuller cursed under his breath.

"My sentiments, exactly," Valentine said. "Now are you going to call your dogs off my house, or should we keep talking until somebody gets killed?"

CHAPTER 25

Negotiating with people with guns was a tricky proposition. One party had to give in and put their weapons down first. That was the hard part. Since Mabel had drawn first, Valentine knew it would put the FBI at ease if she relinquished first. And since the FBI had his house surrounded, he talked her into it.

"Are they going to arrest me?" his neighbor asked.

"Absolutely not," he assured her.

"But I pulled a gun on them."

"They're going to call it a big misunderstanding."

"Really?"

"Yes."

"So you're not a traitor?"

Valentine's face burned at the mention of the word. Fuller had never explained that. Someday he was going to pin the man down and find out why his agents had said that.

"No, I'm not a traitor."

"So his men won't be searching your house, then?" she said.

Valentine smiled into the receiver. Searching the house was the last thing Fuller wanted his agents to do. He'd told Fuller the photographs of him and the hooker were on the hard drive of his computer. His agents would certainly look there, and the cat would be out of the bag.

"Absolutely not," he said.

"All right," Mabel said. "I'm putting the Sig Sauer back in the refrigerator. Now I'm closing the refrigerator door. I suppose my next step is to release these two young men."

"Not yet. I'm going to hang up, and then you're going to get a call from Director Fuller. He's going to want to speak to Reynolds. Put the cell phone next to Reynolds's ear, and listen in. I'll be listening in as well."

"How will you do that?"

"I've got Fuller on the other line."

His neighbor's voice dropped to a whisper. "Oh, Tony, I'm so sorry this happened."

"There's no need to apologize," he said. "You did what you thought was right."

As Mabel hung up, she tried to hide the smile on her face.

"Looks like our bosses have reached an agreement," she announced.

Reynolds and Fisher said nothing. Yolanda let out a sigh of relief, and sat down at the kitchen table. The chair was old and creaky. A startled expression crossed her face. She glanced at the back door as if expecting it to come crashing down and a SWAT team to enter the house.

"It's all right," Mabel said. "They're leaving. Tony fixed everything."

Yolanda went to the window over the sink. Parting the curtains, she peered outside at the neighbor's house and said, "You're right. He's climbing down off the roof." She walked into the living room with Mabel behind her. Through the front window they saw the car with tinted windows that had been parked in the driveway speed away. Yolanda put her arms around Mabel and began to cry.

"There, there," Mabel said.

Yolanda's cell phone chirped. Mabel pulled it from her pocket. "Hello?"

The caller identified himself as Director Fuller of the FBI and asked to speak to Special Agent Reynolds. Mabel remembered Fuller from his picture in the newspaper. Blond and handsome, his only flaw was his mouth, which was too thin for his face.

"He's right here," she replied.

Going into the kitchen, she put the cell phone next to Reynolds's ear, then listened as Fuller told Reynolds that the bureau had acted on bad information, and that the job was to be aborted. Reynolds closed his eyes and muttered under his breath.

"Yes, sir," Reynolds said. "I understand. We'll leave the premises once Ms. Struck releases us."

Looking at Mabel, Reynolds said, "Director Fuller would like to have a word with you, if you don't mind."

"Of course," Mabel said.

Putting the phone to her ear, Mabel listened as Fuller apologized for what had happened. His voice was flat and unemotional, the way so many law enforcement people were. Taking the hand-cuff key from her pocket, she released Reynolds and his partner.

Valentine listened to Fuller apologize to Mabel, then hung up. As he pushed himself out of the chair, a strange thought occurred to him. His house had been raided by the FBI.

His house. The FBI was probably the best law enforcement agency in the world. They could be world-class jerks and arrogant as hell, but it didn't belie the job they did. They were pros, which meant there had been a really good reason for them to raid his house. His business card, and a gym bag that resembled one he'd purchased six months ago, had been found at the murder scene. A coincidence? Someone much smarter than him had once said that there are no coincidences in police work.

His business card, his gym bag.

He picked up the phone and redialed his house. The phone lines had been restored, and he heard Mabel's cheery voice say, "Grift Sense. Can I help you?"

"Just calling to see how you and Yolanda are doing."

"Oh, how thoughtful of you. We're making out fine. Those two FBI agents turned out to be real gentlemen. They apologized up a storm and actually took the garbage out when they left. It was quite a shock."

"Glad you didn't shoot them, huh?"

"Listen to you!"

"Look, I need a favor."

"Your wish is my command."

"Go into my bedroom and open up my closet."

Mabel put him on hold. When she picked up a few moments later, she was talking to him on the speaker phone in the bedroom. "All right, I'm opening up your closet. Oh my, would you look at this mess."

Valentine had never left a mess a day in his adult life. "What are you talking about?"

"Dirty clothes. They're shoved in the corner in a pile. There's a dirty jock strap, a dirty judo uniform, and a T-shirt with holes in the armpits that you *must* throw away."

"Is my gym bag there?"

He heard Mabel shuffle some things around.

"Why no," she said. "It's gone."

He sat back down and for a long moment stared at the phone. Only one person would throw his dirty clothes on the floor and take his gym bag without asking.

Gerry.

He glanced up. Nick was standing in the doorway, ready to go downstairs and bang some heads.

"I need to run," he said. "I'll call you later."

CHAPTER 26

When Pash and Gerry returned from Pahrump, they found a much different-looking Amin waiting for them at the motel. His beard and mustache were gone, and he'd trimmed his hair. It was short and choppy, and looked like the punk kids you saw walking around. He'd also changed his wardrobe, and now wore chinos and a striped rugby shirt.

"You get laid?" Amin asked his brother.

Pash took off his windbreaker and sat on the bed. "Yes. It was wonderful."

"I hope you wore a rubber."

"I did not have a choice. The woman put it on me."

Amin made a face like he couldn't imagine anything more disgusting. He was a handsome guy, and Gerry guessed he had no problem getting action when he wanted to. Pash, on the other hand, was always going to have to pay for it.

"They also wash you down," Pash threw in for good measure.

"You let a strange woman wash your penis?"

Pash flashed a smile. "Oh, yes. With antibacterial

scrub. When it starts to tingle, it actually feels quite good. There is one drawback, though."

"What's that?"

"Whenever I smell Betadine, I get an erection."

Amin let out a rare laugh. Pash had promised to soften him up so Gerry could sell his idea of card-counting in "easy" casinos. Seeing his opportunity, Gerry pulled up a chair and launched into his sales pitch.

First, he explained the concept of how he planned to use his father's information to target casinos, and saw Amin nod in agreement. Then he went into the numbers. Three hundred grand apiece was his first year's estimate.

"These casinos you describe are small," Amin said. "Surely they'll notice such large losses."

"My father has access to the daily financial sheets of every casino he works for," Gerry said. "He examines them to see fluctuations in the holds of the various games."

"How does this help us?"

"Certain times of the day the action is heavy, others it's not. You'll only play when the action is heavy and there's money flying around. That way, your winnings won't be noticed the way they would if the place was dead."

Amin steepled his fingers in front of his chin, deep in thought. Then he spoke to Pash in their native tongue. Gerry hated when he did that, and planned to mention it when their relationship got farther along. Amin ended the conversation by standing, and slapping Gerry on the shoulder. "I think we should become partners."

Gerry looked into his eyes. *Amin bought the pitch.* "You're in?"

Amin nodded approvingly.

Gerry nearly let out a shout. "How about I buy you and Pash a steak? I think this is cause for celebration."

Amin glanced at his watch. "We can eat later. There are some friends of mine I want you to meet. Do you mind driving?"

Gerry tried not to laugh. Did he mind driving? Amin was about to make him rich. He'd drive Amin wherever he wanted, and even wear a chauffeur's cap.

"Ready when you are," he said.

Amin sat in the passenger's seat and had Gerry drive through Henderson, then get on Highway 93 and head east. The road was long and ruler-straight. Ten miles outside of town, Amin pointed to an unpaved road sitting off the highway.

"Take that," he said.

Gerry drove down the road in a cloud of dust. Soon a gas station came into view. The building was abandoned and sagged drunkenly to one side. Nailed to its rusted tin roof was a crude, hand-painted sign. BOULDER AUTO RESTORERS. NO JOB TOO SMALL.

Behind the gas station was another tin-roofed

structure. Pointing at it, Amin said, "I'm meeting my friends there."

Gerry spun the wheel, no longer feeling good about things. Friends met at bars and restaurants, not behind abandoned buildings in the desert. Something bad was going down. He drove around back to an auto graveyard filled with car skeletons and pyramids of empty lacquer cans. The air was chemically ripe, and he crushed his cigarette in the ashtray.

A beat-up station wagon was parked in the lot's center. Two stern-faced Mexican men stood beside it. In their thirties, with jet-black hair and complexions the color of pencil erasers. Gerry glanced sideways at Amin. "These your friends?"

"Yes," Amin said.

He parked a hundred feet from where the Mexicans stood. Then glanced at the paper bag sitting on the floor between Amin's feet. He'd assumed it was food that Amin had brought for the trip. Now he knew otherwise.

"You packing?" Gerry asked him.

Amin ignored the remark. Grabbing the paper bag, he climbed out of the car. He started walking toward the two Mexicans and waved. The Mexicans waved back.

Pash leaned between the two front seats. "Is something wrong?"

"You bet there is."

Pash's face begged for an explanation.

"They're border rats. Smugglers. Your brother set me up."

"Set you up how?"

"He asked me to come as backup. In case these guys got any funny ideas."

"You do not trust these men?"

Gerry shook his head. Back when he'd run a bookmaking operation in Brooklyn, a local hoodlum had brought two Mexicans by and tried to talk him into bankrolling a cocaine run out of Mexico. Gerry had listened because he was interested in how these things worked, then said no thanks.

What he'd learned was that border rats had become popular in the smuggling world since 9/11. Bribing border guards to ignore a truckload of cocaine was a thing of the past. Contraband was having to take different routes, and border rats were cheap alternatives. They carried the drugs on their backs, entering the country with illegal immigrants in southern New Mexico's boot heel.

Amin's friends looked menacing. Short and broad-shouldered, with steely glints for eyes and sweatshirts that hung over their belts. Gerry guessed they were packing heat. The Mexicans he'd met in Brooklyn had been.

"How well does Amin know them?" he asked.

"They've met once before," Pash replied.

Gerry spun around in his seat and stared at him. "And Amin is about to give them a bag of money? Is he crazy?"

"You think they'll kill him?"

"Of course they'll kill him."

"But they come highly recommended."

"By who? Pablo Escobar?"

Pash's eyes turned as big as silver dollars. "Oh, no," he muttered under his breath. "Something is wrong."

Gerry stared out the windshield. One of the Mexicans was holding stacks of money in his hands. His partner was pointing at the money and shouting. Gerry didn't have to understand Spanish to get the argument's drift. Amin had delivered less than he'd promised. That happened a lot in drug deals.

Only Amin wasn't apologizing. He needed to fall on his sword and let the Mexicans have their pride restored. Amin was just standing there, talking calmly.

"He's asking for trouble," Gerry said.

Amin took something from his pocket. It looked like a casino chip. He offered it to the Mexicans, finally extending the olive branch. The shouting Mexican knocked it out of his hand, then went for his gun.

Amin lifted his shirt and drew his own piece. He was lightning-fast, and shot the Mexican three times in the chest. The Mexican's gun discharged into the ground. He staggered backward and fell against the skeleton of a car.

The Mexican holding the money was helpless, and looked at Amin as if to say *Now what?* The guy was cool, Gerry thought. Telling Amin with a shrug that he'd settle for less, no harm done. A real businessman.

Amin lowered his gun. He reached for the battered briefcase the Mexicans had brought. Had his fingers on the handle when the Mexican leaning against the car came to life and started shooting. There were bullet holes in his sweatshirt, but no bloodstains. He's wearing a vest, Gerry thought.

His partner ran for cover. The Mexican doing the shooting hid behind the pyramid of lacquer cans and kept letting off rounds. He was a crummy shot, but Gerry knew he was eventually going to hit Amin, who was standing in the open. Then the Mexican would come after him and Pash, and get rid of his witnesses.

"The car," Pash said. "Drive it between them."

Gerry shook his head. That would only get *them* shot. He looked out his window at the cans lying nearby. The labels said PAINT REMOVER. He jumped out and started shaking them. Finding one half-filled, he unscrewed the lid, pulled a snot rag out of his pocket, and made a Molotov cocktail.

"I need a light," he told Pash.

Pash found his cigarette lighter and jumped out of the car. He made a flame appear, and turned the snot rag bright orange.

Gerry came around the car with the burning can in his outstretched hand. Running three steps, he threw the flaming can over his head with all his might. As it soared through the air, Amin, who was crouching on the ground, craned his neck to watch.

The flaming can landed on the pyramid and toppled it. There was a loud *pop!* as everything that was flammable caught fire at once. An orange wall rose up around the Mexican, and he screamed. Gerry could feel the heat from where he was standing. The Mexican ran out from his hiding place covered in flames.

Pash appeared at his side. "The human torch," he mumbled.

They watched the Mexican run into a nearby field, his clothes throwing off black smoke. His partner ran in the opposite direction, the stacks of money clutched to his chest. They got in the car, and Gerry floored it. He jammed the brakes a few yards from where Amin stood. He saw Amin pick up a brown casino chip from the ground. He wondered if the Mexican had realized that it was worth five thousand dollars.

Amin dragged the briefcase across the dirt and got in. Smoke began to pour out of the ground, and Gerry stared at flames that seemed to rise an inch every second. Their motion was sensuous, almost taunting.

"Hold on," he said.

He was doing seventy down the dirt road leading back to Highway 93 when he heard a muffled explosion. Slowing down, he turned in his seat.

Everything behind them was on fire: the abandoned gas station, the auto graveyard, even the adjacent field. Had he not known better, he would have sworn that a giant bomb had just been set off.

Amin touched his sleeve. "Thank you for saving my life."

"You're a lying son-of-a-bitch," Gerry said. "You know that?"

CHAPTER 27

"You realize that I'm ruined," Nick said as they rode downstairs in the elevator.

The little Greek said it like he was commenting about the weather. Only his voice was strained, and Valentine realized he was dying inside.

"The Gaming Control Board will take the assets of the thirty employees who ripped you off," Valentine said. "You can use that to run the casino until you get a loan from a bank."

Nick laughed harshly. "That's not going to happen. Chance Newman and Rags Richardson and Shelly Michael control the banks—they run a few billion bucks through them every year. I'm a small fry. I've got no juice."

Juice. It was the magic elixir in Las Vegas, even more powerful than money. Who you knew, and how well you knew them. And Nick was saying he didn't have any.

"Have you considered selling the place?" Valentine asked as the elevator docked.

"I've had offers," Nick said. "Venture capitalists, banks. Everybody wants to tear the place down, put in a big moron-catcher. Know what I tell them?"

"No."

"I tell them to get lost."

As they got out of the elevator, Nick punched Valentine in the arm. It really stung, and Valentine thought he understood. Nick had accepted that his run was over.

"Let's nail these people ripping me off," he said.

They found Wily in the surveillance control room, hovering before the wall of video monitors. He was watching the roulette table, and Valentine could tell by the hunch in his shoulders that he was on to something.

"Figure out what Fontaine's gang is doing?"

Wily nodded, surprising Valentine by not gloating over it.

"So tell us," Nick said.

"The gang is double past-posting," Wily replied.

Valentine was impressed. He'd only seen the scam once, down in Puerto Rico, where the game of roulette bordered on high art. The San Juan gang had lightened the house by over a million bucks. He decided not to steal Wily's thunder.

"How?" he asked.

Wily pointed at the monitors. Because the roulette layout was large, two cameras covered the action. One camera watched the wheel, while the second watched the layout on which the bets were made. It was impossible for anyone in surveillance to watch both cameras at once, a fact known to most roulette gangs.

"The gang has three members," Wily said. "The dealer, and two women standing at the end of the table."

He pointed at two women playing roulette. Both were dressed like tourists. One was quiet and reserved, the other a blond woman who liked to bang the table.

"The quiet one's past-posting. In the last twenty minutes, she's won five grand. The reason we're not seeing it is because the dealer and the table-banger are distracting us. Watch."

They watched the ivory ball roll around the wheel. As it started to slow down, the dealer announced the betting was over. The ball landed, and they saw the table-banger attempt to place a late bet. The dealer stopped her and politely explained that the betting was over. Then he pushed her chips back.

"You see it?" Wily asked.

"See what?" Nick said.

"The dealer is blocking the camera when he pushes the chips back. The quiet one is sneaking a bet onto the layout behind his arm. No one pays attention to her."

Nick looked at Valentine. "You ever seen this scam before?"

It was the stupidest damn thing, but Valentine found himself feeling proud of Wily. He'd smartened up, something chumps rarely did. So

Valentine lied and said, "Heard about it, but never seen it."

"No kidding." Nick looked at Wily. "If the past-posting is hidden from the camera, how we going to nail them?"

"Was hidden," Wily informed him.

"Let me guess," Nick said. "You sent someone down to the floor with a video cam, and captured the whole thing."

Wily smiled. "Yes, sir. I was thinking of letting the woman leave and having her followed. Who knows. Maybe she'll lead us to Fontaine."

Nick beamed at him. "Good thinking. Tony, the kid's sharp, isn't he?"

A few years ago, Valentine had likened Wily to a dog trying to walk on its hind legs. No more. "Real sharp," he said.

Nick slung his arm around Wily's shoulder. Then he led Wily across the room to a secluded corner and broke the bad news to him. Wily had worked for Nick for seventeen years, which was a lifetime by Las Vegas standards, and Valentine watched Wily's face change as Nick explained that the Acropolis was doomed. Wily kept trying to interject, but Nick wouldn't let him. It was over.

By the time Nick was finished, the head of security was weeping.

At a quarter of four, the thirty people responsible for destroying Nick's empire began to file into the basement meeting room of the Acropolis.

Valentine watched them on the video monitors. The new hires were laughing and joking, unaware they were about to be busted. Nick appeared by his side, chewing a handful of Tums and gulping down water.

"Fucking rats," Nick said. "I wish this was thirty years ago."

"Why's that?"

"In the old days, casinos shot cheaters in the head and buried them in the desert."

Valentine glanced at him. "You ever do that?"

"Who cares?"

"I like to know who I'm working for."

"No. I just had their legs broken."

"That was civil of you."

"Didn't have a choice. There were no surveillance cameras back then. Sometimes you could snap a picture from the catwalk, but it was hard. Usually, it was your word against theirs in court. Juries didn't buy it, and the cheaters walked."

"So you broke their legs to keep them away."

"Just one leg."

"Why only one?"

"I didn't want them becoming cripples. A guy with a cane can get around, find a job, lead a normal life. I've got principles, you know?"

Valentine's eyes returned to the monitor. Wily was in the basement, standing directly in the camera's eye. When all the new hires were present, he would stick a pen behind his ear. That was the signal for Nick to come down without Wily calling him and arousing suspicion.

"How much security is down there?" Valentine asked.

"Twenty of my best guys."

"Remember those martial arts creeps Fontaine sprang on you last time?"

Nick called downstairs and doubled security outside the meeting room. Hanging up, he said, "If they start to tango, you want a piece of one?"

Valentine looked at him like he'd lost his mind. "Me?"

"Yeah. Weren't you a judo champion? The TV movie said you were."

"About a hundred years ago."

"Come on, you're not afraid of these young punks, are you?"

Nick was putting on a brave face, and Valentine tried to think of something to say. He almost told Nick the truth, which was that if you lived long enough, all good things in your life came to an end. On the monitor, he saw Wily stick a pen behind his ear. Nick saw it as well, and hurried from the room.

Five minutes later, Nick and forty security guards rushed into the basement meeting room and announced that the new hires were being held on suspicion of cheating the house.

Valentine was the last through the door. He saw several females start to weep. Other employees lay on the floor and covered their heads with their arms, a sure sign they'd been busted before. A small group of male employees decided to put up a fight and cleared away the folding chairs in the room's center.

Twenty security guards surrounded them, then charged in. They used billy clubs and their hands, and were not gentle. Nick immediately jumped into the melee and began swinging his arms. He was a lousy fighter, but every tenth punch caught an unsuspecting chin and sent someone to the floor. Seeing Valentine, he yelled, "Are we having fun yet?"

It *looked* like fun, only Valentine was in no mood for it. His mind had locked on Gerry. He needed to find him before the FBI made the connection between his son and the gym bag. He wanted to help Gerry decide his best course of action. Maybe it was hiring a good lawyer; or perhaps he needed to turn himself in. Either way, he wanted to be there, and help him decide.

He spied a familiar-looking guy crawling across the floor. It was Albert Moss, the rat in finance who'd cooked the books. He stood in front of the exit, blocking Moss's escape. Moss rose from the floor.

"Get out of my way, " the crooked accountant said.

"No."

Moss tried to take his head off with a punch. Valentine ducked the blow, then grabbed Moss's arm and in one practiced motion flipped him over his shoulder, then slammed his body onto the concrete floor.

Moss lay on his back without moving. Valentine sat on his chest and saw Moss's eyes pop open. He looked older than his photo, with thin, purplish lips and short curly hair more appropriate for another part of his body.

"I can't breathe," Moss gasped.

"I'll let you up, if you tell me one thing."

"What . . ."

"We've figured out all the scams you've got going, except the slot machines. I want to know how you're ripping them off."

Moss's eyes narrowed. "You're . . . Valentine."

"No, I'm Bozo the fucking clown."

"Frank didn't tell me everything," Moss whispered.

"You must have some idea."

"Frank said the slot scam at the Stardust inspired him."

The Stardust slot scam had happened in 1980 and was the stuff of legend. Fourteen million in quarters had disappeared from the casino, and no one knew how. Valentine guessed Moss knew more than he was letting on.

"You're lying."

"I swear, I don't know."

"Where's Fontaine hiding out? "

"I'll tell you," Moss said. "But you've got to let me up."

Moss's face was turning blue. Valentine pushed himself off his chest. The rest of the employees were standing against the wall, having their rights explained to them. It wouldn't be long before they would be cutting deals and ratting each other out.

He watched Moss get up. His head left a pancake-sized bloodstain on the floor, and Valentine winced. He'd never believed in hurting people for the sake of inflicting pain, and wondered if he'd cracked Moss's skull open.

"You want to know where Fontaine is?" Moss asked.

Valentine lifted his gaze. Moss was standing next to him, and had a small knife gripped in his hand. Drawn from his sock, he guessed.

"Frank's with your girlfriend," Moss said, slicing his face open.

CHAPTER 28

Gerry watched the sun set from the Red Roost Inn's parking lot while trying to decide what to do.

The sun had bled through the sky as it dropped behind the mountains. His old man had gotten him in the habit of catching sunsets whenever he could. His father hadn't used to care about that kind of stuff, but becoming a widower had changed him. He savored things now that he'd never paid attention to before.

Gerry smoked his cigarette down to the filter. His father. So many things he'd done in his life had been to defy him, he could see that now. Back when he was a teenager and had started getting in trouble, his father had always rescued him. He'd been his safety net, shielding him from the consequences of his deeds.

He threw his stub onto the pile on the ground. He knew he had to leave Las Vegas. The fact that he hadn't broken any laws in the past few days didn't matter. He'd been in the company of two guys who'd broken plenty of laws, and his association with them was going to kill him. Nevada was different that way. If you took money from the casinos, you were guilty until proven innocent.

Taking out his wallet, he removed his American Express card. He'd lent Amin his card several days ago for some stupid reason, and there was no telling what he'd bought with it. He folded the card until it broke in half. He would call Amex, tell them the card was missing. Then, if any of Amin's purchases came back to haunt him, he could claim his card was stolen. End of story.

Getting photographed with Amin at the MGM's blackjack tables was going to be more difficult to disassociate himself from. He wasn't sure what the solution was, except to ask his father to step in. The MGM was a client, and that would probably help.

He rubbed his arms and felt himself shiver. The desert didn't hold the heat; once the sun went down, the air got really chilly. He considered getting into his car and finding some food, then told himself no. He needed to finish this process and come to grips with things. He needed to purge himself.

Going home to Florida and confessing to Yolanda was a start. He'd hidden a lot of things from her, and he was going to have to come clean or risk her leaving him. She was a doctor, and wouldn't need him to pay the bills and put food on the table. He felt himself start to choke up. God, did he love her.

Then he had to swallow his pride and confess

to his father. There was so much on his slate, he wasn't sure where to begin. Maybe the first time he'd ever stolen money from his mother's purse was a good place to start.

And then, when he was finished spilling his guts to Yolanda and his father, he was going to fly to Atlantic City and look up Father Tom, the family priest. He hadn't taken confession since . . . he couldn't remember the last time. But he needed to do it soon, and open up his soul. He needed to sit in a confessional and, for however long it took, tell his creator all the things he'd done wrong. Being a Catholic, he had an out. He could accept God and ask to be spared from his crimes.

"Or risk eternal damnation," he whispered.

Taking out his cell phone, he got the toll-free number for several airlines. He started calling them, determined to find which one had the first flight out.

While he was on hold with American, he thought about his father again and began to choke up. He wondered how his father had found the strength to put up with him for all these years. It was a strength he knew he didn't possess.

American came through. They had a nonstop flight to Tampa at seven AM with two seats left in coach. He and his father could leave Las Vegas together.

Pash came out of the motel and stood beside him while he gave his Visa number to the booking agent. He offered Gerry a cigarette. Gerry took it, and a light, while the booking agent read his confirmation number back to him. He'd inherited his old man's memory, and burned the number into his head, then hung up.

"You're not cold?" Pash asked.

Gerry shrugged. "I grew up in New Jersey, on the ocean."

"It gets cold there?"

"We used to sing songs about how cold it was. It's colder than a nipple on a witch's tit, it's colder than a bucket of penguin shit, it's colder than an icicle on a polar bear's ass, it's colder than the frost on a champagne glass."

Pash slapped his hands and laughed. Up until that afternoon, Gerry had liked Pash about as much as he could like anyone he'd known for five days. But the shootout at the deserted gas station had changed that. Beneath the Jim Carrey personality, there was a bad person hiding. Trusting him was out of the question, and Gerry stared at the headlights of cars coming down the highway next to the motel.

"I guess you're disappointed in me and my brother," Pash said.

"Yeah, I'm disappointed," Gerry said, blowing a monster cloud of smoke. "I came to you with a legitimate business proposition, and you played me for a chump."

Pash cocked his head and stared at him. "You came to us with a way to make money. We showed you another way to make money. Is that so bad?"

The afternoon had disappeared, and the fractured light reflecting off the motel's neon sign gave Pash a ghoulish quality. Gerry wagged a finger in his face. "Right. Next we'll be robbing banks and shooting guards. No thanks."

"My brother has never shot his gun before. It was just . . ."

"One of those things?"

"Yes."

Gerry inched closer to Pash and breathed on him. An old mobster trick, and a great way to get another guy's attention. Pash shrank a few inches.

"I killed a guy this afternoon saving your brother's ass," Gerry said. "He may have had it coming, but that doesn't matter. *I killed him.*"

"I know," Pash said.

"Some guys will tell you that killing someone is liberating. It wasn't for me."

Pash swallowed hard. "I'm sorry."

"No, you're not."

"I'm not?"

"You're happy I killed that guy. I saved your brother's life. You understand what I'm saying?"

Pash shook his head. He didn't understand at all.

"It's like this," Gerry said. "You can never feel the way I feel about what happened this afternoon. You're going to go on with your life, and eventually you'll forget about it. Me, I'm going to live with it. It's going to hang heavy on my soul for a long, long time."

"Your soul," Pash whispered.

"That's right."

Pash could no longer look him in the eye, and used the fading ember of his cigarette to light another. He gestured weakly with the pack, offering him one. That was all that was left between them, Gerry thought, a fucking cigarette and the thread of a friendship.

"Think about that when you unload those drugs," Gerry said. Then he went into his motel room and slammed the door behind him.

CHAPTER 29

Nick jumped up and down in the nurse's office while Valentine sat on the examining table, getting his face stitched up.

"That was the greatest thing I've ever seen," Nick told the nurse, an older woman with the patience of Job. "First Tony uses these judo moves to take the knife away from Moss—*Pow! Bam! Boom!*—and then he takes him on, mano a mano, and beats the living daylights out of him." He threw an imaginary uppercut in the air. "It was great!"

Valentine winced as the nurse tied the stitches together. Moss had sliced the side of his face pretty good; he was going to need a plastic surgeon to make his puss look normal. He lifted his hand out of a bowl of ice cubes and stared at his badly bruised knuckles. Moss was going to need a plastic surgeon, too.

He watched Nick prance around the room, still throwing punches. For a guy about to lose everything, he was having a great time, and Valentine remembered why he'd always liked him. Nick knew how to live.

The nurse finished stitching him up, then applied a bandage to his wound. "You're going to need to change this dressing twice a day. I'm also going to give you some penicillin. Make sure you take the entire dose, okay?"

She said the words like she knew Valentine probably wouldn't do it. He took the little vial of pills and thanked her. Nick stood a few feet away, delivering a knockout punch to an imaginary foe. Valentine said, "Got anything for our friend?"

"I wish," the nurse said.

Valentine went into the hallway and powered up his cell phone. The pain in his face was making his entire head hurt. He called Gerry's cell, got voice mail, and left a message. He tried to make his voice sound gentle, and saw Nick grimace as he hung up.

"Be a tough guy," Nick said, "and tell him to get his ass over here."

"You obviously never had kids," Valentine said.

"What do you mean?"

"That approach doesn't work anymore."

The nurse's office was on the first floor of the casino, behind the registration area. They walked out of her office and into the gaming area. At Valentine's suggestion, Nick had closed the casino down and put a call into the Gaming Control Bureau. At any moment, a team of GCB agents would swarm through the front doors, throw up yellow tape, and turn the place into a crime scene.

In Las Vegas, getting cheated was bad, but not telling the authorities about it was worse. Nick let out an exasperated breath.

"Looks like a tomb, doesn't it? Here lies Nick Nicocropolis. He never gave in."

"You want that on your tombstone?"

"It's the only thing I want on it."

They walked around the empty casino. There was something sad about the hollow feeling the space gave off, and Valentine was reminded of the time he'd seen a half-sunken ship in a harbor as a kid, and how it had made him cry. He saw Nick stop and pick up a piece of trash from the floor.

"Old habits die hard," he explained.

Valentine wasn't listening. His eyes had locked on the cage sitting in the center of the casino floor. The cage was where customers turned their chips into cash. Normally, the cage was on the far end of the casino, the thinking being that a customer might stop along the way and place a wager.

But this cage was in the center of the casino. It was small, with brass bars and cutouts for two cashiers. A sign said CHANGE FOR SLOT PLAYERS ONLY. Inside were several hundred plastic buckets filled with quarters and half-dollars.

Valentine found himself smiling. So this was how Fontaine's gang was getting coins stolen from slot machines out of the casino. They were converting them.

"You got a key for the cage?" he asked Nick.

"Of course I've got a key," Nick said.

"Open it up. I'm about to make you some money."

Nick fished a key ring from his pocket and opened the cage door. Valentine went in and searched around the cashiers' chairs. He found two women's handbags and poured their contents into Nick's outstretched hands. Both were stuffed with hundred-dollar bills. Nick counted it. Over thirty grand. He grabbed Valentine's arm and said, "You're a beautiful human being, you know that?"

"Thanks," Valentine said.

"Now tell me what was going on here."

"Fontaine's gang rigged the scales in the Hard Count room to show less weight," Valentine said. "Then they stole the difference and brought those coins back into the casino to this cage. The coins were put in buckets and sold to customers, and that money was put in handbags and carried out by the cashiers."

Nick made a face. "You're not going to believe this."

"What's that?"

"Putting this cage in the center of the casino was Albert Moss's idea. He said it would make things easier for the little old ladies who played the slots."

"Little old ladies?"

"Yeah. And I fell for it."

242

They shared a good laugh. Hustlers had been using little old ladies in their scams since the beginning of time. And it still worked.

They started to walk out of the casino when Valentine heard his cell phone ring. He pulled it from his pocket and stared at its face. CALLER UNKNOWN. He imagined Gerry calling him from a pay phone, and answered it.

"Tony? This is Lucy Price."

It was the last person he expected to hear from. Saturday night, and she was home alone. "Can I call you right back?"

"Don't hang up," she said.

"Look, I'm in the middle of something important."

"Please don't hang up."

He frowned. Hadn't she told him off a few hours ago?

"Please."

"Okay, I'm not hanging up."

She sniffled into the phone. "I-I have someone here who wants to talk to you."

"Who's that?"

"Him."

"Who's him?"

"Him, goddamn it."

Valentine thought back to Albert Moss's remark just before he'd cut him: *Frank's with your girl-friend.*

"Fontaine?" he asked.

"Yes," she said.

He looked at Nick and saw the little Greek start to punch the air.

"Put him on," Valentine said.

CHAPTER 30

It was pitch dark when he drove his rental into Lucy Price's neighborhood in Summerlin. Fontaine had threatened to kill her, and Valentine had believed him. Twenty years ago, Fontaine had killed Valentine's brother-in-law in Atlantic City. Stomped him to death on the Boardwalk while a group of other hoodlums had watched. He was different from any other cheater Valentine had ever known, and a true sociopath.

"Come alone," he'd said, "or I'll put a bullet in her head."

So Valentine had driven to Lucy's condo by himself. Nick had offered to send a car of security goons for backup, and he was glad he hadn't taken Nick up on the offer. A few blocks from Lucy's house, a car parked on the curb put its headlights on and pulled out. He was being tailed.

Her neighborhood was quiet, everyone inside eating dinner. Taking out his cell phone, he retrieved Bill Higgins's home number from its memory bank and hit SEND. His friend answered on the third ring. Valentine quickly told Bill what was going on.

"Don't go in there alone," Bill said.

Valentine looked at his watch. Six fifty-four. Fontaine had told him to arrive no later than seven o'clock. The smart thing was to wait for backup. But if he waited too long, Lucy would end up lying on a cold slab in a morgue.

"I have to," he said.

"You know this woman?" Bill asked.

"I met her yesterday."

"You armed?"

Valentine was more than armed; he was a walking commando, courtesy of the cache of weapons Nick kept in his office safe. Valentine had taken every gun he could shove into his pockets. He'd been waiting a long time to pay Fontaine back.

"To the teeth."

"Give me the address."

He told Bill where Lucy lived.

"Stall Fontaine for a few minutes," Bill said. "I'll get backup over there pronto."

It was the closest thing he had to a plan, and Valentine thanked him. Bill raised his voice. "You be careful, hear me?" and then he was gone.

Valentine passed one of the area's many golf courses and spied a kid hitting drives off a fairway in the dark. At Lucy's street he flipped his indicator on. The tail did the same. Making no pretense about following him.

He pulled up Lucy's driveway. The motion-triggered floodlight above the garage door came on.

He got out of the car, feeling naked in the bright light. The tail parked a block away, the driver watching him.

He drew a .38 from his jacket and blew the light out. One shot was all it took, and he felt safe again.

The gunshot got a neighbor's dog barking. He went to Lucy's front door and glanced at his watch. Seven o'clock on the nose. He pressed the bell and stood to one side.

"It's open," a voice inside said.

He grabbed the handle with his free hand and cracked the door open. Light streamed out, cutting a blade in the darkness. He stared inside the condo. Lucy sat on a couch in the living room, facing the door. Fontaine sat beside her, holding a gun to her temple. It was a shitty little .22, just powerful enough to kill her.

Standing beside Fontaine was a straw-haired cowboy. Valentine remembered him from the scam at the Acropolis two years ago. The cowboy had tried to kill him with a lead pipe. He was the only member of the gang to get away.

"I'm coming in," Valentine said.

"Be my guest," Fontaine replied.

Driving over, Valentine had wrestled with how to handle this. One of Fontaine's men would be hiding behind the door. That was a given. How he dealt with him was the big question.

He had two options. He could shoot him, and take him out of the picture. Only shooting blind was risky and a waste of bullets. Or he could use the door to take him out. He couldn't miss with the door.

Using his shoulder, he opened the door very quickly and heard it bang against the man on the other side. He heard the man fall, and quickly stepped inside.

"That's far enough," the cowboy declared.

The cowboy was holding a stainless-steel Colt Anaconda by his side. The gun was thirteen and a half inches of pure menace. Valentine aimed the .38 at the cowboy's chest, and saw a surprised look appear on his face. Like the cowboy had expected him to fight fair.

Valentine pumped three bullets into him. The cowboy staggered backward and fell onto a glass coffee table with a loud crash. He still looked surprised.

"Goddamn you," Fontaine said, rocking Lucy's head with the .22's barrel.

Valentine took a step into the living room. Lucy stared at him, looking terrified and ashamed. He glanced behind the door. Fontaine's man had rolled onto his back and was passed out.

"Lay your gun on the floor," Fontaine said.

"Forget it."

"I'll kill her."

"It's all you'll do," Valentine told him.

Fontaine blinked, the realization sinking in. By sitting on the couch, he'd made himself an easy target. He couldn't jump behind anything, or fall into a crouch.

"Don't play that macho shit with me," he said. "I found your pants in the bedroom. I'm going to shoot your lady. You want that?"

Valentine let the words play through his head. *His lady.* He looked into Lucy's face. She was fighting back the tears, holding herself together.

"No," he said.

"Then put the gun down."

They heard the death rattle of Cowboy's boots as he passed into the great beyond. Valentine tried to gauge how much time had passed. A minute? How much more time before Bill's people or the police showed up? There was no way of guessing, and he said, "I didn't come here to die. Tell me what you want. I'll do it, and you'll let Lucy go, and I'll let you go."

"A horse trade?"

"That's right."

Fontaine chewed it over. The scar he'd gotten in prison made him look gruesome. It was a look he seemed bent on cultivating, his head shorn like a patient in a psycho ward, his eyes bugged out like he was on drugs.

"Okay," he said.

"What do you want?"

"Call Nick and tell him to release my people."

Valentine had expected something like this and played his trump card. "He can't release all of them."

"Why not?"

"Albert Moss is in the hospital."

Fontaine blinked. "You put him there?"

"Afraid so."

A dark cloud passed over Fontaine's face. He didn't care about any of his people except Albert Moss. Moss knew everything; he was the only person the police would need to break to press charges. Letting everyone else go was a smoke screen.

"Have Nick call the hospital."

"And take Moss out on a stretcher?"

"That's right."

"Afraid I left my cell phone in my car."

"There's one on the table," Fontaine said. "I'm going to have Lucy pick it up and slide it across the floor to you."

"Albert Moss isn't going anywhere."

"Do it."

Valentine hesitated. If Moss skipped town, Fontaine was off the hook. As if reading his mind, Fontaine shoved the .22 deeper into Lucy's face.

"All right, I'll call the hospital," Valentine said.

"Give him the phone," Fontaine told Lucy.

Lucy's eyes had filled with tears, but she wasn't letting them come out. She picked up the cordless phone off the coffee table. Her arm tensed.

Valentine had been involved in two hostage negotiations as a cop. In both, an X factor had upset the balance of the situation. In the first, it had been a flock of seagulls flying over a schoolyard. In the second, a pizza boy coming to the door. This time, it was Lucy slamming the cordless phone into Fontaine's face. With her other hand, she grabbed the .22 and raised the barrel to the ceiling. The gun discharged, the bullet causing an explosion of sparks as it hit something metallic.

Valentine did not remember physically moving across the condo and jumping on Fontaine. It just happened. Knocking Fontaine to the floor, he began raining blows onto his shaved head. Lucy stood beside him, holding the .22 by her side while bellowing at the top of her lungs.

"Beat the shit out of him! Do it! He deserves it!"

What a woman, he thought.

Moments later, he heard someone yell "Freeze!" and looked up to see the condo become filled with armed men.

Not cops, Valentine realized as they pulled him off Fontaine and got the .22 away from Lucy. And not Gaming Control Board agents. Both of those groups had to identify themselves upon entering someone's home. These guys didn't.

There were a dozen, each identically dressed in black pants and black sweaters that were hiding bulletproof vests. All had short hair, and looked to be in their thirties. Six were white, the others black. All looked real strong. He guessed FBI.

One of the agents made him stand against the wall and frisked him. Valentine heard a bunch of surprised grunts as the arsenal he was carrying got dumped onto the couch.

"He's clean," the agent finally announced.

"No, he's not," another man said, and grabbed Valentine from behind by the balls. It was a sensation like no other, and Valentine yelped as the man took him by the collar with the other hand, and dragged him across the room. Glancing over his shoulder, he stared into the eyes of Director Peter Fuller.

Fuller pulled him into the spare bedroom and slammed the door. Dressed in black like the others, he looked like an action figure from a comic strip, with bulging muscles in his arms and chest. He hadn't changed much over the years, except for his hair. Once light blond, it had recently turned snow white.

"How would you like to spend the rest of your life in jail?" Fuller said.

"What for? I didn't break any laws."

"Oh, no? Tell that to the guy you shot in the next room."

"That guy is a wanted criminal," Valentine said. "He and Fontaine were holding Lucy Price hostage. Why the hell are you reading *me* the riot act?"

"Because I know you have a blood feud with Fontaine. Frank told me you were gunning for him."

Valentine stared at Fuller in disbelief. "Frank *told* you? Don't tell me you sprang him out of prison and have him working for the FBI."

"That's right."

"Did you know that while he's been working for you, he bankrupted the Acropolis?"

"Can you prove that?"

Valentine thought about Albert Moss lying in the hospital. He was the key, and was probably not going to say anything for a while.

"Eventually, yes."

"Eventually?" Fuller jabbed him in the chest. "Fontaine's been working with the FBI for a month. He hasn't had time to scam the Acropolis." Fuller jabbed him again. "You lied to me this afternoon. The gym bag we found in the stripper's townhouse *is* yours. Your son brought it to Las Vegas. His airline confirmed it."

Valentine's face burned from where Albert Moss had slashed him, but it didn't burn as much as the shame he was feeling. He should have called Fuller back and told him the truth. Only he hadn't.

"I figured it out after we talked," he said quietly.

"Did you know about the gun?" Fuller asked him.

"I knew he purchased one."

"Your son bought a three fifty-seven Smith and Wesson at a Las Vegas gun store. A three fifty-seven was used in the murder of the stripper who had your gym bag. I need to talk to your son immediately. Do you understand?"

Valentine found himself looking into Fuller's face. He hadn't called Gerry a murderer. There was a pleading look in Fuller's eyes, tinged by desperation.

"I'll bring Gerry in. You can grill him all you want."

"Do I have your word on this?" Fuller said.

"Yes."

"You've got until midnight. Then all bets are off."

"I'll bring him. Then will you tell me what this is about?"

Fuller shook his head. "No," he added for emphasis.

Then the director of the FBI marched out of the bedroom.

CHAPTER 31

Valentine walked back into the living room and saw Fontaine standing with a group of FBI agents, shooting the shit. He wasn't handcuffed, and Valentine felt his head start to spin. Fontaine was a career criminal, yet the agents were talking to him like an old pal.

Two agents walked past, carrying the cowboy in a black body bag. The guy whose face Valentine had broken with the door was sitting up, and being given smelling salts by one of the FBI agents. He wasn't wearing handcuffs, either.

Valentine realized Fontaine was staring at him. He returned the look and saw Fontaine smile like a guy who knows he's Teflon-coated. One of the FBI agents said, "Let's go," and Fontaine walked up to Valentine, said, "My scar's bigger than yours," and followed the agent outside.

Valentine went to the window. Parting the blinds with a finger, he watched Fontaine hop into a car waiting by the curb. He had to imagine his feet were nailed to the floor to force himself not to go after him.

★   ★   ★

The remaining FBI agents cleared out of Lucy's condo a few minutes later. Fuller got in Valentine's face one more time and told him not to get any stupid ideas.

Valentine shook his head. He had run out of those.

Standing by the living room window, he watched the FBI agents pull away from the curb in three black sedans. Fontaine sat in the passenger's seat of one car, being treated like a VIP. He let the blind drop and shook his head. The world had gone crazy and no one had bothered to tell him.

In the kitchen he found Lucy pouring herself a glass of wine. She got a Coke out of the fridge and said, "I know you like the artificial stuff, but is this okay?"

He said sure and took a seat at the kitchen table. She served him the can, then sat down across from him. Hoisting the wineglass to her lips, she took a long pull. The drink brought instant relaxation to her face. She lowered her glass and looked at him long and hard. The white in her eyes had turned pink.

"You okay?" he asked.

"Not really," she said. "What happened to your face?"

"The head of finance at the Acropolis cut me."

"Let me guess. He works with Fontaine."

"Yeah. He seems to be the brains behind the operation. He also had tremendous clout within the Acropolis. My guess is, he had the twenty-five grand you won stolen from your room."

Lucy's eyes narrowed. "I hope you beat the shit out of him."

"Come to mention it, I did."

They went back to their drinks. Lucy polished off her wine, then went to the counter and refilled her glass. Watching people drink booze was one of his least favorite things, yet Lucy wasn't bothering him. She deserved it.

She sat back down, this time taking the chair next to his.

"The way you shot the cowboy."

Her words hung in the air like a puff of smoke. He let her finish.

"You've shot people before."

"Yeah. I was a cop."

"How many?" she asked.

"This is the fifth."

"Does it bother you?"

"It will stay with me, if that's what you mean."

"How long?"

He drained his can of Coke and felt the buzz he got whenever he mixed sugar with caffeine. The look in her eyes said she really wanted to know.

"The rest of my life," he said quietly.

She drew her chair closer and put her arms around him in an embrace, drawing his head close to her bosom, holding it there and kissing his crown.

★   ★   ★

257

She bandaged his face in the bathroom. Then, arm in arm, they walked to her bedroom, the movement of their bodies pressed against each other as natural as anything Valentine had ever felt. Like they were floating a few inches off the ground.

In the bedroom, she found a candle, propped it on her dresser, and lit it. It was perfect, he thought. She unbuttoned his shirt, and he stared at the bed, imagined them making love, then him jumping out of bed to go search for his son.

She had his shirt open to his navel, her fingers sifting through his mat of chest hair. In her kiss he felt a smile. He put his arms around her waist and held her.

"I have to go look for my son," he said.

"You're not going to stay?"

"No. I'm sorry."

She heard the hesitation in his voice, and said, "Can't your son wait?"

He shook his head. "He's involved with this."

"Oh, Jesus," Lucy said.

She buttoned his shirt back up, gave him another kiss. They walked into the living room, and Lucy opened the front door for him. The dog that had barked when he'd shot out her light was still barking. No one in the neighborhood seemed to give a damn. He didn't like that, and said, "Maybe you should stay in a hotel tonight."

"Believe it or not, we have a neighborhood watch group," she said.

"Right," he said.

They both found it in them to laugh.

"I've got friends I can stay with, if it will make you feel better," she said.

"Please. I'll call you tomorrow."

She kissed him again, and Valentine said good night.

Pete Longo lifted his head off the steering wheel. He'd fallen sound asleep, and stared now at the luminous clock on his dashboard. Seven twenty-five. Rolling down his window, he sucked down the cool night air, then glanced upward at the blinking stars that were slowly filling the evening sky.

Taking the infrared binoculars off his lap, he found the house he'd seen Valentine go into. Valentine's car was still parked in the driveway, and he breathed a sigh of relief. He hadn't let him slip away. The front door opened, and a couple became silhouetted in the doorway.

Longo stared at them. It was Valentine and an attractive-looking woman. The problem with infrared binoculars was that they didn't allow you to actually see in the dark. They needed light to work, but Valentine and his lady friend were giving him plenty of that.

He watched the woman kiss Valentine good night. She was real passionate about it. He tried to remember the way Kris used to kiss him. Had it been that good?

He decided that it had.

He'd had a lousy time of it since Valentine had broken his nose yesterday. He'd stuffed cotton up his nostrils, taken some aspirin, and figured he'd be okay. Only he hadn't, and had woken up this morning with a splitting headache. He decided he needed a doctor and killed the day running around town, trying to find one willing to see him. The emergency rooms were all jammed with pregnant women and kids that had fallen off bikes, and it wasn't until four that he'd found a two-year intern willing to shine a penlight up his nose.

"Your septum is deviated," the intern said.

"Is that why I can't breathe?" Longo asked.

The intern had taped a butterfly bandage to the bridge of his nose, and nodded. "You need to get your nose fixed by a surgeon. Otherwise, you'll be breathing through your mouth the rest of your life."

Valentine's car was backing down the driveway. Longo reached down to start up his own car, and cursed. The keys weren't in the ignition. He frantically ran his hand across the seat. Valentine's car came down the street, and he lay sideways on the seat and watched the car's headlights pass.

Sitting up, he dropped his hands to the floor. According to Murphy's Law, the keys would have fallen to the most inconvenient spot. Sure enough, he found them lodged beneath the accelerator and the floor mat.

He jammed the keys in the ignition and fired

up the engine. He was thinking about taking a shortcut to catch Valentine and did not see the fist come through his open window.

It caught him flush on the jaw. Pools of black appeared before his eyes. His door was jerked open, and a pair of hands pulled him roughly from the car. He rolled out and landed on the macadam. A thing began to crawl out of his stomach. Dinner.

"Aw shit, he's puking," a voice said. "You shouldn't have punched him so hard."

"He deserves it, fucking Peeping Tom," another voice said.

"How can you be sure he's the Peeping Tom?"

"I just am."

"Look, here's his binoculars," a third voice said.

Longo made himself get sick. It was keeping them from hitting him anymore, and that was a good thing. He cracked an eye and saw three pairs of sneakers standing around him. Neighborhood vigilantes, one of them carrying a baseball bat. He flipped his wallet out of his back pocket, let it hit the ground. It contained the last of his money, and it was the only way he could think of to save his ass.

"Look, he's trying to bribe us," the first voice said.

"Take the money and break his kneecaps," the second declared.

"Aren't you the brave one," the first said.

Longo saw the third man pick up the wallet.

Seeing Longo's gold detective badge, he dropped it on the ground.

"He's a frigging cop," the third man declared.

They did what any smart law-abiding citizen would do and ran like hell. Longo heard the front doors of their houses slam shut.

Soon the neighborhood grew peaceful, and the barking dog quieted down. He slowly got to his feet. His brain had been rattled; he was seeing two houses across the street where there was only one. The good news was, his jaw didn't feel like it was broken.

"Hooray," he whispered.

Longo climbed into the car. Turning the engine on, he hit the AC button and positioned the vents to blow in his face. It was an old trick he'd learned in college, the quickest way to cure a night of drinking.

The cold air felt like invisible ice cubes rubbing on his skin. Sucking up his courage, he dropped the visor above the steering wheel and looked at his face in the lighted vanity mirror.

"Jesus," he groaned.

He had raccoon eyes, a swollen jaw and the undercarriages of his eyes were ringed black. The bad part was, it would look worse in a few hours. A lot worse.

He needed to find an ice pack and a soft bed. He was clutching his wallet in his left hand, and he opened it. They hadn't touched his money, and he had enough for a cheap motel room. Making amends with Valentine would have to wait.

Driving away, Longo noticed a sign: NEIGHBORHOOD WATCHDOG GROUP. He'd always thought neighborhood groups were idiotic. He didn't feel that way anymore.

CHAPTER 32

Gerry took a hot shower in his motel room. His conscience would not let him forget that he'd killed a man a few hours earlier, and a pounding sensation filled his head.

Coming out of the bathroom, he found Pash and Amin in his room, the door that joined their rooms wide open. His hair was still wet, and he flipped it off his forehead the way he used to as a kid. To another Italian, the gesture was as rude as *fuck you*.

"I suppose you want to know what's going on," Amin said.

Gerry nearly told them to leave. Only he wanted to hear Amin's side of things. The room had twin beds. He sat on one while the brothers sat on the other.

"I have a pretty good idea," he said.

"You do?"

Gerry nodded. Amin had taken off his sweatshirt and was no longer packing a gun behind his belt buckle. Gerry said, "You figured out a way to take the money you were making at blackjack and quadruple it. You bought drugs."

"That's right," Amin said.

Pash was looking at the carpet, wanting no part of the conversation. Reading his body language, Gerry guessed that the drugs were Amin's idea. He felt bad for Pash.

"What did you buy?"

Amin seemed confused. "Mexican drugs," he said.

"Coke, smack, or meth?"

"Smack?" Amin said.

"Heroin."

"Cocaine," Amin said. "We bought cocaine."

"How many pounds."

"Seventy-five."

"Uncut?"

"It is pure, if that's what you mean."

Back when Gerry had run his bar, he'd heard about a lot of drug deals, and he knew how much seventy-five pounds of coke would fetch on the street. A telephone number, as some of his patrons liked to say. He fell straight back on the bed and for a long moment stared at the cheap popcorn ceiling. Dead flies were embedded in the popcorn, and he imagined them trying to escape the room, flying suicide runs into the ceiling. He pulled himself up into a sitting position and looked at his partners. Pash was still showing him the top of his head, while Amin held his gaze.

"A third of it is yours, once it's sold," Amin said.

"Not interested," Gerry said.

"I will sell it in a few days, and give you your

share," Amin said. "Cold hard cash. If you want to leave then, you can."

Gerry didn't like the direction the conversation was heading. Amin was crazy—he'd killed a drug dealer. The Las Vegas police would know there were drugs on the street, and put plants out. If Amin wasn't careful, he'd walk right into the hands of the law.

"No thanks," Gerry said.

"But we had a deal," Amin replied.

He had an emotionless way of talking, and it surprised Gerry, considering he'd watched a man burn to death a few hours ago. He said, "You never said drugs were involved."

"Why does that make a difference?"

"It just does."

"But why? It is business. Nothing more."

"You ever see the movie *The Godfather*?"

"No."

Pash lifted his head and whispered something into Amin's ear. Amin's expression changed, and he said, "Oh, the film with Marlon Brando?" He looked at Gerry. "Yes. I have seen that one. It is one of Pash's favorites."

"There's a scene in that movie," Gerry said. "All the godfathers are sitting around a gigantic table, trying to convince Brando to help them sell drugs in New York. Brando has the judges in his back pocket, and the godfathers want him to peddle some influence. Only Brando won't do it. Remember that scene?"

Amin had to think. Pash whispered again, and Amin said, "Yes, I remember it."

"Good. Brando tells the other godfathers that he won't do it. He says, 'Drugs will be the death of us all.' Well, I feel the same way. I've never been involved with them, and I never will be. Okay?"

"But a third of the money is yours," Amin insisted.

Gerry took a pack of cigarettes off the night table and popped one into his mouth. He wasn't going to tell Amin that he was damn straight some of the money was his—he'd saved their asses. Rising, he went to the door, said, "Give it to charity," and walked outside to have a smoke.

Valentine drove back to the Acropolis with his head spinning. He'd nearly jumped into the sack with Lucy Price. The woman had more problems than a Hollywood starlet. He couldn't deny the magnetism he felt when he was around her. But was it enough of a reason to have a relationship with her?

The valet stand at the Acropolis was deserted, and he parked his rental by the front door and ventured inside. A velvet rope had been run across the entrance to the casino, and a sign announced that the place was closed. He stuck his head into One-Armed Billy's alcove. Even Big Joe Smith was gone.

He went to the front desk and rang the bell. A reservationist with a familiar face emerged from the back room. Seeing him, she broke into a smile.

"Hi, Mister Valentine. I hear you kicked some ass this afternoon."

Her name tag said LOU ANN. "It wasn't that big a deal," he said.

"Tell that to Albert Moss. I hear every bone in his face is busted."

"Where is everybody, Lou Ann?"

"Our guests checked out when they heard the casino was closed," she said sadly. "Kind of a glum day. I hear Nick's going down."

"You work here a long time?"

"Since I got out of college."

"What's that? Five years?"

Her smile returned. "Try twenty. You checking out, too?"

"No, I'm here for the duration. I'm looking for my son. His name's Gerry. He hasn't been in asking for me, has he?"

"I've been on duty since this afternoon, and I haven't seen him," Lou Ann said.

He'd promised Fuller he'd bring Gerry in by midnight. Henderson was a twenty-minute drive, and he decided to head out there to track his son down. He hadn't done that since Gerry was in high school, running with the wrong crowd. *The more things change, the more they remain the same,* he thought.

He stepped away from the desk. "Thanks anyway, Lou Ann."

"You want something to eat?" she asked. "The cook's trying to get rid of the food. No reason to let it spoil."

"Thanks for the offer, but I need to run," he said.

"It won't take five minutes. Give the staff some hope, knowing we have a guest."

He didn't know how to refuse a request like that. Lou Ann pointed at Nick's Bar, and he crossed the casino and went in. A dozen employees were sitting at tables, eating. He sat down, and the hostess took his order.

While he waited for his food, he realized that Lou Ann and the other hotel staffers knew that Nick was heading toward bankruptcy and wouldn't have the funds to meet their next paychecks. They'd stayed out of loyalty, a quality that was hard to find these days. Nick had always bragged that he had the best employees; now he understood why.

His cheeseburger arrived with a monster helping of french fries and an onion slice as big as the bun. He asked the hostess to thank the cook. The TV above the bar was on, and as he ate, he stared at the mute images on the screen.

He realized the images looked familiar. It was the same gang of FBI agents he'd met in Lucy's condo. They were standing in the desert beneath the blazing sun. Behind them, a building was burning out of control. He found the bartender and persuaded him to jack up the volume with the remote.

The picture on the screen changed to a blond newswoman clutching a sheet of paper. "Reports differ as to what happened at a deserted auto shop off the Boulder Highway this afternoon," she intoned gravely. "The highway was closed in both directions for several hours, with both the police and FBI manning the roadblocks. At the scene is Action News reporter Lance Peters."

The picture changed to a Hollywood-handsome reporter standing in the desert. Grasping the mike with both hands, he said, "Thanks, Mary. Earlier, I talked with a Henderson Police Department spokesman and learned that there was a gun battle at the auto shop, which left one man dead. His partner, a Mexican illegal, was arrested in town driving a vehicle with an expired license."

The picture jumped back to the female newscaster. "Lance, is it true that the FBI appeared on the scene with dogs and helicopters, and refused to let traffic pass in either direction?"

Back to Lance. "Yes, Mary. There are dozens of FBI agents out here. If I didn't know better, I'd think we had a major catastrophe on our hands."

The picture returned to Mary. "Did you get the opportunity to talk to any of them, Lance?"

Lance's face lit up the screen. "That's when things got hairy, Mary. The FBI refused to answer my questions, and threatened to seize our cameras and recording equipment if we filmed them. I do know that the FBI has taken the Mexican to an undisclosed location and is interrogating him."

The picture went back to Mary. "Sounds like our tax dollars hard at work. In other news, six members of UNLV's baseball team were suspended today for allowing imposters to attend classes for them. The team's coach is appealing the suspension. All six players are hoping to play in next week's College World Series . . ."

Valentine stuffed the last of his french fries into his mouth and rose from the table. Maybe the FBI could get involved with that case as well. They sure had gotten involved with everything else going on in Las Vegas.

He threw down ten bucks for the hostess, then remembered his cell phone. As he powered it up, it started to ring. He stared at its face and felt his heart skip a beat.

His son had finally decided to call him back.

CHAPTER 33

Lying on the bed in his motel room with the lights out, Gerry spilled his guts to his father. He told him everything—from the moment he'd hooked up with Pash and Amin five days ago to the shootout at the gas station that afternoon. His father, God bless him, didn't rush to pass judgment. He just listened, his breathing calm and measured.

"That's all of it," Gerry said, glancing at the clock on the bedside table. Twelve minutes had passed. It hadn't been nearly as bad as he'd thought it would be.

"My gym bag was found in the townhouse of a dead stripper," his father said. "You think Amin killed her?"

"Must have," Gerry replied, keeping his voice below the TV, which he'd turned on to a baseball game, the running commentary a perfect cover. "Pash told me Amin was using strippers to launder chips into cash."

"There's nothing to tie you to this girl?" his father asked.

"No, Pop. I haven't dated or slept with or even

272

kissed another woman since I met Yolanda. I'm clean."

"Good for you," his father said.

The remark made Gerry feel good all over. His father didn't hand out compliments very often, not that he'd done anything to deserve any. But they were nice to hear, and he added them to the mental checklist of things he wanted to do when his own kid grew up.

"So, you want me to go to the FBI," Gerry said.

"Yes," his father replied. "You need to let them hear your side of it, pronto."

"What if they don't believe me? What if they think I bought the gun and shot this girl?"

"I can prove you didn't," his father said.

"You can?"

There was a click on the line, indicating his father had another call.

"Hold on, Wonder Boy, I'll be right back."

His father put him on hold. Wonder Boy. His father hadn't called him that in a long time. One summer when he was a kid, they'd vacationed at a resort in the Catskill Mountains, and his father had taught him a mind-reading trick called Second Sight. His father would stand on one side of the room, holding a coin given to him by a spectator in his fist. He'd say, "I want you to think hard. Please . . . be quick."

"You're holding a quarter," Gerry would say. "The date is nineteen sixty-five."

The trick was a real fooler. It was based on a

simple code. *I* stood for the number 1. *Am* for the number 2. *Can* for the number 3. Other simple words stood for the numbers 4 through 9, and 0. By stringing the right words together, his father could relay the coin's value, and date, in a single sentence.

They had done the trick for every guest at the resort. One of the older guests had christened him Wonder Boy, and the name had stuck. He heard his father come back on the line.

"Was that Mabel? How's Yolanda doing?"

"I wasn't talking to Mabel," his father replied. "It was a woman I met."

Gerry perked up. "She got a name?"

"Lucy Price."

"You like her?"

"I met her yesterday."

"Does she like you?"

"It seems that way."

Gerry threw his legs over the side of the bed. He'd been hoping his father would start courting again. He'd hung out with a female wrestler for a while, but that had been a grief thing. "Good for you, Pop," he said.

He heard his father breathing into the phone, and guessed he didn't want to talk about it. Gerry said, "So how can you prove that I didn't kill this stripper?"

"Easy," his father said. "Nevada requires its gun stores to have surveillance cameras in case of robbery. That means there's a picture of whoever bought the three fifty-seven with your credit card."

Gerry smiled into the receiver. Leave it to his old man to save the day. He glanced at his watch. It was a few minutes past eight. "I'm going to pack my stuff and check out. I'll meet you at nine-thirty."

"Why so long?" his father asked suspiciously.

"Pop, it's Saturday night. Traffic is going to be horrible. I'll meet you at the Jokers Wild casino on Boulder Highway. There's a small theater inside the lobby."

"Why that dump?"

"There's an act playing there you have to see."

"This is no time to be seeing acts," his father scolded him. "The FBI wants to talk to you."

"You said we have until midnight."

"Why push it?"

"Pop, this will take ten minutes. You won't regret it. Trust me."

He heard his father breathing into the phone.

"The Jokers Wild it is," his father said.

Gerry hung up feeling good about things. There wasn't that much in his life except Yolanda to feel good about, but his father could do that to him. Sometimes, his father could be the best person in the whole world.

He got his suitcase from the closet and opened it on the bed. He put his dirty clothes on one side, his clean on the other. Sandwiched between them, he put the Gucci loafers he'd bought in a casino gift shop. He'd seen them in the store's window, and even though he was broke he knew he had to have them. From the bathroom he got his toilet kit, and he was done.

He went to the door and stopped. Should he say good-bye to Pash? Deep down, he still liked the guy—even if he was a chip off his brother's block in the lying department. Better not, he decided. There was no telling how Amin might react.

He put his ear to the wall that separated their rooms. Pash and Amin were on the other side, engaged in a heated conversation. Their TV set was on, and he realized they were watching the same baseball game.

He had an idea, and turned up the volume of the set in his room. It would blend in with their set; he could leave without anyone being the wiser.

He opened his door. A gust of night air blew into his room and made him shiver. A highway ran parallel to the inn, and he saw globes of yellow light float mysteriously by, the headlights disembodied from their vehicles. He could hear boom boxes and people trash-talking in cars.

He took a deep breath. It was time for him to face the music. He crossed the gravel lot, his shoes crunching loudly. His suitcase was heavy, and halfway to his car he started to drag it. Popping the rental's trunk, he hoisted the suitcase off the ground and threw it into the back.

He heard footsteps. Glancing over his shoulder, he saw Amin coming up behind him wearing a grim look on his face. He didn't think Amin was stupid enough to try something out in the open, and he started to walk around to the front of the car.

Amin called his name.

"Not interested," Gerry said.

Amin yelled at him. Gerry slowly spun around and saw Amin standing ten feet away. Amin had stuck the .357 behind his belt buckle. Gerry glanced over his shoulder at the hundreds of cars passing by. Whoever had said there was strength in numbers hadn't been kidding. He looked Amin in the eye.

"Go ahead and try something," he said.

CHAPTER 34

Valentine had taken Gerry's call standing outside Nick's Bar. Hanging up, he tried to remember where the Jokers Wild was situated on the Boulder Highway. He thought it was halfway to Henderson, on a deserted stretch of desert. A real down-and-dirty kind of place. He could only imagine what his son wanted to show him.

His cell phone was ringing, and he stared at the caller ID. It was Bill Higgins. He felt his jaw tighten. Bill had betrayed him. There was no other explanation for the FBI appearing at Lucy's house. The bad part was, Bill knew that he and Fuller hated each other.

"Hey," he said.

"We need to talk," Bill said.

"I'm busy."

"This is about your son. How soon can you get to my house?"

Valentine frowned into the phone. He had no intention of driving to Bill's house tonight, and started to tell him so. Bill cut him short.

"You need to hear this, Tony. I don't want to see your boy getting hurt."

Valentine heard the warning in Bill's voice. Bill's house was due south, Jokers Wild southwest. Fifteen minutes max from one to the other. "I'll be right over," he said.

Bill's partner, Alex, greeted him at the front door. Alex was a veteran ATF agent, a tall, gravel-voiced outdoorsman who spent his weekends rappelling in the mountains.

"What happened to your face?" Alex asked.

"A cheater over at the Acropolis cut me."

"Pay him back?"

"In spades."

Alex smiled and led him to Bill's study. Tapping on the door, he said, "Tony's here," then walked away. Valentine went in. The room's light was muted, the shades drawn. Bill sat behind his desk, wearing the same clothes from the day before. His TV was on, the image frozen. It was a surveillance tape, and showed an Ivy League guy in a Brooks Brothers suit playing blackjack. His stacks of chips reached just below his chin. If Bill was watching him, he was either a card-counter or a cheater.

"Have a seat," Bill said.

Valentine sat across from the desk and watched Bill rub his face with his hands. He hadn't shaved, and his stubble was predominantly gray. He was up for retirement in a few years, and Valentine guessed he'd take the same route as most Gaming Control Board directors—to the private sector, where he'd make three times the salary and deal with half the headaches. He lowered his hands, and Valentine saw that his eyes were bloodshot.

"You and I go back a long time," Bill said. He let the statement hang for a few seconds. Then he said, "I'm about to tell you some things that could get me fired."

"I appreciate that."

Bill put his weight on his elbows and leaned forward. "Remember that letter you wrote two years ago, criticizing the FBI for demanding that every casino in the country start profiling Middle Eastern gamblers?"

"Sure."

"Do you remember why the FBI asked the casinos to do that?"

Valentine dredged his memory. "There were two reasons. The first was that the FBI had information about a Middle Eastern gambler in the U.S. with ties to the 9/11 attackers. The second was that a Middle Eastern man was seen the morning of 9/11 about a mile from the White House. He showed a gas station manager a five-thousand-dollar casino chip. The manager thought it was suspicious, and reported it.

"The FBI thought the two stories might be linked. They asked the casinos to play Big Brother, and scrutinize every Middle Eastern gambler. I heard about it, wrote the FBI a letter, and reminded them there are five million Middle

Easterners in the U.S. Profiling every one who plays in a casino is a waste of time."

"You're aware the FBI dropped the idea."

"Yes. What does this have to do with my son?"

"The FBI found the guy," Bill said. "Your son's been seen with him."

Valentine thought back to Gerry's description of Amin and Pash.

"Jesus," he said aloud.

There was a stack of photographs lying on Bill's desk. Bill flipped the top one over. It was a surveillance shot of a Middle Eastern man, early thirties, playing blackjack. "This guy popped up in a homicide investigation in Biloxi last month. He befriended a gambler he met in a casino, used the guy's credit card to buy stuff, then skipped town when things got hot. Before he ran, he murdered the guy and tried to make it look like a suicide.

"A homicide detective saw similarities in the case to another gambler suicide in Biloxi. Thinking he might have a serial killer on his hands, he sent the information to the FBI's Behavioral Science Division. The FBI matched the case to four other gambler suicides they'd been investigating in Reno, Atlantic City, New Orleans, and Detroit.

"The FBI showed the photograph to the gas station manager in Washington. He confirmed that it was the same guy he'd seen the morning of 9/11. The FBI sent the photograph to every casino in the country, asked them to be on the lookout."

Bill flipped over a second photograph. It showed

two people standing outside a Strip casino called Excalibur. One was the Middle Eastern man, wearing shades and a baseball cap. Beside him was a pretty blond woman.

"Last week, a casino here spotted the guy and alerted the FBI," Bill said.

Valentine pointed at the blonde. "That the stripper who was murdered?"

"Yes."

Bill flipped over the last photograph on the desk. Valentine stared at it, and felt his face grow flush. It was the same man, this time wearing an elaborate disguise. He was sitting at a blackjack table. In the seat next to him was Gerry.

"This photograph was taken last night at the MGM Grand. The FBI believes your son is in mortal danger. They also think you're protecting him. Fuller called me a little while ago. I told him that if you promised you'd bring Gerry in, you would."

Valentine struggled for something to say.

"No need to thank me," Bill said. "This can't be easy for you."

"How does Fontaine figure into this?"

Bill frowned. "The FBI got a hold of this guy's phone bills and discovered he has a network of associates around the country. They listened to some calls and realized he was talking in a complicated code. Fontaine is a master at cracking ciphers, so the FBI sprang him out of prison. I was against the idea."

Valentine looked at the clock on Bill's desk. It was a few minutes past nine. It was going to take fifteen minutes to reach the Jokers Wild, and he didn't want to be late. His son had gotten into trouble before, but never anything like this.

He rose from his chair. Bill stood as well, and handed him the surveillance photograph taken outside the Excalibur.

"You didn't get that from me," he said.

Valentine folded the photograph and put it in his pocket. "The FBI think I'm somehow involved because I wrote that letter two years ago, and then my son shows up with this guy."

"I told Fuller it was a coincidence."

"Did he believe you?"

Bill shrugged. "Hard to say what Fuller believes. He's paranoid. He's gotten the bureau all screwed up because of it."

"You're telling me," Valentine said.

Bill started to walk him out of the study. Valentine stopped in the doorway. The frozen face on Bill's TV had finally struck a bell.

"That's Karl King," he said.

Bill walked back into the room. "Know him?"

"He's a card-counter. One of the best."

"You're kidding. He hardly ever looks at his cards."

Valentine found the remote and resumed the tape. He stared at the other players, then the spectators standing behind the table. A regular joe smoking a cigar caught his eye. He stood behind King stiff as a statue. Counters had come up with many ways to camouflage their skills. Valentine said, "The guy with the cigar is doing the counting and passing the information to King."

"How?"

"He has a computer strapped to his leg. See how he's got his hand stuck in his pocket? He's entering the cards' values into the computer."

Bill stared at the screen. "How's he passing the information?"

"The computer does that with a radio signal. King wears a transmitter in his ear. The information is sent by Morse code."

"But the casino's RF detector didn't pick anything up," Bill said.

Every casino had an RF detector. Used to detect illegal radio frequencies on the casino floor, they were pointed down at the players from the ceiling.

"The signal is going through the back of King's chair," Valentine explained. "That's why the RF detector isn't catching it. The frequency is too short."

"How do you know so much about this?"

"I busted King's students a few months ago."

"His students?"

"He's a professor at MIT."

Bill walked him to the front door of the house. They shook hands, and Valentine thanked him for his help. Bill had a funny look on his face.

"What's wrong?" Valentine said.

"How do I stop King?" Bill said, clearly exasperated. "I can't tell the casinos to have security walk the floor and point RF detectors at everyone."

Valentine slapped his friend on the back. Sometimes the most obvious solutions were the ones everybody missed.

"Change the chairs the players sit in to ones with solid backs," he said. "That should put an end to it."

CHAPTER 35

Leaving Bill's neighborhood, Valentine turned his rental right onto Las Vegas Boulevard. In the distance, he could see the neon spectacle that was Las Vegas at night, the casinos burning up hundreds of thousands of kilowatts trying to outshine each other.

Traffic was bumper to bumper, and he crawled ahead while staring at a green laser beam coming out of the tip of a pyramid-shaped casino called Luxor, the light ruining an otherwise flawless sky. Turning on the car's interior light, he removed the surveillance picture from his pocket and drove with it on the steering wheel.

Was it his fault that this guy hadn't been caught? He hated to think that it was, but still didn't believe the FBI's approach had been the correct one. Profiling people based on skin color was a throwback to the dark ages. There were better ways to catch criminals.

He drove with the picture on the steering wheel, staring him in the face.

★   ★   ★

At nine twenty-five he pulled into the Jokers Wild parking lot. The casino sat on a deserted stretch of the Boulder Highway. A rinky-dink marquee boasted nickel slot machines and single-deck blackjack.

He ventured inside. There was a theater just off the lobby. People were lined up for the nine-thirty show. Had Gerry said he'd meet him by the theater, or inside? He didn't remember, and decided to stick his head inside the casino.

The gaming area was a low-ceilinged room with enough cigarette smoke to make breathing dangerous. It was packed, and he elbowed his way through to a pair of double doors. Opening them, he entered a bingo parlor. A caller in a plaid jacket stood on the stage.

"Folks," the caller said, "it's time to get up from your seats. Come on, you can do it. Don't want the support hose to cut off our circulation!"

Valentine returned to the lobby. Gerry had said that he wanted him to see an act in the theater. He'd made it sound like something special. Was his son already inside, waiting for him? He bought a ticket and went in.

The theater was filled with rough-looking people chugging beers. He walked up and down the aisles but didn't see his son. The lights dimmed, and he went and stood by the exit. Over the PA, a man's booming voice said, "Ladies and gentlemen, welcome to Jokers Wild, the entertainment capital of Las Vegas—"

"Right!" a guy in the audience with a ponytail yelled.

"—and maybe the world. Tonight we're proud to introduce two premier novelty acts. Get ready to laugh and be amazed, to hold your sides and not believe your eyes. The show is about to begin!"

"Get on with it," Ponytail yelled.

"Our first act is a man who needs no introduction. You've seen him on Johnny Carson, heard his voice in a hundred TV commercials. Here he is, the master of mirth, the one, the only . . . Hambone!"

A spotlight hit center stage. The crowd did its best to make some noise. An old guy with a face like a basset hound shuffled out. Walking into the spotlight, he shielded his eyes with his hand.

"Turn that fucking thing down," he hollered.

The spotlight dimmed, and the old guy lowered his hand. He wore a tuxedo, or rather the tuxedo wore him, his shoulders sagging so badly that it seemed his clothes were the only thing keeping him from falling to the floor.

"So how you folks doing this evening?" he asked.

"Better than you," Ponytail replied.

Hambone threw his arms out in surprise. "Holy cow! I didn't know this was Jerry Springer! Hey buddy, you ever help a comic before?"

"No!"

"Well, you're not helping one now. Shut up!"

The crowd started laughing. Valentine saw a man enter the theater, and he tapped him on the shoulder. The man turned around. It wasn't Gerry.

"Sorry."

"A funny thing happened on the way to the show," Hambone said. "I got here! But seriously folks, it's tough when you've got Celine Dion singing down the street. Anyone know how much money she's making a week?"

"Two million bucks," someone said.

"Two million bucks," Hambone repeated. "But it's not steady!"

A woman in a red dress appeared on stage. She wore her hair like Snow White and weighed about two hundred pounds. Holding up an envelope, she said, "Telegram for Hambone!"

"That's me," the comic said. Snatching the envelope, he tore it open. "It's from the William Morris Agency. Oh, boy. It says, Hambone—stop. Saw the act—stop, stop, stop, stop . . ." He crunched the telegram into a ball and tossed it over his shoulder. "Everyone's a comic!" Turning to his assistant, he said, "What's your name?"

"Twiggy." She had a voice like air slowly escaping from a balloon. "Hambone, is it true you were once a boxer?"

"That's right."

"How many fights did you have?"

"A hundred and one."

"How many did you win?"

"All but a hundred."

"Ever make any extra money boxing?"

"Sure. I sold advertising space on the soles of my shoes."

"I heard you had back trouble."

"It's true. I had a yellow streak up and down my back."

"Why did you quit?"

"Couldn't make hospital expenses."

It wasn't long before the crowd turned hostile. Arm in arm with his assistant, Hambone shuffled off stage, immune to the audience's taunts and jeering. Valentine checked the time. Nine forty-five. He would give his son fifteen more minutes, then drive to Henderson and start looking for him.

There was something wrong with the curtains, and the next act had to set up in front of the audience. Valentine found himself smiling as Ray Hicks and Mr. Beauregard, the world's smartest chimpanzee, came on stage. Two months ago, Hicks had saved his life in Florida, and they had become friends. This was why Gerry had picked the Jokers Wild to meet, he realized. To surprise him.

Hicks wore a canary-yellow sports jacket, baggy black pants, and a porkpie hat. He was funny looking, only no one in the audience was paying attention to him. They were looking at Mr. Beauregard, who wore a magnificent tux with a shiny satin cummerbund. As the chimp glided across the stage on roller skates, his eyes settled on Valentine's face. A happy noise came out of his mouth.

"Good evening," Hicks said, holding a microphone. "My name is Ray Hicks, and this is Mister Beauregard. Several years ago, while traveling with my carnival in Louisiana, I found Mister Beauregard in a pet shop, abused and underfed. I bought him for five hundred dollars."

"Louisiana?" Ponytail shouted. "They shoot mad dogs there, don't they?"

"I planned to teach Mister Beauregard a few simple tricks," Hicks went on, "and put him in my carnival. But when I tried to train him, I discovered that Mister Beauregard had already been to school."

A large chest sat stage center. It was the act's only prop, and the chimp flipped open the lid and removed a beat-up ukulele. He strummed the instrument with his thumbless hand.

"Someone name a song, any song," Hicks proclaimed.

"Free Bird," Ponytail called out.

Mr. Beauregard started playing really fast, the music instantly familiar. Ponytail and his girlfriend stomped their feet, as did others in the crowd. "He's good," someone said.

"Another song," Hicks said.

"The theme from *Friends*," someone called out.

Hicks said, "Mr. Beauregard, do you know the theme from *Friends*?"

The chimp skated to the edge of the stage. Suddenly there was music.

"Yeah," the person who made the request said.

"It has often been said that animals communicate on a different level than humans, and perhaps can tap into thoughts," Hicks said. "Impossible? Just watch. May I have a volunteer from the audience?"

Ponytail hoisted his girlfriend's arm into the air. The spotlight found her, and she reluctantly went up. She was a big woman, and looked like she slept in the road. Hicks coaxed her into revealing her name.

"Bitch," she said.

A chalkboard was wheeled out. Hicks positioned the chalkboard so it was out of Mr. Beauregard's line of vision, then handed Bitch a piece of chalk.

"Please write the name of a song on the chalkboard," he said.

Bitch wrote KNOCKING ON HEAVEN'S DOOR.

Mr. Beauregard was playing the song before the last letters were on the board. It had a slow, easy pace, and someone in the audience clapped along.

"Another, please," Hicks said.

Bitch wrote COCAINE. Mr. Beauregard nailed it again. This time, there was real applause. Ponytail stood up in his seat and said, "Give that woman a sugar cube!"

Bitch jumped off the stage like she was diving into a mosh pit. She ran after her boyfriend with tears streaming down her face and the audience howling. It was an ugly scene, and Valentine heard a voice over the PA announce that the show was over.

★   ★   ★

"I thought I saw your face in the audience," Hicks said, ushering Valentine into his dressing room a few minutes later. "Like my dear mother was fond of saying, it ain't much, but we call it home."

The dressing room was a pit, the plaster walls so badly pocked it looked like they'd been riddled with a machine gun. Mr. Beauregard sat in a leather director's chair. He had his skates off and was puffing on a cigarette.

"I'm looking for my son," Valentine said. "You haven't seen him, have you?"

"Gerry?" Hicks tossed his porkpie hat on a chair, revealing a few loosely combed strands of white hair across his freckled scalp. "He came by the other day with his two friends. They didn't stay very long."

"Something happen?"

"Mr. Beauregard did not like your son's friends. I believe the feeling was mutual."

Valentine looked at the chimp. Hicks claimed he had special powers. Valentine didn't believe that, but he knew that the night Hicks had saved his life, Mr. Beauregard was involved. He'd *smelled* him standing nearby, only Hicks had later told the police otherwise, and Valentine had gone along with him. He removed the surveillance photo from the Excalibur, and showed it to Hicks. "This one of my son's friends?"

Hicks squinted. "My vision is not what it used to be." Taking the photo from Valentine's hand, he showed it to the chimp. "Mister Beauregard, was this one of them?"

The chimp looked at the photo and hissed.

"Yes," Hicks said.

Valentine put the photo away and looked at his watch. It was just before ten. Maybe Gerry had gotten stuck in traffic and was out in the lobby. "I need to run. How long you in town for?"

"Until we decide to leave, " Hicks said. "We're four-walling."

"What's that?"

"We rent the theater, then set our ticket price based upon a certain number of people coming to each show. Unfortunately, I did not factor in the drawing power of Celine Dion. Did I, Mr. Beauregard?"

The chimp removed a rubber knife from his jacket and plunged it into his heart. Falling back on his chair, he let his tongue hang out the side of his mouth. Hicks said, "I have my carnival to return to if we decide show business isn't to our liking."

Valentine said good-bye and shook his hand. Mr. Beauregard was still playing dead. Hicks said, "Mr. Valentine is leaving. Let's not be rude."

Mr. Beauregard sat up in his chair. Reaching into his jacket, he removed a cigar wrapped in plastic and offered it to Valentine. Valentine had always enjoyed a good smoke, and slipped it into his pocket. He watched the chimp dig out a pack of matches and hand them over as well.

"I guess he wants me to smoke it right away," Valentine said.

"I believe he does," Hicks said.

CHAPTER 36

Valentine checked the lobby. Then he walked through the casino and got readdicted to smoking without having to light up. He even looked inside the bingo parlor again. His son had pulled a no-show.

He walked outside to the parking lot. It was nothing new. Gerry had been breaking his promises to him for as long as he could remember.

He got into his rental and saw his cell phone lying on the passenger seat. He'd left it on, and the phone was blinking and beeping. He grabbed it off the seat and went into voice mail.

"Hey, Dad, Wonder Boy here," his son's voice rang out. "Look, something's come up. I can't make it over tonight. I'll call you later, Dad. Bye."

Valentine took the cell phone away from his ear and stared at it, his anger clouding his vision. *Something's come up?* What the hell was Gerry thinking? His son knew the FBI was looking for him, and that he'd put his ass on the line to help him out. If he'd been sitting beside him, Valentine would have strangled him.

A car's horn made him jump. The parking lot

was packed, and in his mirror he saw a burly guy in a pickup truck, hoping to grab his spot.

"Hey Pop, you leaving?" the guy asked.

Valentine shook his head and watched the pickup drive away. The guy had called him Pop. Gerry called him Pop, just like he'd called his own father Pop. Gerry *never* called him Dad.

Valentine replayed the message.

"Hey, Dad, Wonder Boy here . . ."

His son was trying to tell him something. He thought back to the code they'd used in the Second Sight act when Gerry was a kid. Then he remembered: *Dad* had been part of the code. *Dad* meant Gerry hadn't understood him, and needed help.

Dad meant trouble.

He burned down the Boulder Highway to Henderson where his son was staying. Digging out his wallet, he extracted the slip of paper with the Red Roost Inn's phone number and punched it into his cell phone. The night clerk answered. Valentine asked to be transferred to his son's room.

"He checked out," the night clerk said. "Actually, his buddy checked out for him."

"Describe the guy who checked my son out," Valentine said, standing in the motel's dingy office ten minutes later, having broken every speed limit and run every red light on the drive over.

The night clerk was walking testimony to the

evils of alcohol, his face a mosaic of busted gin blossoms, his eyes runny and dispirited. He scratched his unshaven chin, thinking. Valentine tossed down twenty bucks to prod his memory along.

"Middle Eastern, five-ten, about a hundred and seventy pounds," the clerk said. "Not a bad-looking guy, except he was always scowling. He and his brother shared a room."

"How long they been here?"

"Couple of weeks."

Valentine removed the surveillance photo from the Excalibur and laid it on the desk.

"That him?"

The clerk gave it a hard look. "Yup."

A ledger sat on the desk. Valentine flipped it open and heard the clerk squawk.

"That could get me fired," the clerk said.

Valentine tossed him another twenty. Then he scanned the names in the ledger. Two stood out. Amin and Pash Amanni. Pointing, he said, "This them?"

"Sure is."

"Let me see their credit card imprint."

"Didn't use one." The clerk removed a flask from a drawer. The money had put him in a celebratory mood, and he took a pair of shot glasses from the same drawer and slapped them on the desk. He unscrewed the flask with his teeth.

"You a drinking man?" he asked.

Valentine felt something inside him snap. The

shot glasses shattered as they hit the floor. The clerk jumped back like he'd been struck.

"Hey mister, I was just trying to be—"

"I don't care what you were trying to be. I need to find these guys. Anything you can remember before you get drunk would help."

Valentine put his hand on the flask. The clerk swallowed hard, realizing he wasn't getting any hooch unless he cooperated. He scrunched his face up, giving it some effort.

"Come to think of it, there were a couple of things," he said.

Amin and Pash Amanni had liked to eat pizza. They also went to the movies a lot. Those were the two things the clerk remembered.

It wasn't much, but better than nothing, and Valentine killed the evening visiting every pizza shop and movie theater in Henderson. At each he showed Amin's surveillance photo to the help, asked if anyone recognized him.

None of the ringed and pierced employees did.

By midnight he felt ready to drop from exhaustion. Sitting in a strip mall parking lot, he ate a slice of pizza that tasted like cardboard with catsup. He washed it down with a soda, told himself he had to keep looking. If Amin knew he'd been photographed in the MGM the night before, he was probably staying away from Las Vegas. That left Henderson as his only real hiding place, unless he was camped out in the desert.

Valentine realized he was dying for a smoke. He'd gone cold turkey a year ago, and didn't get the cravings for nicotine unless he was under stress. He pulled Mr. Beauregard's cigar from his pocket, peeled away the plastic, and passed it beneath his nose. The tobacco was dry, but still smelled wonderful.

He fired up the cigar with the rental's lighter and filled his mouth with the great-tasting smoke. It lifted his spirits and calmed his nerves at the same time.

He saw the lights go out in the pizza parlor. Other stores around Henderson were probably closing as well. Which left fewer places for Amin to hide.

He started up the car and was backing out of his spot when he heard the explosion. It was right in his face, and very loud. It snapped his head back, and he saw nothing but eternal blackness. *Your life just ended,* he thought.

The banging on his window brought him back to the real world, and Valentine stared at the kid who'd served him the pizza standing beside his car. He rolled his window down.

"Hey mister, you all right?" the kid anxiously asked.

Valentine touched his arms, and then his face. Everything felt fine.

"Yeah, I think so," he mumbled.

"What happened?"

"I honestly don't know," he replied.

The kid sauntered off. Valentine inspected the car. The windshield wasn't broken, nor were any of the windows. He turned on the interior light and stared at his reflection in the mirror. His lips and chin were covered in black soot. It slowly dawned on him what had happened. Mr. Beauregard had given him an exploding cigar.

Valentine thought back to the chimp handing him the pack of matches. He hated to be played for a fool, and thought about calling Ray Hicks, and giving him a piece of his mind. Then his cell phone rang.

He stared at the luminous clock on the dashboard. It was twelve-oh-five.

"I need more time," he told Fuller.

"You just ran out of that," the director of the FBI replied.

CHAPTER 37

Hog-tied and gagged, Gerry lay across the backseat of Amin's rental car and watched the sun break over the horizon.

Dawn was different in Las Vegas. Before the sun ever came up, the sky put on a show, turning from black to magenta to a magnificent dark blue. The changes were gradual, yet also severe, as if the colors were being sucked from the desert.

Soon sunlight flooded the rental, and he heard Pash and Amin stir in the front seats. They had driven into the desert around eleven o'clock, parked behind a deserted building, and promptly gone to sleep. Gerry hadn't slept at all, his heart pounding so hard he thought it might explode.

Amin rubbed the cobwebs from his eyes, then climbed out of the rental and walked away. Lifting his head, Gerry looked through the side window and saw Amin standing twenty yards away, pissing on a cactus. He kicked the back of Pash's seat.

"Wake up," he said through his gag.

Pash turned around and stared at him. His happy-go-lucky expression had been replaced by one of mounting dread. "Be quiet," he whispered.

"Not until you tell me what's going on."

Pash reached over and tugged his gag down. "Be quiet, or my brother will put a bullet in your head."

"The truth," Gerry said. "I think I deserve that."

"My brother will kill you, do you understand?"

"Big fucking deal."

That hit Pash hard. "You are not afraid of dying?" he asked.

Not as much as you, Gerry nearly said. Before he could reply, Pash turned back around. "My brother is returning. Please shut up."

Gerry lifted his head. Amin was still draining the monster. During the night, he'd realized he might die not knowing what the brothers were up to, and he said, "Come on. I have a right to know."

"How so?" Pash said, staring straight ahead.

"I saved your lives yesterday, didn't I? Just tell me the truth."

"Stop it. Please."

"You're not drug dealers. I figured that out."

Pash stiffened like a thousand watts of electricity had been jolted through his body. His chin dropped down and touched his chest, and Gerry realized he was fighting back the overwhelming urge to cry. "How did you know that?" he asked.

"You didn't sample the merchandise."

Pash lifted his chin and looked over his shoulder into the backseat.

"Please explain."

"The meeting with the Mexicans," Gerry said. "You gave them cash, and they gave you drugs.

Only you didn't try the drugs, or test them with chemicals. For all you knew, they could have sold you cornstarch."

A guilty look spread across Pash's face.

"What I can't figure out is, what the hell did they sell you?" Gerry said. "Amin got a beat-up briefcase. It was too small to be filled with weapons. So what was in it?"

Pash was trembling, as if the secret were burrowing a hole in him. He reached between the seats and readjusted the gag over Gerry's mouth.

"I am sorry this is happening," he said.

Valentine dragged himself through the Acropolis's deserted lobby. He'd driven around Henderson until three AM, then stopped at an all-night gas station for a coffee and a jelly doughnut. The next thing he remembered was waking up in his car at nine o'clock with a pancake-sized coffee stain on his shirt.

He heard someone call his name. It was Lou Ann, the pleasant receptionist he'd chatted with yesterday. He shuffled over to the front desk.

"I've got some terrific news for you," Lou Ann said.

Terrific news? He thought he'd run out of that. He waited expectantly.

"Your airline found your luggage," she said.

On the scale of one to ten, it was a minus two. Then he remembered that the shirt he was wearing was his last clean one. That made it a plus two.

304

"Great," he said. "Where is it?"

Lou Ann removed a piece of paper from the counter and read from it. "Your suitcase was in Portland. The airline is routing it to Los Angeles. It should be here sometime tomorrow."

He thanked her and went to the elevators. While he waited for a car, he took out his cell phone and stared at its face. No messages. No Gerry. For all he knew, his son was in another city, or buried in the desert. He'd called Bill Higgins twenty minutes ago to see if the FBI had maybe found his son. Bill had said they hadn't.

The elevator doors parted. As he stepped in, a hand clasped his shoulder. He spun around and stared at Wily. He was so tired, he hadn't heard him approach.

"Mind some company?" Wily asked.

"Only if you don't mind my yawning."

Wily said he didn't. As they rode up to the penthouse, Valentine removed Amin's photograph from his pocket and showed it to the head of security.

"Ever see this guy before? He's a card-counter."

Wily studied the photo. "No, but he shouldn't be too hard to track down."

Valentine didn't think he'd heard Wily right. The doors parted, and they got out.

"How you going to do that?"

"Easy," Wily said. "The casino subscribes to FaceScan. They have the face of every known card-counter in a database in their computer. I'll give them your picture, see what they turn up."

Valentine had a feeling the FBI had already tried that, but there was always the chance they'd missed something. He slapped Wily on the arm.

"Anyone ever tell you how smart you are?"

Wily feigned embarrassment. "Look, there's something I need to talk to you about. As a friend."

"What's that?"

Wily hemmed and hawed. Valentine didn't think he could have made a speech if his life depended upon it. Finally, Wily gave up, and walked down the hallway to Valentine's suite. "Give me your key," he said.

Valentine gave him the plastic key. Wily swiped the door and pushed it open.

"This is what I want to talk to you about," he said.

Valentine entered the suite. The living room was filled with flower arrangements, their fragrance strong enough to knock over a horse. A card was propped up on the coffee table, addressed to him. Picking it up, he tore the envelope open.

It was a Valentine's Day card with a big heart in its center, only his name had been added to the front. A Tony Valentine's Day card. It made him smile, and he opened it and read the note.

I THINK I'M FALLING IN
LOVE WITH YOU

Wily told him to sit on the couch, then got two Diet Cokes from the mini bar. Valentine held the card in his fingers and stared at Lucy's proclamation of love.

Wily made the couch sag and handed him a soda. Valentine took a long swallow. He'd read that the artificial sweetener in Diet Coke stimulated the body's craving for sugar, and was bad for you. It was a shame it tasted so damn good.

Wily cleared his throat. "Look, Tony, what I'm going to say isn't easy. But you've got to hear it. For your own good."

"Go ahead."

"Lucy Price is bad news."

"You think so?"

"Yes. Know what her nickname is?"

"No."

"The Blowtorch. She burns everyone she gets near."

Valentine put the card on the coffee table. "I really don't want to hear this right now, okay?"

Wily took a long pull on his soda and stared at him. "Know how many times I've wanted to say that to *you* over the years? About a hundred. Know why I didn't? Because I realized that everything that comes out of your mouth is true."

"Are you suggesting I shut up and listen?"

"Yeah," Wily said. "Hear me out."

"Go ahead," he said.

Wily put on his serious face. "It's like this. Lucy Price couldn't stop gambling if her life depended on it. She's lost everything. House, car, family. Six months ago, her husband took their kids and moved to Utah. He got a job and sent her an airline ticket. She won't join him."

"Who told you this?"

"Her husband did. He used to work here. He begged her to get help, but Lucy wouldn't go. She doesn't think she has a problem. She's a lost cause."

"Don't say that."

"You like her, don't you?"

Valentine thought about it. "I'd like to," he admitted.

"Don't."

"You make her sound like a leper."

"The casinos in Las Vegas have a program for compulsive gamblers. If a person with a problem asks us, we'll bar them when they come in. Over a thousand people have signed up. It started up in Canada, works great."

"So?"

"Lucy wouldn't sign up," Wily said.

"You tried?"

"About a dozen times."

Valentine finished his soda. What a wonderful time he was having in Las Vegas. He'd lost his son, gotten his face slashed, and now this. He stared at the open card sitting on the coffee table. I THINK I'M FALLING IN LOVE WITH YOU. Did Wily know how precious those words were? Wily had a wife, probably got to hear sweet nothings whenever he wanted. He didn't know what it was like to be alone.

Wily glanced at his watch, then rose and went to the door. Taking the surveillance picture of Amin from his pocket, he said, "FaceScan's office is on my way home. I'll drop this off, ask them to run it through their computer."

"Thanks. I appreciate it."

"Call them in a couple of hours. They get backed up on weekends."

"I'll do that."

Wily's fingers were on the doorknob. Lowering his voice, he said, "I'm sorry, Tony, but I had to tell you," and walked out of the suite.

CHAPTER 38

Valentine drove to Lucy Price's condo in Summerlin thinking about his conversation with Wily. Wily had called Lucy a lost cause. He didn't believe that. No one was truly lost. That was the one thing he'd learned growing up Catholic. There was always a shot at redemption.

Pulling into her driveway, he realized he should have called, and let Lucy know he was coming. After what had happened last night, she'd probably gone and bought a gun. He saw the front door open. Grabbing the paper bag off the passenger seat, he climbed out of the car.

Lucy stayed in the doorway. Her skin did something magical in the daylight, its glow soft and mysterious. He came up to her and she kissed him.

"Did you find your son?"

"Still looking. I had to come and see you. Thanks for the flowers."

"After last night, it was the least I could do."

She led him inside. The condo smelled of fresh coffee and burned toast. She offered to make him scrambled eggs, and they went into the kitchen. He sat at the breakfast table and placed the bag between his feet. As she fixed breakfast, he found himself staring at her furniture and kitchen appliances. All of it was old and beat-up. Every compulsive gambler he'd ever known lived like this. He tried not to think about it.

"Hope you don't mind them runny," she said, ladling the eggs onto a plate.

"Not at all. Got any Tabasco sauce?"

"Sure. I think it's pretty old, though."

She found the Tabasco in a cupboard and sat down. Years of eating crummy diner food had gotten him addicted to Tabasco, and he sprinkled it on his eggs. With his foot, he pushed the bag across the linoleum floor so it touched her chair.

"This for me?"

He nodded. "It's *all* for you."

She made a face, then picked the bag up from the floor. She opened it and let out a shriek. The bag fell from her hands, its contents spilling onto the floor.

"Oh, my God! Oh, my God!" Lucy grabbed his arm. "It's my twenty-five thousand dollars, isn't it? Isn't it?"

He nodded and kept eating. It was actually the money Chance Newman had paid him two days ago for demonstrating Deadlock. He'd decided that it wasn't a coincidence that Chance had paid him the same amount that had been stolen from the safe in Lucy's hotel room.

"You got it back from them, didn't you?" she asked.

Another nod. The eggs were terrible. He kept shoveling them into his mouth, wanting her to do all the talking.

"I'm not going to ask you how," she said, her face glowing. She picked up the stacks of bills from the floor and held them tightly against her bosom. "Do you know what this means, Tony? Do you know what this means to me?"

She kissed him, then jumped to her feet, kicked off her flip-flops, and danced around the kitchen like a ballerina, pausing to do an occasional pirouette, the stacks of money slipping from her grasp. He put his fork down and smiled.

"It means you can get your life in order," he said.

She stopped in the middle of a spin. "What's that?"

"It's what you said to me on the balcony. The money was going to help you get your life in order."

"Is that what I said?"

"Yes. Now you can."

She laughed. The sound was harsh as it escaped her lips. "It means that my luck's changed, that's what it means. It means that Lucy Price is back."

The eggs were doing a number on his stomach. He wiped his mouth with a paper napkin and stood up. The moment of truth was at hand, and he could feel his legs shake.

"I want to talk to you about something," he said.

Lucy picked up the money from the floor and put it into the bag. Done, she rose.

"What's that?"

"I want you to do something for me."

A dreamy look spread across her face. "Whatever you want," she said.

"I want you to enter into a Gamblers Anonymous program and start going to meetings. They hold them every night. You've got to address this problem."

It was as if he'd slapped her across the face. Lucy stepped back until she was leaning against the kitchen counter, looking at him like he was the most horrible person alive.

"What problem? What are you saying?"

"Your gambling problem, the one you can't control."

"Who said I have a problem?"

"I did."

"What makes you the expert? You're not a shrink."

"I've worked in casinos most of my life. I can recognize a gambling problem when I see one."

"I'm down on my luck. So are a lot of people."

No, he thought, *you're desperate.* It was why she'd let Fontaine talk her into being his shill. Deep down, she'd probably sensed the deal was too good to be true, only her situation had clouded her judgment.

"You need help," he said.

313

"Don't fucking lecture me," she said angrily.

"That's what I want."

"No. Go to hell."

"Please. For me."

Her face had gone red, and she shook her head violently. The Lucy he knew was gone. This was Lucy the gambler. From his jacket, he removed the Valentine's Day card he'd found in his suite and propped it beside his plate of food. Then he looked at her.

"I'm leaving," he said.

"Are you going to take the money back?"

"It's yours," he said.

She crossed the kitchen while staring suspiciously at him. Then she snatched up the bag with the ferocity of a mother pulling her child from a rushing stream. He waited, always the optimist when it came to things of the heart.

"Good-bye," she said.

CHAPTER 39

The sound of someone banging on her front door awakened Mabel from the deepest of sleeps. She lifted her head off her pillow and found a dead phone lying on her chest. Beside it was a pad of paper and the things a desperate casino boss had asked her to write down last night. Had she gone to sleep while the casino boss was talking to her? She honestly didn't remember.

Climbing out of bed, Mabel threw on a bathrobe and walked barefoot down the cold hardwood floors of her house. "Hold your horses," she called loudly, and ducked into the bathroom.

A minute later, she cracked open the front door. Yolanda stood on the stoop, dressed like she was going on a trip. In her hand was a suitcase. Mabel threw the door open and said, "Did your water break?"

Yolanda shook her head. "No, but it's time. Can you drive me?"

"Are you dilating?" Mabel said, backing down the drive five minutes later.

"No, everything's normal."

"Then how—"

"I just know," Yolanda said.

Just about everybody in Florida went to church on Sunday, and the traffic out of Palm Harbor was miserable. Mabel drove the speed limit, taking Route 19 to State Road 60 then heading east over the causeway to the mainland.

"But how do you know?" Mabel asked.

Yolanda drank from a bottled water. "My mother told me I would have a dream. She said a truck would come to my house. A man would open the back, and the truck would be filled with apples. She said I would smell the apples in my dream. If the apples were green, it was a boy. Red, a girl."

"And you had this dream last night?"

Yolanda raised her eyebrows and smiled. She could do that, and tell you exactly what she was thinking. Mabel grabbed her hand and squeezed it excitedly.

"What color were they?"

"Red. It's going to be a girl."

The hospital Yolanda had chosen was called St. Joseph's, only everyone called it St. Joe's. It was a long drive from where they lived, but Yolanda had checked around and been told it was the best. That, and she'd found the right doctor, a white-haired Russian gentleman with a twinkle in his eye and the gentlest of hands. Those hands, she had decided, would bring her child into this world.

"Did you talk to Gerry? Does he know?" Mabel asked when they were on Dale Mabry Highway and only a few miles from the hospital.

"He hasn't called since yesterday," Yolanda said.

"Oh," Mabel said.

A wailing ambulance blew past, and traffic stopped altogether. Mabel threw the car into park. She glanced at Yolanda and saw the corners of her mouth trembling.

"What's wrong, dear?"

"There was another part of my dream," she said.

"Please tell me."

"The man with the truck gave me an apple. I went into our house to show Gerry. Only he was gone, and so were his clothes and all his things. It was like he'd disappeared."

Cars were moving again, and Mabel tapped the accelerator. Reaching across the seat, she took Yolanda's hand and held it all the way to the hospital.

Amin pulled up Bart Calhoun's gravel driveway and saw his teacher's mud-caked pickup truck parked in the garage. Calhoun had not impressed him as the type who spent his Sunday mornings in church. He killed the engine and took several deep breaths. He did not like this part of it. Calhoun had *helped* him. But it was necessary.

Amin looked up and down the street. The neighborhood was not fully developed, and Calhoun's closest neighbor was a quarter mile away. He opened his door and glanced sideways at Pash. His baby brother looked terrified.

"Promise me you will not let me down."

Pash stared at the dashboard as if hypnotized.

"Answer me," Amin said.

"I will not let you down," Pash whispered.

Amin glanced in the backseat at Gerry, still bound and gagged. "What about him?"

"He is not going anywhere."

"What if he tries to escape?"

"I will beep the horn to alert you."

Pash's lips were trembling. Amin put his hand on his brother's knee and said, "The end of one journey is at hand, while another is about to begin."

Amin started to climb out. In his mirror, he saw Gerry staring at him. Reaching between the seats, he smashed his fist into Gerry's stomach. Gerry curled into a fetal position, his gag muffling his screams. Amin had killed five different men whose identities he'd stolen in the past two years, and their final moments had ranged from defecating on themselves to crying like babies.

"If you try to escape, I will come out and shoot you. Understand?"

"Yes," Gerry spit through his gag.

Amin adjusted the .357 in his pants so the handle hung over his belt buckle. He covered the weapon with his sweatshirt and got out of the car.

He was smoothing the sweatshirt out when Calhoun answered the door. His teacher was unshaven, and there was lint in his buzz cut. Like he'd just woken up, Amin thought. Only Calhoun's eyes were alert. He squinted at Amin.

"What's up?" Calhoun asked.

"Pash and I are driving to Laughlin to play blackjack," Amin said. "I wanted to ask you a couple of questions to help avoid the surveillance."

There was a hesitation in Calhoun's response, a split-second delay that wasn't normally there when he spoke. A screen door separated them. Calhoun kicked it open with his foot.

"Want some coffee?" he asked as they crossed the house and entered the converted garage that served as Calhoun's classroom.

"No thanks."

Calhoun flipped the fluorescent lights on, and their brightness momentarily blinded Amin. He walked painfully into a desk and heard Calhoun's pace quicken. His teacher was heading for his office.

Amin followed him, fingering the .357's handle beneath his sweatshirt. His teacher's office was Spartan. A desk, and a swivel chair with busted leather. On the desk sat an ancient PC. Its screen saver was on, and showed tropical fish swimming in a deep blue ocean.

Calhoun took the chair and slapped his elbows on the desk. The desk was covered with flash cards that he used to test his students.

"What seems to be the problem?" Calhoun asked.

Amin hesitated. His teacher had already forgotten their conversation.

"Pash and I are going to Laughlin."

"Oh, that's right. Why do you want to go there? The casinos are all burn joints. Make a big wager, and management will sweat your play like there's no tomorrow."

Amin stiffened. Calhoun had his legs under the desk, and was moving them. His teacher was a cowboy. From what Amin had seen in the movies, cowboys were prone to doing stupid things.

"We need a break from Las Vegas," Amin said. "You mentioned during class that the facial recognition equipment in Laughlin was easy to beat. You got interrupted and never explained how."

Calhoun smiled at him. "Most of the casinos in Laughlin use the same surveillance cameras they had ten years ago. Walk through them fast enough, and the lens can't pick up enough information. I've got a book on which casinos in Laughlin have them."

"You do?"

"Sure. Want to see it?"

"Yes."

Calhoun shot his hands under the desk. Amin hesitated, then jumped back, the shotgun blast coming straight through the desk and missing his head by a few inches. The flash cards exploded into the air.

Calhoun frantically tried to reload. Amin drew his .357 and pumped four bullets into him. His teacher's chair was on wheels, and he flew straight back, hit the wall, then fell off the chair onto the floor.

Amin came around the desk. Calhoun lay on his back. His eyes had a flicker of life in them. His lips parted, and Amin realized he was trying to say something.

He had always liked Calhoun. His teacher was what Americans called a man's man. He knelt down and placed his ear next to his teacher's lips.

"Fuck your mother," Calhoun whispered.

His teacher died before Amin could shoot him again.

Amin took the swivel chair and sat in front of the PC. The computer looked like the first one ever made. He clicked the mouse to erase the screen saver. The underwater scene vanished, and he found himself staring at an FBI MOST WANTED poster. In its center was a picture of him, standing on the sidewalk outside the Excalibur. He scrolled up and found a note from the sender.

Bart, every casino in town got this last night. Ever see this guy before?

Amin read the poster and swore in his native tongue.

The FBI had tied him to the murders in Reno, Detroit, New Orleans, Biloxi, and Atlantic City. It didn't have a lot of information, but it said just enough—*last seen in Las Vegas, armed, traveling with his brother*—that he knew he'd made the right choice. He couldn't run anymore, nor did he want to.

321

He got off the Internet. Calhoun's computer had a wordprocessing program called WordPerfect, and he booted it up. The computer was slow, and he banged it several times with his hand, thinking it might speed it along. Finally, the program appeared on the screen. Hitting the CAPS LOCK button, he typed:

AMIN SHOT ME. GOING TO LA.
PLANNING SOMETHING HORRIBLE.
MUST STOP HIM.

Amin reread the message. Satisfied, he pushed the chair away from the desk. Pash's passion for the movies had come in handy. Amin had seen enough scenes where dying people wrote notes to believe this one would pass. It was just dramatic enough.

On the bullet-scarred desk sat a cordless phone. He picked it up and punched in 911. The call went through, and an operator said, "Police emergency. Can I help you?"

"Help," he said hoarsely into the phone.

"Sir? Are you all right?"

"He . . . shot me," he said.

"Who?"

"Amin. Going to LA. Must stop him . . ."

"Sir? Sir!"

"Going to do . . . something bad."

He knocked the receiver off the desk, then listened to the operator's frantic attempts to get him back on the line. He glanced at his watch. It was ten thirty. It would take ten minutes for the cops to arrive, another ten for them to piece things together and alert the FBI. He glanced down at Calhoun's lifeless body lying beside him.

"Fuck *your* mother," he whispered.

CHAPTER 40

Valentine left Lucy's condo and, having no place else to go, drove up and down the Strip. It was a depressing place on a Sunday morning, and he listened to the clatter-and-cling of slot machines rattling out the casinos' open doors while imagining Lucy at a machine, blowing the money he'd given her.

It was depressing to think about. Finding a jazz station on the radio, he prayed for Sinatra or any of the old crooners to lift his spirits. Louis Armstrong came on, asking what did I do, to be so black, and blue? A sad song, but he hummed along anyway.

Someday, when he was lonely and feeling sorry for himself, he would kick himself over this. He could have struck up a long-distance relationship, seen Lucy when he wanted, and gone with the flow. He could have pretended the gambling problem didn't exist. It was how a lot of couples lived their lives.

Only he couldn't live that way. He couldn't live within a lie. It was the way he'd always been, and he was a fool to think he could change it.

★　　★　　★

324

At eleven o'clock he called FaceScan.

Wily had said it would take them a few hours to compare Amin's picture against their database of known counters. Maybe they had found something the FBI had missed.

He got FaceScan's number from information, called it, and got a recorded message. The message gave the company business hours and their address. They were just off Sahara Boulevard, and only a few miles away.

Five minutes later, he pulled into FaceScan's parking lot. The company worked out of a five-story steel-and-glass monolith. There were several dozen reserved FaceScan spaces in the parking lot. All of them were taken.

The lobby was filled with surveillance cameras. He picked up the house phone and called the company's receptionist, the extensions listed on a laminated sheet beside the phone. A recorded message answered. Hanging up, he started calling the extensions on the sheet. The fifth one answered. A friendly-sounding guy named Linville.

"This is Tony Valentine. I was hoping you could help me."

Linville came into the lobby a minute later. Midforties, glasses, a neat beard, he pumped Valentine's hand and said, "I used to work surveillance for Bally's. Your name came up a lot. It's nice to meet you."

Linville looked like the kind of guy who'd pull

off the highway and help you with a flat. Valentine explained the situation and Linville brought him inside, took him to the second floor, and led him through a warren of cubicles where the company technicians worked. Each technician sat in front of a blue-screened computer fielding requests sent from casinos with suspected card-counters.

They came to an empty cubicle, and Linville pointed at the chair and said, "This is where Monte sits. He handles the Acropolis, so I'm going to guess Wily brought your photograph to him. I just saw him a minute ago."

Linville stood on his toes and looked over the tops of the cubicles for Monte, then shook his head. "He's probably helping someone. Sunday mornings are rough. Sometimes we back each other up, especially when a casino is dealing with a team of counters."

The clock on the wall said eleven twenty. Valentine could feel his opportunity slipping away. Linville sifted through a pile of papers on Monte's desk and found the picture of Amin near the top of the stack, with a Post-it note attached to it.

"This your guy?" he asked.

Valentine nodded.

"You know how to use a scanner?" Linville asked.

Valentine nodded again. Moments later, he was sitting at Monte's computer, getting a quick primer from Linville on how to navigate his way through FaceScan's software program. It had many similarities to ACT, the database management system he used at home, and he quickly felt comfortable with it.

"Yell if you have trouble," Linville said. "I'm right down the hall."

Valentine ran Amin's picture through the scanner, then downloaded it into the computer. For a guy who hated everything electronic, he'd gotten adept at using computers. He typed in the necessary commands and leaned back in Monte's chair as FaceScan searched its database of card-counters for a match.

The technicians were a noisy bunch, and he listened to them talking to each other. There was a lot of cursing, and it didn't surprise him. He'd done a lot of cursing on Sunday morning back when he was a cop. Every casino had downtimes in their surveillance department when not enough technicians were working. Most of these downtimes occurred on Sunday mornings.

A message appeared on the screen.

No match found for your selection.

He scratched the stubble on his chin. Bill had said Amin was a known counter. FaceScan had every known counter in the world. It didn't make sense. He ran Amin's photo through the program again, and got the same message.

"Huh," he said.

He found Linville helping a technician on the other side of the room. A minute later, Linville was standing over him, staring at the computer screen.

"You're sure he's a known counter?"

"According to the GCB he is."

"Anything else on his record?"

"He's murdered five people."

Linville exited FaceScan's database and brought up another program. It required him to submit a password, and he typed his name backward, then hit ENTER. On the screen appeared the home page for the FBI. He navigated through the site until he finally reached the bureau's search engine.

"FaceScan and the FBI share a lot of information," he explained. "They use our database, and we occasionally use theirs. The guy you're looking for should be in their database. If not, he's the invisible man."

Linville left. Valentine went through the process of scanning Amin's picture again, then asked the bureau's search engine to compare it to its database of known criminals. A box came up on the screen with a message.

Be patient. This could take a minute or two.

Leave it to a government agency to tell someone to be patient. He left the cubicle in search of coffee. His lack of sleep was catching up with him, and he felt on the verge of dropping on the nearest couch.

He found a coffee machine in the employee lounge. Thankfully, it took dollar bills. He bought a double espresso and felt his eyelids flutter the moment he sucked it down. Caffeine put his brain into another gear, and he walked back to Monte's cubicle with a spring in his step.

The screen was flashing. The FBI's search engine had made a match. He sat in Monte's chair. He was finally going to learn something about the son-of-a-bitch who'd kidnapped his son. He clicked the mouse on the button on the screen. A message appeared.

This is a restricted area. Please enter your password.

He typed Linville's name backward, and hit ENTER. A page appeared on the screen. It was an FBI MOST WANTED poster. In the center of the poster was the same photo he was carrying around in his pocket. Next to it a SPECIAL ALERT had been posted at 2:00, Eastern Standard Time. That was only twenty minutes ago.

He quickly read the alert and felt a jolt to his nervous system as strong as the double espresso. The FBI had determined that Amin was a terrorist, and planning a major attack somewhere near Las Vegas.

CHAPTER 41

Valentine got in his rental, took Sahara to I-15, and headed south toward Bill Higgins's house. He did seventy most of the way, his eyes peeled on the empty highway. The sickening sensation he'd felt reading the FBI's poster would not go away.

He needed a comforting voice to talk to, and decided to call Mabel. When she didn't answer her house line, he tried her cell.

"I'm at St. Joe's with Yolanda," his neighbor said.

He nearly swerved off the highway. "She okay?"

"She went into contractions ten minutes ago. The doctor is here, and he's concerned she's going into labor too soon. She's not due for another three weeks."

Valentine pulled onto the shoulder, threw the rental into park, and shut his eyes. Taking a deep breath, he said, "But she's okay so far?"

"So far, yes," Mabel said. "The bad news is, she knows Gerry's in a lot of trouble. She had a dream that told her so."

"A dream?"

"I know, it's goofy, but she's convinced it's a premonition."

Valentine swallowed the rising lump in his throat. "It's going to be okay," he said.

"These people Gerry's associated with are very bad, aren't they?" his neighbor said.

"Everything's going to be fine."

"Oh, Tony, the evidence is right there. Gerry sent Yolanda a box of money, and he bought a gun with his credit card, and—"

"Did you hear what I said?" He realized he was shouting, and lowered his voice. "It's all going to work out in the end. Please, trust me on this."

"But, Tony—"

"Please, Mabel. Please."

"Is that what you want me to tell Yolanda?"

He imagined Yolanda in labor, and the thoughts that were going through her mind. "Yes. That's exactly what I want you to tell her."

"Whatever you say," his neighbor said.

Walking up the path to Bill's house, he picked up the Sunday *Las Vegas Review-Journal* lying in the grass. The headline was about six UNLV baseball players accused of not attending classes. Beneath their pictures were the words TSK! TSK! TSK! Before he could ring the bell, Bill opened the door and took the paper from him.

"Must've been a slow news day," he said.

They went to his study. Bill tossed the newspaper into the garbage, then rested his cane against the desk and took a chair. Valentine remained standing, his eyes vacantly staring at his friend's face.

"So you know what's going on," Bill said.

"Yeah. Who told you?"

"The FBI monitors whoever goes into the classified area of their site. They called Steve Linville at FaceScan and asked him why one of his employees was in there. Linville told them it was you."

"Any sign of my son?"

"Nothing," Bill said. "Your boy hasn't communicated with you?"

"He left me a voice message last night," Valentine said. "He used a code to tell me he was in trouble."

Bill ran his fingers through his hair. It was a signal that cheaters often used to signal each other there was "heat" and trouble on the horizon. He wondered if Bill recognized the irony in the gesture.

"Why didn't you tell me last night that the FBI thought this son-of-a-bitch was a terrorist?" he said.

"Because last night, the FBI didn't know that he was a terrorist," Bill replied.

"What changed?"

"Sit down, will you? You're making me nervous."

Valentine pulled up a chair and sat down. "Feel better?"

"Yes." Bill's eyes were watery from lack of sleep, and he rubbed them. "Remember when I told you how the FBI linked two murders in Biloxi to four other gambler suicides?"

"I remember."

"When the FBI was looking at the information, they saw something else. The cities where the gambler suicides took place were Biloxi, Detroit, New Orleans, Reno, and Atlantic City. These same cities have something else in common."

"What's that?"

"In the past two and a half years, caches of high-grade explosives have been found in each one. With the explosives were sophisticated detonators and mercury switches. In each city, the FBI got an anonymous tip that led them to the explosives before they were used. In New Orleans, they found a van with the stuff lining the interior walls."

Valentine felt another jolt to his nervous system. They were starting to scare the hell out of him. He placed his hand on his chest and felt his ticker. Its beat was slow and steady. His nerves, he decided.

"You okay?"

"I'll live. When did the FBI link the explosives to the murders?"

"This morning," Bill said. "There was a shootout yesterday at a gas station outside Henderson. A Mexican died. His partner got pulled over by the highway patrol. A K-Nine dog sniffed vapors in his truck. The partner broke down this morning and admitted selling explosives to a guy matching the suspect's description."

"What kind of explosives?"

"Triacetone triperoxide, also called TATP. It's what that guy Reid had in his basketball shoes when he tried to take down the jet right after 9/11."

"How much did they sell him?"

"Seventy-five pounds. If it were detonated all together, it would take down an entire city block."

Valentine closed his eyes, then slowly opened them. "You think he's planning to hit Las Vegas?"

"That's the general consensus."

"I talked to my son last night. I know things about this guy the FBI might not know."

"Did you tell Fuller?"

"I tried last night. He wouldn't listen."

"You want me to call him?"

"Yes."

He watched Bill dial the phone. He'd wanted to find Gerry before the FBI did, but he knew now that that was no longer the most important thing. The FBI had to find Amin, and they had to do it fast. Even if it meant his son ended up getting hurt.

"Peter, this is Bill Higgins," Bill said into the phone. "I've got someone here who I think can help your investigation."

CHAPTER 42

Longo woke up Sunday morning feeling like he'd slept with his head stuck in a vise. Like an idiot, he'd gone and gotten a six-pack of beer the night before, sat in front of the TV in his motel room, and polished it off. His body ached from the beating he'd taken, so he'd gotten drunk, hoping the alcohol would wash his misery away.

It had worked, and he had slept like a dead man.

But then he'd woken up with the world's worst headache. Staggering into the bathroom, he'd stared at his reflection in the vanity and groaned. The lumps and bruises on his face were reminiscent of the white boxers on ESPN who couldn't fight. Throw in the broken nose, and he was the picture of a palooka.

He couldn't deal with it. Not so early in the morning. So he'd taken a handful of ibuprofens and washed them down with the remains of a beer. Soon his head was spinning. Lying on the lumpy bed, he'd returned to dream world.

At eleven o'clock the phone on the bedside table rang. Only a handful of people knew he was here, all of them cops. Longo raised the receiver expectantly.

"What's up?"

His caller was an undercover narcotics detective named Hotchkiss.

"I've been calling you for an hour," Hotchkiss said belligerently. "Where the hell have you been?"

Longo sat up in bed. "Out jogging. You got something for me?"

"Yeah, I found your guy."

Before he'd gone to sleep, Longo had called every cop in Las Vegas who owed him a favor, and asked them to help him track down Valentine.

"Where is he?"

"Right now, he's on Las Vegas Boulevard, heading back into town."

"You got a tail on him?"

"No," Hotchkiss said, "a helicopter."

Longo smiled. Narcotics had a great way to track suspected dealers. They would put tiny reflectors on the hoods of their cars and watch their movements from the sky. "How did you find his car in the first place?"

"A sheriff saw him driving the Strip this morning. He followed him to the FaceScan building and tagged his car."

Longo's smile grew. It made his face hurt, but he didn't care. He was going to finally give Tony Valentine his due. Nothing in this world could have made him happier.

"Your guy just turned into the Acropolis," Hotchkiss said.

There was a pause, and Longo guessed Hotchkiss was watching the action through the computer in his office, the helicopter sending him back a live feed.

"What's he doing?"

"He left the car by the valet and went inside. I heard the place is closing down."

"How come?"

"Got ripped off by a gang of cheaters."

Longo slowly rose from the bed. His head felt like a balloon, and his legs were rubbery. He sat back down and said, "Thanks for the information. Thanks a lot."

Longo ingested another handful of ibuprofens, then tore open a Little Debbie cupcake he'd bought the night before and wolfed it down. This time, the pills didn't knock him sideways, and he dressed himself in yesterday's clothes, then got his Glock .45 from the dresser. He slipped it into his shoulder harness, then went into the bathroom and combed his hair. He heard a knock on the door. Raising his voice, he said, "I'll be out of your way in a few minutes."

Another knock. This one louder, and more determined. He went to the door and stuck his eye to the peephole. It was his wife, Cindi. He pulled his face away.

There was a curtained window next to the door.

Cindi's face appeared behind the glass. Her eyes peeked through the opening in the curtain, and saw him.

"Pete. Please open up. I want to talk to you."

His wife. Jesus Christ. He couldn't let her see him like this.

"Pete? Do you want me to kick this door down?"

She would, too. Cindi was tough as nails. Her father had been a judge, and the genes had been passed down. Longo undid the chain and threw the deadbolt. Then he stepped back, hoping his face would be obscured by the room's shadows.

Cindi came in, saw him, and did her best not to scream.

"Oh, my God," she said. "What happened to your face?"

"I walked into a jet engine," he replied.

They stared at each other for a long minute. Cold air invaded the room, his wife having left the door ajar, as if knowing she might want to escape. Finally, she found it in her to speak, the words coming out slow.

"Your detective friend Jimmy Burns told me you were here, if that's what you're wondering. I went and saw him this morning. I figured you'd probably seen him, and he'd know what you were up to.

"I asked Jimmy if he knew why you had the affair. I figure Jimmy's been a cop a long time, he probably understands these things. Jimmy said,

338

'Yeah, I know why,' and he showed me your girl-friend's picture."

Longo couldn't deal with this, and stared at the floor.

"Look at me, Pete."

He lifted his eyes and stared at his wife. She looked no different than when they'd met in college twenty-odd years ago. He'd loved her a lot back then. So what had changed? Him? Her? Or was it just the world?

"She was beautiful," Cindi said.

Longo felt like he'd been kicked. Why was she doing this to him?

"Don't," he said.

Cindi edged closer. She offered a faint smile. *I won't hurt you,* her face said. She put her arms out and encircled his waist. "I looked at that picture, and said to myself, *Looks like Pete found his cabana boy. Or should I say girl.*"

Longo saw a twinkle in her eye. He'd once brought home a bottle of rum called Cabana Boy. On the bottle's label was a picture of a handsome, well-proportioned guy in a bathing suit. Cindi had swooned over the bottle all night.

"You're not mad?" he said.

"Of course I'm mad, you dickhead. What I'm trying to say is, I understand. Hell, if I was a guy, I'd probably screw her, too."

Longo couldn't help it, and started grinning. The first time they'd met, she'd cracked him up with the things she'd said. He felt her squeeze his waist.

"Jimmy told me this woman was using you," Cindi said. "She was laundering stolen casino chips, and you were her protection."

"Jimmy said that?"

"Yes. He said she was caught doing it up in Lake Tahoe and got two years' probation. She was a bad person, Pete."

Cindi was really holding him. They were the odd couple—him six-one, her nearly a foot shorter—and he rested his chin on her head, and felt her heart beating against his ribs. "I couldn't . . . help myself," he whispered.

"I'm willing to give our marriage another shot," she said after a moment. "Go see a counselor, and get some stuff off our chests. I won't hold this against you."

"You won't?"

"No. But you have to promise me one thing."

"Whatever you want."

"You'll never do this to me, or the girls, again."

He kissed the top of his wife's blond head. He used to love Cindi so goddamn much that he'd never thought he could love anybody else. Loved her with all his heart, and all his soul. And now she was giving him a chance to do it all over again.

"Never, ever," he said.

"Say it, and not have your fingers crossed," Cindi said.

Longo grinned so hard, it made his face hurt. Putting his lips to her ear, he said, "On my mother's grave, I'll never be unfaithful to you, or my family, ever again."

Cindi looked into his eyes. Searching for something, and finally finding it.

"Let's get out of this toilet," she said.

CHAPTER 43

Gerry sat upright in the backseat of the rental, still hog-tied. He'd convinced Amin that he wasn't going to scream, and Amin had removed the gag.

They had left Bart Calhoun's house an hour ago. Amin had driven around Las Vegas, then gotten onto I-15 and headed west toward the California state line. A mile before the line, he'd pulled into the parking lot of an old-time casino called Whiskey Pete's. He parked at the back of the lot, a hundred yards from the other cars. He'd not spoken a word since coming out of Bart Calhoun's house. Gerry watched him get out of the car, and walk to the casino. *It's now or never,* he thought.

"Know what they call this place?"

"What," Pash said, watching the casino.

"A sawdust joint."

Pash adjusted the mirror so he could watch Gerry and Whiskey Pete's entrance, at the same time. "Why's that?"

"Back in the forties, every casino had sawdust on the floor, so they called them sawdust joints.

342

Then a gangster named Bugsy Siegel came to town."

Pash's face came alive. "Didn't Warren Beatty make a movie about him?"

"Yeah. Bugsy Siegal was also the Moe Green character in *The Godfather*."

"Moe Green. The mobster who got shot in the eye?"

Gerry nodded. It was working; Pash was acting human again. "Bugsy Siegel bought the Flamingo, and turned it into a swanky club. It was the first casino in town not to have sawdust on the floors, so they called it a carpet joint."

Posh smiled. "A carpet joint. Very good."

"Look. You like the movies. Ever watch any Westerns?"

"Oh, yes. John Wayne is my favorite."

"In the Westerns, they always give a dying man a last request. How about giving me one, and tell me what the hell is going on."

Pash's lips snapped shut. Gerry leaned forward, and thrust his head between the front seats. "Look, Pash. I don't want to die not knowing the score. Understand?"

Pash exhaled deeply, his eyes glued on Whiskey Pete's entrance. "The score?"

"The truth, the skinny, the facts. Come on. You owe me."

"You really want to know?"

"Yeah."

Pash spent a moment gathering his thoughts.

When he spoke, his voice was without emotion. "All right, my friend. Here is the score. You know of the events of 9/11."

Gerry blinked. "Sure."

"Well, there was a second group of terrorists, who were dedicated to destroying important buildings and structures throughout the United States. My brother was the leader of that group."

Gerry felt like he'd been hit in the head with a brick. He fell back in his seat.

"It is true," Pash said. "My brother and I are Pakistani. My brother was recruited in college, and trained at Osama bin Laden's camp in southern Afghanistan. At night, bin Laden liked to show movies. Do you know what his favorite was?"

Gerry shook his head.

"*Independence Day*. When the alien spaceship blew up the White House, everyone in the camp would stand up and cheer."

"Fuckers," Gerry swore under his breath.

Pash took a bottled water off the seat, had a sip, and offered him the bottle. When it was declined, he screwed the top back on. "Amin came here in nineteen ninety-nine under a student visa and spent two years buying plastic explosives. Even though he was a foreigner, he found people willing to sell them to him. Ex-CIA, drug dealers, white supremacists. He amassed enough to fill a small van.

"He also helped the men in his group obtain explosives through the money he made card-counting in casinos. Those men were in Atlanta, Chicago, Los Angeles, and Philadelphia.

"The morning of 9/11, my brother drove into Washington, DC. He was in contact with his group through his cell phone." Pash paused to stare at him. "Do you know anything about plastic explosives?"

Gerry felt himself shudder. "No."

"They have to be detonated by another bomb. My brother had three hand grenades tied to his waist. He planned to drive down Pennsylvania Avenue, knock down the fence, and drive across the lawn to the White House. He had enough explosives to level the building and everything around it."

Gerry thought back to that day. He remembered nothing about a truck in the capital, and said, "What stopped him?"

"A confluence of events," Pash said. "The man in Los Angeles got stuck in traffic. He panicked and called Amin. My brother parked several blocks from the White House and tried to calm him down. Then he called the others in his group and heard panic in their voices. They were all young and very afraid.

"One by one, the men quit. On the radio, Amin heard that the towers had been hit. He got back onto Pennsylvania Avenue and saw that the police had cordoned off the street. He drove to Virginia and ditched the truck."

Pash turned around in his seat. His eyes were wet and shiny. "Now I will tell you something else. I am not a terrorist. I'm an elementary school teacher. I came here two years ago, looking for my brother. I hadn't heard from him, and was afraid he was sick. I didn't know what he was doing.

"I tracked him down, and he told me the truth. Right then, I knew he was doomed. Either the police would kill him, or he would die in prison. His life was over. And so was mine."

"You could have run to Canada, or Mexico," Gerry said.

"Before 9/11, yes. Not now. The smugglers will turn us in. Even they hate us."

"So you went on the lam with him."

"Yes. We went on the lam."

Pash stiffened. Gerry stared through the windshield. The midday sun had thrown a glare on the glass, and he saw Amin's faint outline as he came out of Whiskey Pete's.

"Now you know," Pash whispered.

Gerry watched Amin approach the car. He had always seemed different, and now Gerry knew what it was. Amin was in league with the devil.

CHAPTER 44

Amin got into the rental. Removing the .357 from beneath his sweatshirt, he placed it between the seats so the barrel was pointing at Gerry's chest.

"Some friends of mine are going to come out," he said. "When they come to the car, I want you to smile and act normal. Understand?"

Gerry stared down the barrel's eye. If his hands had been free, he would have eaten a bullet just to get them around Amin's neck.

"Whatever you say."

A minute later, two Middle Eastern guys in monochromatic waiters' uniforms walked out of Whiskey Pete's back entrance. One was tall and skinny, the other short and extremely fat. Amin flashed his brights. Both men waved.

They disappeared in the parking lot, then drove up in a blue Chevy Intrigue and parked alongside Amin's rental. The tall one was driving, and had a big smile on his face. Amin rolled down his window.

"Thank you, again," the tall one said.

The shorter one leaned across the taller one's

lap. "Yes! Thank you for renting this car for us. We have always wanted to see Los Angeles."

"Good," Amin replied.

"When will you be leaving?" the taller one asked.

"Later today. I have some business to take care of."

The tall one removed a slip of paper from his shirt pocket. "This place we are to meet you at, Grauman's Chinese Theatre. Is it easy to find?"

"Grauman's is where famous movie stars put their hands in wet concrete," Amin said. He jabbed a finger in Pash's direction. "My brother will tell you the names of every movie they've ever been in."

"Wonderful!" both men said.

"I almost forgot," Amin said. "I need you to take something to Los Angeles for me."

"Of course," they said.

Amin pressed a button on the dashboard that opened the trunk. To Pash, he said, "The suitcase is in back. Go put it in their car." He glanced in the back at Gerry. "I will watch him."

Pash turned to stone. "Do they know?"

"*Of course not,*" Amin said through clenched teeth.

"But why—"

"*It is safer this way.*"

Pash went and got a battered suitcase from the trunk. He strained putting it into the backseat of the Intrigue. Gerry realized it was the same suitcase Amin had bought from the Mexicans the day before. Explosives. The Mexicans had sold him explosives.

Pash returned to the car, breathing heavily. The waiters departed, the tall one beeping the horn as he exited the lot.

"Why are we going to Los Angeles?" Pash asked.

"Las Vegas is no longer safe," Amin said. "The FBI know we're here. It is only a matter of time before they track us down." He placed his hand on Pash's knee. "We will go to Los Angeles and finish our mission. All right?"

Pash nodded stiffly.

"What's that?" Gerry shouted, no longer able to control himself. "Blowing up a few thousand innocent people? Is that your mission, you crazy lunatic?"

Amin jerked the .357 from between the seats. Turning around, he leaned through the seats and flipped the gun so he was gripping the barrel. His eyes met Gerry's.

"Yes," he said, raising his arm.

Gerry started to curse him, then saw a thousand stars explode before his eyes.

CHAPTER 45

Valentine returned to the Acropolis because he didn't have anyplace else to go. The valet stand was deserted, and he parked at the front door. Inside, a receptionist informed him that he needed to be out of his room by three o'clock.

"We're shutting the place down," she said sadly.

He took the elevator to the penthouse. Lucy's flowers were still in his suite. He filled two garbage pails with them, then grabbed a soda from the mini bar and went out onto the balcony. It was a picture-perfect day, and hordes of people mobbed the Strip. He watched them while drinking his soda.

He played the last two days over in his head. He'd bungled so many chances to help Gerry. Had he done it on purpose? Or had he been hoping that Gerry would work things out for himself?

He found himself remembering the day Gerry had been born. He'd been a little screamer, with lots of curly black hair. It had been the happiest day of his life.

When he'd found out Yolanda was pregnant, he'd

thought that being a grandfather would bring him the same kind of joy. If Gerry died, he wondered if he'd be able to look at his grandchild, and not ask himself if he could have handled this differently.

Gerry opened his eyes and thought he was dead. It was pitch dark, and he couldn't feel his arms or his legs, or for that matter any part of his body. *You've gone straight to hell,* he thought. But then he smelled gas fumes and tasted the gag in his mouth.

He tried to move his arms, and realized his wrists were still tied behind his back. A picture formed in his brain. He was in the trunk of the rental. What mobsters called a dead fish. Still alive, but just barely.

Don't quit, a voice in his head said.

He took several deep breaths, then brought his arms down behind his back. If he could just bring his arms in front of him, he could untie his wrists with his teeth. He remembered a childhood magic book that had explained how escape artists did it. The description in the book had made it sound easy.

Lowering his arms, he tried to bring his wrists down below the soles of his feet. He stretched his arms until he thought he was going to scream.

No go.

He shut his eyes. The book had also said that escape artists could dislocate their shoulders. The book had warned him not to try it at home.

Gerry wedged his wrists beneath the soles of his shoes. Biting into the gag, he pushed down with his legs. The pain was excruciating. He thought about the suitcase Pash had put in the trunk of the waiters' car. How many innocent people would end up dying because of that suitcase? Hundreds? Thousands?

He pushed some more. He heard his right shoulder pop, then his left. Again he tried to bring his arms around. There was enough room now, and he smiled through his tears as he brought his hands up to his face and pulled the gag away.

He breathed hard and felt his heart calm down. Bringing his hands to his face, he tried to undo his wrists with his teeth. The twine would not loosen.

He frantically felt around the trunk. He needed something sharp to cut the twine with. Only the trunk was empty.

He felt his panic return. What was he going to do? He could scream, but then Amin would pop the trunk and kill him.

Then he had an idea. Jamming his fingers into his pocket, he found his cell phone and pulled it out. Fumbling in the dark, he hit every single button until it powered up.

You're not dead yet, he told himself.

"Do you have any idea where you are?" Valentine asked his son. He could hear the fear in Gerry's voice, and felt himself start to tremble.

"I just heard some voices," his son replied. "One guy giving another guy directions. They were pretty far away. I think I'm at a gas station out on I-15. I remember seeing one when we drove out here. It's about twenty miles before Whiskey Pete's casino."

"Did you call 911?"

"Not yet. I wanted to call you first."

That was dumb, Valentine thought. *Sweet, but dumb,* and he said, "I'm going to call the cops, then call you right back."

"Wait," his son said.

"Gerry, there's no time."

"I want you to do something. I want you to tell Yolanda how much I love her."

Valentine swiped at his eyes with his hand. "You're not going to die."

"Promise me, Pop."

Valentine felt his chest heave and his throat constrict. "I'll tell her. Then I'll call you right back."

"Thanks, Pop. I love you."

"I love you, too."

"Oh, shit," his son said.

"What's the matter? Gerry? *Gerry?*"

The line went dead. Valentine frantically dialed his son's cell number, and got put into voice mail. He hung up, waited for a dial tone, and punched in 911. Gerry wasn't going to die, he told himself. Gerry wasn't going to die.

While he waited for an operator to come on, he

found himself staring at the sky north of Las Vegas. Hordes of giant black locusts were gathering and descending upon the city. It was like watching something out of a science fiction movie. Down below, he saw everyone on the street staring at the sky as well.

As the hordes got close, he realized what he was looking at. It was a squadron of Apache military helicopters from nearby Nellis Air Force Base. He covered his ears as they passed over his balcony, then watched them make a sharp turn and head southwest.

Toward Whiskey Pete's, he thought.

CHAPTER 46

The gas station Amin was parked at had a convenience store. At 12:10, he went inside and killed a few minutes browsing through the crowded magazine rack. Normally, he hated these places. They were always run by smiling Arabs.

At 12:14, he took two bottled waters out of the cooler and went to the front of the store. A mountain of a man was at the register. His name tag said EARL. All the other customers in the store seemed to know him. Amin got on line to pay.

At 12:16, he put the waters on the counter, and Earl rang them up. From his wallet he removed a hundred-dollar bill and saw Earl frown.

"It's the smallest I have," Amin said.

Earl snapped the bill, then held it up to the fluorescent light. Amin tried not to act insulted. He stared down at the stack of Sunday newspapers next to his feet. A headline caught his eye. He put the newspaper on the counter.

"This, too," he said.

At 12:17, he got back in the car. He'd parked near the car wash. There was a pay phone on the back of the building. Seven minutes was plenty of time, he thought. He handed Pash a water. His brother unscrewed the top and took a long swallow. Amin indicated the trunk with a tilt of his neck. "Did Gerry give you any trouble?"

"No," Pash said. "He was quiet."

"Good." Amin started the engine. Then he stared at his younger brother. Pash looked very nervous. *He did it,* Amin thought. But he had to ask. Just to be sure.

"Did you call them?" Amin asked.

Pash's head snapped. "Who?"

"You know."

"No, I don't."

"The police."

"What are you talking about?"

"Did you call the police while I was in the store?"

"Come on, be serious," Pash said.

Amin grabbed him by the arm and squeezed his younger brother's biceps so hard that it made his eyes bulge. "The charade is over. I know what you did."

"What are you talking about?"

"You called the police in New Orleans and Biloxi and Detroit and the other cities, and told them where the explosives were hidden. It wasn't someone in the network, like I first suspected. It was you."

"I didn't—"

Amin grabbed the back of Pash's head and banged it into the dashboard.

"Don't lie to me, or I'll break your fucking neck."

Pash pushed away, his eyes wide with fear. "Is that what you think? That I betrayed you?"

"Yes! You called the FBI and used some kind of code to tip them off. Somehow you made them know each time that the threat was real. Didn't you?"

Pash took several deep breaths. "I only told them about the explosives. Never you."

Amin raised his hand to strike him. Pash grabbed his hand. For a moment, they wrestled in the front seat of the car.

"Why must you kill innocent people?" Pash said. "What will it prove?"

Amin stopped fighting and glared at him. With his head, he pointed at the newspaper lying on the seat between them. *"Read it,"* he said.

Still holding his brother's wrists, Pash stared at the front page. The headline was about six baseball players who'd gotten caught cheating, but were still being allowed to play in a big game. "So?" he replied.

"Yesterday, a young Palestinian couple were killed by Israeli gunfire in the Gaza Strip. In Iraq, a family was shot in their car when the father didn't stop at a checkpoint. Those stories aren't in the newspaper. Take a look if you don't believe me."

Pash let go of his wrists. "If they're not in the newspaper, how do you know they actually happened?"

"I saw them on the Internet."

Pash stared at the headline. He shook his head.

"It is wrong," he said. "But killing innocent people solves nothing."

"Did you, or did you not, call the police while I was in the store?"

Pash gave him an exasperated look.

"Yes," he said.

"Did you tell them about the explosives in the suitcase in the rental car?"

"Yes."

"Did you tell them anything else?"

"I told them the waiters were going to Los Angeles."

"Good," Amin said.

Out on the highway, a police cruiser raced past, its siren blaring. Another followed, then another. The sirens pierced the Sunday-morning quiet, only to be drowned out by a squadron of air force helicopters passing overhead. Like the police cruisers, they were following I-15 toward Los Angeles.

"You . . . wanted me to call them?" Pash asked.

Amin looked sadly at him. He had tried to make Pash understand that by coming to the United States, he was part of the jihad. Only Pash had never accepted his reasoning.

"Yes," Amin said.

"Why?"

Amin grabbed the paneling on his door and pulled it away, revealing the bags of TATP lining the interior. The deception hit Pash like a punch in the stomach, and he recoiled in horror.

Pulling out of the gas station's lot, Amin drove the car back toward Las Vegas.

CHAPTER 47

Valentine followed the cruisers down I-15 doing a hundred miles an hour. Whiskey Pete's was an old-fashioned casino about a mile from the state line. Gerry had said the gas station was twenty miles before Whiskey Pete's. By his estimation, that put the gas station twenty miles from Las Vegas.

He watched the miles fly by on his odometer. The desert landscape was flat and unforgiving, and he looked for any break on the horizon. Then he saw a Shell station sitting off the road. It had a car wash and a convenience store, and he made his brakes screech pulling up to the front door. Through the front window he saw a big guy behind the register give him a mean look.

He ran inside. There was a line at the checkout, and everyone on it was staring at him. For the first time, he became conscious of how he looked. Unshaven, his shirt stained, his mouth hanging open.

"You can't park there," the guy at the register said.

He took the picture of Amin out of his pocket,

unfolded it, and held it up between his hands. He showed it to the guy, and those on line.

"Any of you seen him?"

"Earl, ain't that the guy gave you the hunnert?" a man on line asked.

Earl reached across the counter, took the photograph out of Valentine's hands, looked it over, handed it back. "Yeah. He was just in here. You looking for him?"

Valentine felt his heart going faster than the engine of his car. Outside, another police cruiser passed, and he said, "Yes. So is everyone else. Including the helicopters."

Earl gave him a no-nonsense stare. "Who is he?"

"He's a terrorist," Valentine said.

Earl came around the register. Normally, guys who stood behind registers stood on phone books to make themselves look taller. Earl didn't need a phone book. He placed a giant paw on Valentine's shoulder.

"You ain't bullshitting me, are you? I got a brother over in Iraq."

"I'm not bullshitting you," Valentine said.

Earl led him outside, pointed at I-15. "Guy pulled out a few minutes before you pulled in. Green car, I think it was a Taurus. Went thataway."

Earl was pointing east, back toward Las Vegas.

"Are you sure?" Valentine asked.

"Positive. You probably passed him on the road."

The police cruisers and army helicopters were going the wrong way, and Amin had been sitting here, watching them pass by. Valentine thought about the crowds of tourists he'd seen walking the Strip earlier. Men, women, and kids. Thousands of them. He grabbed Earl by the arm.

"I need a gun," he said.

Earl had a hunting rifle and a four-ton pickup truck. He drove like a bat out of hell down I-15 toward town. Valentine sat in the passenger's seat with the rifle in his lap. He tried 911 on his cell phone and got a frantic busy signal. In disgust, he threw the phone on the floor and examined the rifle. It was a Remington Model 700 .270 with a Leupold scope. He'd gone hunting once in the Catskills and used the same gun. It was a good open-range weapon, known for long-distance, flat-trajectory hits. Half a mile up ahead, he saw a police roadblock made up of several cruisers, and guessed the police were doing the smart thing and cordoning off the city. Earl slowed the truck.

"You see the car?" Valentine asked.

The big man looked in both directions. "Nope."

"If they wanted to get to downtown, is there another way?"

"Not on pavement," Earl said.

"How about dirt roads?"

"Sure. They could take a dirt road and loop around."

"Show me."

Earl got on a street with a DEAD END sign, and Valentine saw him flip a switch that put the pickup into four-wheel drive. At the street's end, he jumped the curb, crossed someone's private property, and was soon driving across the bumpy desert.

The midday sun was blinding, and Valentine strained his eyes looking for the vehicle Earl had described to him. He remembered Bill saying that the explosives found in New Orleans were fitted inside a car. *The car* is *the bomb,* he thought. Earl pointed at a distant bluff and said, "I think we can see them from up there. If this is the way they came."

Earl was asking him a question, wanting confirmation.

"Is that the way you'd go?" Valentine asked him.

"Yeah, it's the quickest."

"Then take it."

Earl floored the accelerator, and the pickup shot into the air like an animal released from a cage. They hurtled across the desert, Valentine grabbing the oh-shit bar by his head and holding on for dear life. A bad thought flashed through his head. He had not asked Earl if the rifle was loaded.

The Model 700 had an internal box magazine and could hold four bullets, plus one in the chamber. If the gun was fully loaded, that gave him five chances to take Amin down.

As they neared the bluff, Earl slowed down, and Valentine pulled the bolt back and checked. Only three bullets in the magazine, none in the chamber. He felt his body lurch forward as Earl slammed on the brakes.

They both jumped out of the pickup. The elevation was no more than thirty feet. Nothing but sagebrush and half-ugly land that would someday probably hold lots of identical-looking houses. Earl grabbed him by the arm and pointed.

"There. Over there."

Valentine cupped his hand over his eyes. A quarter mile away, a car matching Earl's description was driving through a half-finished housing development. The car's wheels were caked in brownish red dirt. He lifted the Model 700 to shoulder height and got the occupants in the crosshairs of the rifle's telescopic lenses.

"That's them?" Earl asked breathlessly.

Valentine stared at the driver, then his passenger. Both Middle Eastern males. He lowered his line of vision and looked at the trunk. He imagined Gerry lying in back.

"Is it?" Earl demanded.

"Yes."

Earl banged the side of the pickup with his fist. "Shoot the bastard!"

Valentine found the back of Amin's head. He knew that the rifle's bullet was going to do more than kill Amin. It would go straight through him and hit the engine or, worse, hit the plastic explosives lining the interior. The bullet was going to make the car explode, killing his son. He lowered the rifle.

"What the hell you doing?" Earl bellowed. "You're letting them get away."

"My son's in the trunk," he whispered.

Earl wrestled the rifle from his hands, aimed, and let off a round.

"Fucking shit," he screamed.

The gun's retort echoed across the desert. Amin veered off the road and jumped a curb. He knew he was being hunted, and drove the Taurus toward a finished development filled with prefab houses and Japanese imports in the driveways.

Earl let off another round. Dirt flew up around the Taurus.

"Shit," he screamed.

Valentine thought of Yolanda back in Tampa, about to give birth, and remembered it like it was yesterday, his son's head popping out of his wife's womb, screaming at the world. The greatest moment in his life, for sure.

"I love you, Gerry," he whispered.

Then he grabbed the rifle out of Earl's hands, aimed at the back of Amin's head through the telescopic lenses, and fired the last bullet.

CHAPTER 48

Nick sat in his office in the Acropolis, staring at the casino's ledgers lying on his desk. He had come to Las Vegas in 1965, and opened the Acropolis two years later. It had been a helluva run.

He heard a delicate cough and looked up. Wanda was standing in the doorway, dressed in a red leather mini skirt and stiletto heels, his favorite outfit.

"Hey, baby," he said.

He hadn't seen her since yesterday. Too busy figuring out how much Albert Moss had screwed him out of. Good old Al had run him right into the ground. His cash reserves were gone, his credit allowance at the bank depleted.

"Can I come in?" Wanda asked.

"Of course, baby."

Wanda didn't walk into a room: She made an entrance. Nick rose from his chair and watched her come around the desk. Taking his hand, she led him across the office.

"Where are we going?"

"To the big picture window. I have something wonderful to tell you."

He needed some good news. She picked up a remote and pushed the button that automatically drew back the picture window's blinds. Sunlight streamed into the room.

It was a gorgeous day. Down below, one of the last of his employees was standing on a ladder, scrubbing his ex-wives with a mop. He was going to leave the fountains on for as long as he could, just to piss everyone in town off.

"Hold my hands," Wanda said.

Nick obliged her. An ancient gold coin hung around her neck, and he smiled. He'd given it to Wanda the night he'd proposed. It was the only coin that hadn't disappeared when his employee had hidden his treasure.

"Remember when you gave me this coin," she said, "and told me how you believed it was magic. Do you?"

Nick smiled. "Yeah, baby."

"Well, it really is. I'm pregnant."

He gulped hard, then lowered his eyes and stared at her wonderfully flat stomach. "I thought . . . you couldn't have a kid."

"That's what the doctors said. My first husband and I tried everything—in vitro, artificial insemination—and they kept coming back saying it was me, I couldn't be a mommy. Well, they were wrong, Nicky." She touched the coin dangling above her magnificent breasts. "The coin was magic. I'm going to have a baby."

Nick stared at the coin. His father and grandfather had been sponge divers in a town called Tarpon Springs. Some nights they would come home and give Nick coins they had plucked off the ocean floor. *They're magic,* they had told him.

He put his arms around her waist. "You sure?"

"Yeah. You're not . . . mad, are you?"

He shook his head.

"I thought . . . maybe you wouldn't want a baby."

"Your baby I want," he said.

She squealed and jumped up and down and kissed him all at the same time. She was acting like it was the greatest day in her life, and he decided to wait, and tell her later that he'd lost the casino. Holding her in his arms, he felt a tremendous explosion rip the air.

"Oh, my God, Nicky! Oh, my God!"

The whole building was shaking, and they watched the picture window bow like it was made of putty. Amazingly, it did not break, and they stared at the enormous black cloud rising in the western sky.

The cloud quickly blocked out the sun. Down on the street, terrified tourists were running for cover, with people being trampled and hurt. Nick wanted to do something, but wasn't sure what he was supposed to do. He looked at Wanda. She was crying.

"Nicky—what's happening?"

He wished he knew. Going to his desk, he picked up the phone and began punching in numbers.

He knew everyone in the Metro LVPD who was important. All the police lines were busy, and he slammed down the phone.

"I want you to go home," he said. "Stay in the house, and don't come out until I call you."

Wanda's face was pressed to the window. She wasn't moving.

"Did you hear me?"

She turned from the window. "Oh, Nicky," she cried.

"What's wrong?"

"It's . . . it's . . ."

"What?" he said.

"Magic," she said.

Nick hurried over to where she stood. Down below, the employee on the ladder had fallen onto the statue of Bambi, his second wife. The statue had broken at the waist, and hundreds of shimmering gold coins now lay in the fountain's turquoise water.

CHAPTER 49

Valentine blinked awake. He was lying in the pickup's shadow, and Earl was standing over him, holding the Remington with one hand. Earl's lips moved, but he couldn't hear what he was saying.

"Can't hear you," he said.

Earl knelt down and put his mouth to Valentine's ear. "Mister, what the hell was in that car?"

Valentine pushed himself into a sitting position. The last thing he remembered was shooting Amin in the back of the head. The Taurus had banged against an embankment and flipped over. He'd started to run, believing he could still save Gerry. Then a brilliant white light had enveloped him.

He stood on shaky legs, staring at the deserted lot where he'd last seen the Taurus. It was gone, replaced by a black, smoldering crater as wide as two football fields. His eyes shifted to the housing development Amin had been heading for. The windows on every house were gone. Many of the closer houses had lost their roofs. The destruction looked horrific, and he saw a line of neighborhood people standing at a fence, gaping at the crater. Earl's massive hand touched his shoulder.

"I'm sorry about your boy," Earl said in his ear.

Valentine went and leaned against the pickup. Stared at the ground for a long while and listened to himself breathe. He'd done what he had to do.

"You going to be okay?" Earl asked loudly.

"No," he replied.

Earl got on his cell phone and tried to dial 911. All the lines were busy, and Valentine heard him call his gas station. Suddenly, he acted excited, made Valentine get in the pickup, and gunned it across the desert. Valentine knew he should stay— the police would eventually show up, and want to ask a thousand questions—but Earl was having none of it.

Soon they were back at the gas station. One of Earl's employees was standing by the front door. Earl jumped out. Valentine's hearing had come back, and he heard Earl say, "Where is he?"

The employee pointed at the car wash on the other side of the station. Earl came over and opened up Valentine's door. Grabbing Valentine by the arm, he said, "Come on."

Valentine followed him, feeling like he was in a dream that he was never going to wake up from. They walked around the car wash, and Valentine saw two men he recognized from earlier, on line at the cash register. They were standing over another man, who lay on the ground. Valentine felt his heart leap into his throat. His son.

Valentine pushed the two men aside without thinking, got on his knees, and saw that Gerry was breathing. He told God right then that he was going back to church again, and he cradled his son's head in his arms and heard him groan.

"Something's wrong with his shoulders," one of the men said.

The other man had put his jacket beneath Gerry's head, and Valentine lowered his son's head onto it. There was a mean-looking bruise on his temple, and his eyes were cloudy, but otherwise he looked absolutely beautiful.

"Hey, Pop," his son whispered. "You stop them?"

Valentine told his boy that he had. Gerry smiled.

"Way to go."

"How did you end up here," Valentine asked.

"Pash . . . pulled me out of the trunk," his son said.

Gerry was having trouble speaking, and one of the men ran to the convenience store, got a bottled water, and soon had it beneath Gerry's lips. His son thanked him.

"Was Pash the other one in the car?" Valentine asked.

Gerry nodded. "Yeah. Amin's brother. He pulled me out of the trunk while Amin was inside the store. Told me he was sorry, and conked me in the head."

"What's wrong with your shoulders?"

"Popped them out of their sockets freeing my arms," Gerry said.

"They hurt?"

"Like a son-of-a-bitch."

Valentine heard the sound of approaching sirens. Earl walked around the car wash, and Valentine heard him calling to the driver of the police car that had just pulled into the gas station. He saw his son grimace, and realized it had nothing to do with how he was feeling. It was time for Gerry to tell the police everything that had happened.

His son motioned to him, and Valentine knelt down in the dirt.

"Closer," his son said.

Valentine realized Gerry didn't want the other men hearing what he was about to say. He lowered his head, and brought his ear next to Gerry's lips.

"I know this is going to sound stupid," he said.

"What's that?"

"I really liked Pash. I'm sorry you had to kill him."

Valentine felt himself shudder. He saw a blue uniform come around the car wash, heading straight toward them. In a whisper he said, "You'd better not tell the police that."

CHAPTER 50

Except for Amin and Pash, no one had died in the blast.

The bomb had ripped a hole in the earth worthy of a falling meteor, the explosion strong enough to be felt as far away as Los Angeles, and now the newspapers and TV stations and Internet news services were calling it a miracle.

Several thousand windows were shattered— including those in casinos over five miles away— and a hundred houses within the blast's immediate radius were damaged, their gas and water lines rupturing, forcing the immediate evacuation of their occupants. The cost was estimated at twenty million dollars, not including the loss of revenue the casinos experienced from being temporarily shut down.

Even the two Pakistani waiters whom Amin had tricked into driving to Los Angeles were spared. They had pulled off at a truck strop on I-15, and were inside the building relieving themselves when the Apache helicopters swooped down and riddled their rental car with over a thousand rounds of ammunition.

An elderly lady named Alice Sweet was found dead in her house several miles away from the blast, but the Clark County coroner quickly determined that she'd passed away peacefully in her sleep the night before, and had died from natural causes.

But many could have died. The media brought in their experts and showed what the bomb would have done had Amin made it into the city, and detonated seventy-five pounds of TATP in a closed space. Besides killing thousands of pedestrians, the explosion would have taken down a block's worth of buildings. The estimated loss of life was put at over fifty thousand people.

It was the theme of Mayor Oscar Goodman's speech during a news conference that afternoon. Standing before a room packed with reporters, he had called Las Vegas the luckiest city on earth, and praised the military, police and firemen who'd responded to the emergency so quickly. Then, he'd taken off his glasses, and thanked a retired cop named Tony Valentine.

"I've been told that this man has single-handedly saved the city's casinos millions of dollars over the years from cheaters and thieves," the mayor said. "And now, he's saved the city itself. How do we thank him? I don't honestly know. Maybe we should all go out and place a bet in his name."

Valentine had listened to the mayor's speech in Gerry's hospital room at University Medical

Center, and had wanted to throw something at the television. Placing a bet in his name was the last thing he wanted people to do. Gerry, who had just woken up, stared at the TV and started laughing.

"Maybe they'll name a street after you," he said. "Or a slot machine."

"Very funny," Valentine replied.

A pair of stern-faced uniformed cops stood outside the door. Once Gerry was feeling better, they were going to formally arrest him. He was tied to everything Amin had done in the past week, and was facing multiple criminal charges that could put him in prison for the next thirty years of his life.

In desperation, Valentine had called everyone he knew in Las Vegas. So far, only one person had offered to help him.

"You talk to Mabel?" Gerry asked expectantly.

"Ten minutes ago," he said.

"Any news?"

"Yolanda's still in labor. It's going to be a girl."

"How does she know?"

"Yolanda had a dream with red apples in it."

They sat in silence for a while and stared out the window at the beautiful afternoon. It was not hard to imagine what might have been, and more than once, Valentine saw his son wipe a tear away from his eye.

"I always wanted a girl," he said quietly.

CHAPTER 51

Nick did not believe in wasting time. He had his lost treasure appraised that afternoon, showed the appraisal to his bank, and was granted a line of credit that allowed him to open the Acropolis that night. Then he called Chance Newman and demanded a meeting with him, Shelly Michael, and Rags Richardson for the next day.

"Your office, ten sharp," Nick said. "No lawyers."

"Why should I meet with you?" Chance replied.

"I've got something that belongs to you," Nick said.

Nick appeared in Chance's office the next morning with Wanda draped on his arm. He wore basic hoodlum attire: black slacks and shirt, silver necktie, and a black sports jacket with silver buttons. Wanda wore a Nancy Sinatra–vintage pink jumpsuit. As she was introduced, Chance, Shelly, and Rags rose from their chairs. Each wore a pin-striped suit and carried a sullen expression on his face.

"My pleasure," she purred.

The men returned to their chairs. Nick reached into his pocket and removed the Deadlock cheating device Valentine had given him over breakfast that morning. It hit Chance's desk with a loud thud.

"Being our casinos are next door to each other, it's not surprising that I sometimes get deliveries for you," Nick said. "I got that little baby in a package from Japan. I believe it's called Deadlock."

The three casino executives looked stricken. Each had gone through a rigorous examination when applying for his casino license. No criminal activity of any kind was allowed. Owning a sophisticated cheating device could get their licenses taken away.

"Now, I suppose you could argue that you purchased Deadlock in order to educate your surveillance techs," Nick went on. "Only there's this little problem called Frank Fontaine. The FBI picked him up this morning and threw him back in jail. If I tell the FBI about Deadlock, and they ask Fontaine what he knows, well, you boys could be royally screwed."

"Nick!" Wanda said disapprovingly.

"Sorry, baby."

"I should hope so," she said.

Nick smiled at his bride. He'd promised Wanda to stop swearing. Wanda believed the baby could hear him, and would develop bad habits.

Shelly Michael cleared his throat. "Let me guess. You want to make a deal."

Nick's smile grew. "Let's call it a business arrangement."

Rags shook his head. To his partners, he said, "I'd rather take my chances in court than get fucked by this clown."

Nick wanted to belt him. Hadn't Rags seen how sensitive Wanda was to vulgarity? He decided to hit him where it hurt, and said, "What's the name of your company? BE BOP SHABAM Records?"

"That's right," Rags said.

"Or is it BE BOP SCAM Records?"

Rags glared menacingly at him. "What did you say?"

"You heard me," Nick said, puffing out his chest. "You got this great thing going, don't you? You take these ghetto rappers, release their CDs to other ghetto kids, and they go gold in two weeks. You go to the chains, show them the sales figures, and they order a million copies for their stores. That's the game, isn't it?"

Rags said, "Yeah, so what's your point?"

"The point is, those kids aren't buying music CDs. They're buying Hershey bars with altered bar codes. The sales numbers are faked. You're a fake. You want to take me to court? Do you?"

Rags shrank in his chair, his bluster gone. "No."

"I didn't think so. Maybe while I'm at it, I'll tell everybody how Chance bankrupted his software company in Silicon Valley, and how Shelly's law firm struck a secret deal with the feds so none of the partners had to go to jail."

Shelly and Chance both closed their eyes.

"You boys think I lasted thirty-nine years in this town by being a dummy?" Nick said, his voice rising. "I know everything about everybody. So we can deal, or we can fight. It's up to you."

Chance opened his eyes. "What do you want?"

Nick held up two fingers. "Two things," he said.

"Name them."

Nick clicked his fingers, and Wanda removed a rolled sheet of paper from her handbag with the aplomb of a game show hostess. Nick unfurled the paper. It was a crude rendering of a pedestrian walkway connecting the Acropolis to the three men's casinos. The sketch included stick people and a smiling sun. Wanda had even signed it.

"In the spirit of cooperation, and the betterment of mankind, I propose that our casinos be linked," Nick said. "It will be good for *everyone's* business."

Chance groaned as if confronting his worst nightmare.

"I'll take that as a yes," Nick said.

"Are you going to get rid of those awful statues?"

"They're being demolished as we speak," Nick replied. "I'm replacing them with ones of Wanda."

Shelly Michael stared at the sketch. "What else do you want?"

Nick went to the window. During breakfast, he'd asked Valentine how he could thank him for saving the city. Tony had only wanted one thing.

"A favor for a friend," he said.

In the glass, Nick saw the three men exchange looks.

Shelly said, "You going to explain?"

Nick had greased plenty of palms over the years, but he still didn't have the juice to accomplish what Tony had asked him for. That was going to take help. He tapped his fingers on the glass, then turned to look at the three men.

"It's a little sticky," he said.

CHAPTER 52

Lois Marie Valentine was a tiny thing, just under six pounds, but she had a voice like the fat lady in the opera, and Yolanda's doctor said she was perfectly healthy. Gerry could not stop holding her, his wife lying in bed, looking like a truck had run over her, the labor lasting thirty hours.

"I'll never do natural again," she'd declared.

Valentine sat in a chair beside Yolanda's bed, staring at his granddaughter. Other people's babies looked like larvae, never your own. Two days had passed since he'd shot Amin, and it was nice to finally be home. He pushed himself out of the chair.

"I'm getting coffee," he said. "Either of you want anything?"

"No thanks," Gerry and Yolanda said.

He left, and Gerry put his daughter on the bed so they could both look at her. In her tiny face, he saw traces of his mother, and it made him feel things in his heart he'd never felt before. Yolanda touched his arm.

"Gerry, what's going to happen?"

"Nothing," he said, stroking his daughter's hair.

"But Mabel said you were in trouble. That you might end up going to jail for helping the terrorists win money at the casinos, and for buying explosives. She said the district attorney wanted to throw the book at you."

"He changed his mind."

"He did?"

"Yeah. I'm free," he said quietly.

"You are? Really?"

He met her gaze, hearing the mistrust. He was going to have to win that back, however long it took.

"Really," he said.

"How did you manage that?"

His daughter let out a scream that lifted the hair on his head. Yolanda lifted her off the sheets, and she instantly went quiet.

"My dad got these three casino bosses to fix it with the DA's office," he said. "The charges were thrown out this morning. The judge wasn't too happy about it."

"What did he say?"

"He gave me a real tongue-lashing. Told me never to step foot in the state of Nevada again. We went straight from the courthouse to the airport. I think my father was afraid the judge was going to change his mind."

Yolanda took his hand and squeezed it. "Oh, my God, that is so wonderful."

"Tell me about it."

"What about your job? Is your father going to let you stay in the business?"

Gerry looked at the floor. It was tile, and he saw his reflection in it. If the guy looking back at him wasn't the luckiest guy on the planet, he didn't know who was.

"He's going to give me another chance," he said.

Valentine stood outside the hospital's rear entranceway, smoking a cigarette. He had picked up a pack two days ago and been puffing away ever since. Mabel came out and stood beside him.

"Sorry to be a party pooper, but that's bad for your health."

He raised the cigarette to his lips and inhaled deeply.

"A crew from a local TV station is in the reception area," she said. "They found out you were in town. They're very persistent."

He took another deep drag on his cigarette. His name had gotten splashed across every newspaper and TV news show in the country, and now everyone thought they owned a piece of him.

"You're going to have to talk to them eventually," she said.

He watched the cigarette's smoke curl around his head. He didn't like the newspeople, and had decided he was going to avoid them for as long as he could. They threw around the word *hero* too easily. They thought he was one, only he wasn't. Shooting a man in the back of the head with a high-powered rifle wasn't what heroes did. Heroes broke down airplane doors and fought armed assassins with their bare hands; heroes were soldiers who went to war, and didn't come home.

"What would you like me to tell them?" Mabel asked.

His cigarette was almost gone. He dropped it on the ground and crushed it out. He looked across the parking lot and saw there was a rear exit to the street. Great.

"Will I see you later?"

He nodded.

"I called the plastic surgeon who replaced your ear. You have an appointment next week for him to look at your face."

He nodded again and dug his car keys from his pocket.

"I've got your favorite lasagna frozen. I'll put it in the microwave, get some Cuban bread from the supermarket. Would you like a salad?"

It all sounded great, and he guessed it showed in his face. Mabel smiled, and as she turned to go back inside the hospital, he remembered something.

"Wait," he said.

His neighbor turned around expectantly. Valentine removed the gold coin Nick had given him from his pocket. He'd bought an elegant eighteen-karat chain for it at an airport kiosk, and now he fitted it around her neck.

"It's from a sunken treasure," he explained.

Mabel held the coin up to her face. It was old and worn and absolutely exquisite. She saw Tony walk away, and called after him.

"Will you tell me the story behind this?"

Valentine found his '92 Honda Accord in the parking lot, unlocked the door, then turned to face her. It had been the longest five days of his life, and he was ready to put them behind him. He would revisit the memories, but not for a very long time.

"Someday," he said.